Doppelganger

a novel

Simon Heath

For my family, book lovers all.

Chapter 1

Frank, Marcia and George all take their morning coffee break at 10:30 am. Every morning of the week they look at their watches, put down the phone, save the document they are working on and stop what they are doing for fifteen minutes. Frank is usually on conference calls from the moment he steps into the office at 7:30 until this first break. George, a software engineer, rarely leaves his desk. Marcia smokes. The shop associates at the Timothy's and the Tim Horton's, where Frank and Marcia buy their coffees, respectively, announce the beginning of the rush based on their arrivals.

Every day, this fifteen minute break has its own personality, which reflects the state of time on that given day. Time ebbs and flows and expands and contracts, like every other bit of matter on the planet. On the whole, it averages out. Over the course of a day, a year, a life, it settles in to the neat compartments of seconds, minutes and hours. It follows a rhythm throughout the course of the day, slowing down between two and four in the afternoon and two and four in the morning, approximately.

None of this affects the workings of the world or the unfolding of people's lives beyond the occasional feeling that time has slowed to a standstill, or that a watched pot never boils.

Time is gravity's sister. The gravitational pull of the sun and the moon balance each other out, on average, and give us the natural rhythms the world follows. Time, like gravity, has a sun and a moon, two sides that tug at us as we move through the world. There are, however, patterned occurrences where time splits open for a brief instant before slipping quietly back into its natural path. Like a total eclipse, where two gravitational fields line up and combine their forces to tear the ocean out of its basin, the flow of time will sometimes open to reveal the other side of life, the upside down reality that flows unnoticed alongside our every waking moment.

Today, on Frank and George and Marcia's coffee break, time opens up. Like a river that comes across an island in the middle of its current, time splits and then flows on, leaving the water unchanged.

Frank

Frank wears a dark suit because it's always acceptable. He is a professional of indeterminate age. Wings of grey at his temple. He drives a Saab, slightly outside the norm of the standard grade middle-tier executive BMW. He is a Vice President of Systems Operations, one of 115 other Vice Presidents in the company. Twenty Senior Vice-Presidents, of which he plans to become in the next year or two. He presents well.

He buys lottery tickets because they offer a slight jolt of energy. He buys these underground. Where he parks and buys CDs and most of his Christmas presents and picks up steaks for dinner on his way home. Frank is a good man. He is married and has two children, goes to church on Sundays and keeps his work life buttoned up in a briefcase when he leaves the office.

Completely at odds with his appearance, Frank likes to choose activities that push the limits of safety. He regularly drives his Saab at speeds of 135-150 km/hour. Last month he spent an extra three days following a business trip in New Mexico parasailing. His favourite sport is boxing. Of these three facts, his wife is only aware that Frank likes boxing, which she chooses to overlook as a by-product of Frank's lower middle-class upbringing. It comes from the same place as the Cheese Whiz and celery

Frank will indulge in when allowed to make his own lunch.

Today he is buying a coffee at Timothy's. It is his morning break. He's pouring the excess coffee out of a Styrofoam cup and into the grate to leave room for the cream. As he rights the cup and reaches for the cream, Frank looks up and through the pane of glass with the Timothy's logo on it and directly into the eyes of a man who is identical to him in every way. The man is carrying a bouquet of roses. Frank's mouth shapes itself into a perfectly round "O" of surprise. He startles and spills scalding hot coffee onto his hand, which causes him to jump and drop the entire cup of coffee. The cup bounces off the edge of the counter, splashing hot coffee all down the front of his suit pants. Frank springs back, too late. He looks down and sees the large stain running down his pants and a puddle of coffee spreading across the floor. When he looks up again, the man is gone. Frank is immediately surrounded by a group of concerned well-wishers and friendly helper-outers, who he pushes past, leaving the spilled coffee on the floor and a second, untouched cup on the cream and sugar counter.

The man with the roses sees only his reflection in the window and keeps moving toward the escalators that will take him under the street to the north, straight to the elevators of the office tower where he works, and up to the empty office where he has arranged to meet the woman with whom he is having an affair.

Frank has run out to the large open concourse area. Sunlight shines through the glass-paneled second floor and breaks the uniformity of the underground halogen lighting. He stands for a moment in the concourse with a large wet stain that begins at his belt, encompasses his groin and continues down his left leg. His hair is ruffled and his breathing is erratic. He turns in a full circle, runs to the fountain where he can see up to the mezzanine, runs back the other direction past the Timothy's Coffee where a blue-aproned associate is mopping the floor by the cream and sugar counter.

"Exactly", he mutters to himself. He catches sight of his reflection in the window of The Gap and realizes how quickly a man's appearances can dissolve into those of a lunatic. He pulls his Blackberry out of its holster, dials, waits a minute, then asks his assistant to inform any callers that he is running behind. Even underground, the reception is perfect, five bars. Why can't they fix that dead spot on the drive to and from work? Every day he sees the bend in the highway coming, has to end the call, re-dial. How hard can it be? Frank smoothes his hair and goes to pick up his dry-cleaning, which is ready at the convenient underground location.

George

George is above all a collector. He has collections of: hockey cards, coins, stamps, model airplanes, first-run 1950s detective novels, Star Wars action figures still in the box, beer bottle caps, autographed music CDs and an extremely detailed knowledge of computer systems and networks. All of these collections at various times help George to sleep at night. He lies in bed and counts them, sorts them, lingers over items that he is particularly fond of. This is what makes him endearing. What makes him somewhat tragic is that in his heart of hearts, he believes that one day all these collections will add up to something.

George's least favorite time of the day is the elevator ride up to the 40th floor of the office tower he works in every morning. When he arrives at the tower, he has to go underground to wait at the bank of elevators servicing floors 40-58. There are six elevator shafts. He stands in anticipation of which elevator will arrive first, gauging by the floor each elevator is on, the time of day and the number of people waiting. Since starting his job seven years ago, he has a 72% accuracy rate. It has been increasing steadily over the years, from 64% when he first started to his current average successful prediction rating of 85%. The difference hasn't been in the accuracy of his calculations. Over the years, he has learned to trust his instinct.

When the doors open, George always rushes to get in before remembering to allow the ladies who may be waiting to go in first. If he remembers, and chivalrously ushers the ladies in, he then has to ride the entire way up with the itching feeling he gets when someone is standing directly behind him. If he forgets, and charges in first, everyone by the door is forced to exit the elevator when he gets to the 40th floor, his floor being the first in the numbers this elevator serves. His favorite position is in the middle of the right-hand side of the car.

The most important reason for George's dislike of the morning elevator ride is that he is afraid of heights and this daily routine is a constant reminder of the fact that he is forced to spend 31.5% of his year forty stories above the ground. When he is at his desk or in Frank's office looking through the binoculars at activities in neighboring office towers, it doesn't bother him so much. It doesn't seem real when the people look like ants and the cars, beetles. But in the elevator, George is very conscious of the cables and winches that are carrying him floor by floor up and out of the real world and into this alternate universe.

Because of this fear of heights and subsequent dislike of elevators, George, unlike almost everyone else on the floor and very unlike Frank, drinks the coffee available from the machine at the employee kitchen area instead of the superior roasts available at the Timothy's on the concourse level. Sometimes Frank will offer to bring him one back when he goes down for his morning break. It is on these occasions that George will pass the time waiting in Frank's office by picking up the Bushnells Frank has sitting on one of his shelves, and scanning the windows of the neighboring office towers. There is very rarely anything of interest to see. There is very rarely any physical movement in offices. People are in their cubicles sitting at their computers or talking on the phone. Lately, there have been renovations on three entire floors of the office tower across the way, leaving precious little activity for George to watch during the fifteen minutes it takes for Frank to return with the coffees.

Today is different.

Marcia

When Marcia was a girl growing up, she was the gullible one. Now she's head of Learning and Development for HR with a large financial firm. She chose human resources because she believes in people.

Marcia lives alone in a downtown loft space with oak timbers that span the 12' cathedral ceilings. She lives 8 blocks from the office tower where she works. The living space is open, light and her mortgage is the same as rent would be. She doesn't drive, because it's bad for the environment. She has signed up for an Autoshare program, so that when absolutely necessary, she has convenient access to a vehicle for less than $10 an hour. She's always late, which means that, like she did today, she takes a lot of cabs. Marcia likes living downtown. When she goes to the cottage, as she does every summer, she gets restless and irritable, trapped in that great expanse until she can get a ride back down to the city. A large part of Marcia's frustration is that she knows these things about herself but continues to follow the same patterns anyway.

Right now Marcia is taking her morning break. She goes to street level because it is Secretary Day, which she had forgotten until she arrived at work this morning, and is buying a dozen roses from the man who sells them from buckets in front of the hospital. She is in part doing this because she smokes. Only 5 or 6 a day and very light, very slim ones, angel farts her mother calls them. But smokes nevertheless. She tries to keep this from her colleagues, as she feels it sends a negative image.

She walks above ground back to her office tower, taking enough time to finish her cigarette. As usual, her break is taking longer than fifteen minutes. The time it takes to ride the elevator down 32 floors, go back up to ground level, smoke a cigarette 10 meters from the entrance and then try to accomplish anything else is always closer to twenty minutes. While Marcia knows this, she continually pushes herself to fit within the fifteen minute allotment, because it's nobody's fault but her own that she smokes. She has a choice. Today, she is already running late when she stops to buy some dissolvable Listerine tablets because she is about to meet the man she is having an affair with. This purchase takes longer than she expects, as there is a man arguing with the woman across the counter over the price of public transit tickets. This particular convenience store refuses to offer the reduced rate offered when tickets are bought in denominations of five. The man grows angrier and more urgent as the rumbling of the approaching streetcar grows louder. He changes his tack and asks for change for his ten dollar bill. The woman behind the counter refuses to make change without a purchase. The man turns to Marcia, trying to drag her in as an ally. He eventually uses his ten dollar bill to buy one ticket, gets his change and sprints up the street to where the streetcar is already starting to move past the stop.

Marcia emerges from the convenience store, glances at her watch and sees with irritation that it is 10:57.

"Hey lady, spare some change?" A punk with a pit bull, chain for a collar. Torn cardboard sign that reads Will Fight Globalization for Change.

She is about to mutter something apologetic, when she reads the sign and snaps her mouth shut, feeling taken in, her sympathies falsely played upon. She hurriedly takes six steps south before hearing a loud dull smack off to her right. This sound is followed by another, louder sound of glass and metal meeting, followed by screeching car tires and the inevitable honking that accompanies anything out of the ordinary in the downtown grid. At the same time that she hears these things, Marcia feels something splash against her thigh, as if a nearby car has sped through a puddle. While all of these sensory inputs register in different areas of Marcia's brain, they are combined temporally into the same instant. Marcia looks down, past the bouquet of roses in her hand across her grey skirt which is now lightly spattered with blood, along the pavement, up the length of a grotesquely twisted body and into the eyes of the man she was hurrying to meet.

Marcia begins to scream.

Chapter 2

At 10:45am on this Monday the 27th of April a man and a woman are meeting in an empty office on the 38th floor of their workplace. This is the third week of their affair. They have agreed to meet in this office, which will belong to the man once the construction is complete and the institutional re-org takes effect. The office is currently empty. The man has brought the woman a dozen red roses.

The scene is a simple one: it is just two people making love. What gives it its intensity are all the things that make it wrong: his wife, the time of day, the empty office, their professional relationship.

When they enter the office he pins her to the door with his body. He opens his mouth and bites the woman's throat. She has her head thrown back so that her neck is strong and taut. She hesitates for an instant, aware of the cigarette that must still be on her breath. As the man slides his mouth up her neck, she grabs his face in her hands and draws his lips into her open mouth. With the kiss, she feels her insides melt and she wraps one nylon-covered leg around his thigh. The man undoes her blouse with one hand, feels how the silk slides against her skin. As the blouse drops away to reveal her lace bra, the man drops his mouth to the soft upper curve of the woman's breast. A moan rushes out with the woman's breath.

The man pulls away and leads the woman to the floor to ceiling window that faces north across the city. He holds the woman's arms spread out above her head as he pushes his body into hers. The man slides down the woman's body with his mouth, removing first her bra, then her skirt. He is kneeling now, pulling down the woman's skirt as his mouth moves from her stomach to the hollow curve inside her hip. His hands cup the woman's buttocks as she moans and pushes against the glass behind her. She draws him back up, slides her hand into his pants. It is the man's turn to moan as she draws his penis out of his briefs. The woman, in turn, goes to her knees, as the man looks out over the city.

On the 40th floor of the office tower directly north of this tower, a man is scanning the windows with a pair of binoculars. He moves across each floor systematically. When he reaches the 38th floor, he sees notices two figures, stops, goes back. The man's penis stirs as he sees the figure of a woman in the unmistakable act of giving a man a blowjob. The man continues to watch as the couple begins to make love against the window. The man turns away from the window and speaks to someone inside the office. A second man appears next to the first and looks at the couple making love. The second man then moves away from the window.

The woman now has her back against the window; one leg wrapped around the man's, his head cradled in her arm. She is looking over his shoulder into the room. The man faces north towards the office tower that contains the two men. The woman sees an empty room except for a print from the corporate art collection left hanging on the office's south wall. It is an Inuit print showing four igloos and three Inuit men carrying home strings of fish. There is red, blue, green and yellow cable hanging out of a hole in the grey wall. As the man approaches orgasm, he places both hands against the window pane, one to either side of the woman's head. He tilts his head back seeing pure blue sky as he starts to come. At the peak of his orgasm, he looks through the pane of glass and directly into the eyes of a man who is identical to him in every way. The man's mouth shapes itself into a perfect "O" of surprise. The man on the outside seems to slow momentarily as the two identical men lock eyes. He then continues his plunge towards the ground.

The man's body has started to shake slightly, and while disappointed that it has ended so suddenly, the woman pulls him even closer and pulls the lobe of the man's ear gently into her mouth. The woman loosens her grip on the man's neck and begins to stroke the soft hair there. He is pushing away from her now, not gently, and rubbing his face with one hand, becoming aware of his nakedness.

"Frank, honey, are you alright?" Marcia is stroking the back of the man's neck gently and kissing the base of his neck.

"I'm fine. Just cold all of a sudden." The man is still shaking and feels an urgent need to cover his naked body. As their minds return, shame begins to set in, as it always does, and the lovers part company swiftly, with only the most cursory of kisses.

The encounter, in its entirety, lasts twelve minutes.

:)

At 10:50 am, the doors to the elevator on the 40th floor slide open, and Frank walks out carrying three garments in light plastic drycleaner bags. He rustles slightly as he walks down the corridor of chest level workspaces, filled with his direct reports on hands-free headsets. As he passes each team member, he or she looks up from their monitor, smiles at Frank and returns to his or her conversation. Frank, even in this heightened state of agitation, is mindful to make direct eye contact with each team member and smile slightly as he passes. This happens in exactly the same way every day, except that today it happens five minutes later than usual. Frank's dry-cleaning is covering a large dark stain on his suit pants. The skin under his suit pants has turned red where it was scalded a few minutes earlier by 170°F coffee. The skin under the elastic of Frank's Calvin Klein mid-thigh briefs is the worst off, where the coffee trapped against his skin has given Frank second degree burns.

Frank opens the door to his office, enters, closes and locks the door, hangs up his dry-cleaning and drops his pants with a sigh of relief. He hooks both thumbs under the elastic of his briefs and drops them to the ground, too. He leaves his shirt and tie in place and begins to unwrap the fresh suit.

"You gotta check this out!"

Frank freezes, his naked buttocks facing his desk and behind that his office's south-facing window.

"They're doing it right up against the window!"

Frank slowly turns away from the door and into the office at the same time George drops the binoculars he's been holding to his face and turns away from the window and into the room. Their eyes meet for a moment and then travel down the length of the other man's body, registering the reality of the situation; Frank seeing the binoculars in George's hand, George seeing Frank's naked genitals. Neither man understands what is happening. Both men turn again, George back facing south out the window and Frank facing north into the wood grain pattern of his office door.

"What're ya doin', Frank?"

"I, Jesus, I forgot you were here." Frank is fumbling with the flimsy plastic covering his suit, which makes a sound like rain. "I spilled coffee on my pants. I forgot you were here." He is now putting on a clean, dry pair of pants.

"How'd you do that?"

"It's weird, but I could have sworn I saw my double. This guy looked exactly like me. It surprised me so badly I spilled the coffee."

"I didn't know you went commando. Bit of a shock, seeing you standing there."

"I don't. The coffee burnt me."

"You can sue for that, you know. Woman in the States took McDonald's to court 'cause she burnt herself. She won."

"I know. I read about that."

"You dressed? Because you really gotta see this."

By this point Frank is, in fact, dressed. He is wearing a new pair of pants, the same shirt and tie, and a new suit jacket, which clashes slightly with the tie. He is not wearing underwear. He crosses the ten steps from where he was standing to where George is sitting, still peering through the binoculars. George hands Frank the binoculars, which Frank holds to his eyes. He grasps each barrel firmly and moves them farther apart until the divided image becomes a single circular field.

"Straight across. They're doing it against the window. I mean, Jesus, look at it. How stupid is that? They're 40 stories up! Crazy."

This scene goes to the heart of everything that irritates Frank about George. Like one of the local gossips content to sit back and comment on how others live their lives, rather than living their own.

"George, you've seen me jump against these windows a hundred times."

"I know. It gives me the creeps every time."

Frank gives a motivational speech to his team that ends with him jumping against the window. The first time, this has a powerful effect, a sense of awe at the willingness of their VP to throw himself on the line for the business. A fear and the nagging question, "Would I do that?" George has been part of Frank's team for several years now and has seen the speech multiple times. Each time he hears the speech, he hates Frank just a little more.

"The glass up here is shatterproof. Think about it. It has to be. Otherwise some bird could smack into a window and your air pressure for the whole floor is gone."

Frank is standing still, watching through the binoculars. George is becoming agitated and is moving from the chair, over to the east wall and back to Frank. They both stand staring out the window for a full 30 seconds, Frank through the binoculars, George without.

"Here, stop looking through the binoculars. Look at the building. It's this huge, flat surface, right? And then you zoom in with the binoculars and there's these two people doing it right against the windows. Makes you wonder what else is going on right under your nose that you can't even see."

Frank puts down the binoculars on his desk, which is an L-shaped unit that starts at the window and covers a third of the west wall and then curves into the centre of the room. There's the background hum of his computer tower, a buzz from his monitor and the regular chime announcing the arrival of new e-mail. Otherwise, there is silence as Frank pushes his real leather office chair into the curve of his desk, crosses the ten steps back to the door of his office. He buttons the top two buttons of his blazer.

"You know what I mean?" George is still standing in front of the window, close to Frank's desk.

"No, George, I never know what you mean. What I do know is that you're always going to be the guy watching through the binoculars. You're the guy who waits for me to bring you your coffee because you don't like elevators. You're the guy in the movies who they tell to "Wait here." You know what happens to that guy, George? When the bad guys show up, he cowers in the corner, muttering something pathetic and then they shoot him. And the worst part is, the movie goes on, and honestly? No one gives a shit. Not the characters in the movie, not the people in the audience waiting for the next special effect, no one. The one they care about is the person who takes action, not the person who decides to 'Wait here.' Do you understand what I'm saying to you George?"

George pauses slightly before answering, swallowing the anger. "I'm not sure that I do, Frank."

"Life is about taking risks, George, when are you going to learn that?"

"Not the risk-taking speech, Frank."

"Faith is the knowledge that if you leap, you will either land on solid ground or you will learn to fly."

"I've heard it a thousand times, Frank."

"Well you obviously haven't been listening. Watch."

Frank takes three large strides across the office and launches himself at the floor to ceiling, wall to wall window. When he pushes off with his final stride, both arms are stretched wide and his head is thrown back, like he's going for a celebratory chest bump with his gloating reflection. It happens in a second. George, who is still standing by the window says and does nothing except watch, as he was told to do.

There is no subdivision of the sequence that leads to Frank falling 40 floors to his death. True to his word, the glass does not shatter. Rather, the full window leaves its stationary position and adopts the trajectory of the body hurled against it. Frank continues to move straight forward through space until gravity begins to bend the shape of his flight into a graceful arc. The window follows a similar, though smaller arc.

Because George is standing by the window, he is able to watch Frank fall the first 15 stories before he disappears from sight. He is left standing at the edge of a hole in a 58-storied building. Inside the building alarms are sounding. Outside the building there is the roar of air. George is caught between these two realities. The only feeling he has is that of being cold.

Behind George alarms are now sounding throughout the building. He picks up the binoculars off Frank's desk and holds them to his eyes. He adjusts the barrels until the divided image becomes a single circular field and focuses on the 38th floor of the building across the way. He wonders if the lovers had seen Frank's fall, or if they had been too involved in their own passion. But they too are gone, and George, standing at the edge of a hole which divides two realities, feels more loneliness than he has ever felt before.

Hands are hammering at Frank's door. His body hit the street below some time ago. The sound has been going for some time, but George has only just become aware of it. George puts down the binoculars and looks at his watch. 10:57. He turns and walks the ten steps to the office door, unlocks it, and crumples unconscious into the arms of Frank's assistant Bernadette.

Inside the alarms continue to sound. Outside the wind continues to roar.

Chapter 3

The 40th floor is swarming with people. There are four police officers, the Director of Communications from Centre Capital, two Senior Vice Presidents from HR, Centre Capital legal representation, Insurance Inspectors, City Inspectors, Fire Inspectors, a detective from 55 Division, building maintenance people and IT Security specialists who have come in to lock down all the computers on the floor. The security-card doors on either side of the elevators have been sealed off with yellow Police Line – Do Not Cross tape.

The hole where the window was has been covered by a thick plastic sheet which flaps slowly and loudly in the wind. Light shines dimly through the sheet in a milky glow. The power to Frank's office is off and this glowing hole in the wall is the only source of light. This, combined with the slow thunderous flapping of the sheet has created an otherworldly feeling. Most of the investigation of the office proceeds in silence, with only the occasional hushed conference between parties.

Police have examined every square inch of the office, paying detailed attention to the window, frame and casement. The entire assembly, window pane and casing, had come out. The 8 foot by 12 foot window was secured with thick bands of silicone, recessed behind aluminum flashing. That flashing is now ripped and twisted, the screws holding it in place gone. A thin, smooth line of silicone is all that is left behind, the rest having remained attached to the window. Little can be recovered at the point of impact, the window having finally shattered into small glass cubes when it landed, crushing the trunk of an idling cab, sending the shaken cabbie to the emergency room for minor cuts and bruises. A miracle that no one was killed.

At street level, an officer can be seen photographing the crushed window. He stoops to one knee to take the picture. When he stands, he looks at the debris, cranes his neck all the way back to look up at the tower for a moment, then slowly shakes his head before going back to work. This slow shake of the head can be seen repeated over and over by officers, witnesses and curious bystanders.

After thoroughly examining the office, the detective from 55 Division spends close to an hour asking George questions.

"What was your relationship to the deceased?"

"Describe what happened as you remember it. Please include everything, even if it seems irrelevant."

"Why were you in Mr. Lewis' office with the door closed?"

"Can you tell me about these binoculars?"

"Nice office. What does a guy like this make, if you don't mind me asking?"

The detective makes eye contact with George twice during that hour. Once at the beginning, to form an initial assessment of the person he is interviewing. The second time is after hearing George's account of the event.

"He just threw himself at the window? Why would he do that?"

When the detective ends the interview, he thanks George, gives him his card and says, "Thank you George. If you think of anything that you might have overlooked, give me a call. I'm sorry about this. I know it's hard to lose a friend."

George takes the card and puts it in his shirt pocket. It feels strange to have Frank referred to as "his friend". He supposes it's true, that they were friends, had been since childhood, but it rattles around when he hears it all the same. He opens the door to Frank's office and steps out, feeling a flood of relief as if he had just stepped out of a grave. Gathered around the door is a group of people from the floor who decided to stick around: Frank's assistant, Bernadette; his three Directors; and a visibly shaken junior programmer who just joined the team and had been scheduled to meet with Frank later that day. The rest of the floor is at a bar downstairs having cocktails.

George walks past the group. He keeps his head down and only glances up when he feels Bernadette's hand on his back. "Are you okay, George?"

"I'm going home, Bernie. I'll call in. I don't know... I don't know. I'll call in."

"Okay, George. Here, take this card. It's a management firm we're partnered with. They do all sorts of stuff, including high-level corporate emergency response. If you need someone to talk to, they can help. They're very discrete and very low-key. And Centre Capital already has them under contract. Frank worked with them on leadership. Get them to send me the invoice."

George takes the card, slides it into his pocket next to the detective's and walks past the deserted warren of cubicles to the elevator. At the elevator, George pushes the down button which glows warmly. His game of guessing which elevator will arrive first only works on the main floor where the car's location is displayed. Up here it's simply a matter of waiting.

The elevator – far left north bank – arrives and George steps into the empty car. He pushes 1 and the button with two arrows ▶ ◀ pointing towards each other. As the door is closing, George sees a man standing with his back to him, looking into the open door of Frank's office. His profile, the beige khakis, something about the man seems agonizingly familiar, like having a word or a name on the tip of his tongue. George thinks about stopping the doors, going to ask the person what he's doing there, then thinks better of it. The last thing he wants is to talk to anyone, or worse, share a long elevator ride down with someone else.

The doors slide closed and George corrects himself. The last thing he wants is to be in an elevator by himself.

The second the doors close, George is struggling for breath. His chest is pounding and the sound of it fills his ears. He starts to sway and has to reach out a hand to steady himself against the wall of the car. He starts talking to himself, saying things like, "There's no reason to panic. There's cables and brakes and emergency back-up systems designed by engineers. This is safe." He conjures a mental picture of the mechanical, electrical and software systems required to allow this elevator car to operate smoothly and efficiently, without interruption of service. But the image of Frank's body falling into space and the sucking sound of air being drawn past him are stronger and send his blood pumping too fast through his veins. This battle between engineering diagrams and the final image of Frank's death is all inside his head, building louder and more urgent until he lunges at the Emergency Stop button on the elevator. The car shudders to a slamming halt, sits, then suddenly drops another foot, slamming George to his knees. The car is quiet. The humming and the smooth sensation of movement have stopped. George stands and listens. In the distance he can hear other elevator cars moving. He can hear a clanging followed by a whoosh of air. He is listening to the interior workings of the building. Like being trapped in someone's chest cavity, listening to the blood and the lungs and the heart.

From the outside, from the security camera perspective, it is simply a normal-looking employee who inexplicably reaches out and pushes the button that stops the elevator.

"Is there a problem, sir? Can you hear me, sir? Do you need help? Are you having a medical emergency? Sir? Security has been sent to your location."

"I would like to get out of the elevator, please. I'm sorry for the trouble. I just don't want to be on an elevator anymore. I would like to get off the elevator."

"I can do that from here, sir. I can move you down to the next floor and open the doors from here."

"I'd like to take the stairs."

"I understand, sir. I am going to have to wait until security arrives at the floor and then I am going to ask them to escort you down. You will be on the 27th floor when the doors open."

"Thank you."

George stands and waits. He is suddenly calm. He knows that releasing him is a simple procedure. A small glitch in an otherwise smoothly ordered system. He is slightly embarrassed by his actions, but he knows that shortly he will be home watching a movie on satellite, that on his way home he can either stop and get a chicken at the rotisserie down the street from his condo, or he can order in. He will often order East Indian food when he's had a bad day. Either way, this incident in the elevator will be forgotten, swallowed by other events, like an object on the beach is swallowed by sand.

"Mr. Stevens?"

"Yes." How did they know his name?

"I'll be taking you down to the 27th floor now. There's a security officer waiting for you there. He will escort you to the lobby."

"Thank you"

The elevator starts with a jolt, slowly descends 6 feet and opens.

"I hope you're feeling better, Mr. Stevens."

George steps out of the elevator. There is a blue-uniformed security guard standing in the pine, brushed-metal and glass reception of SmithGreenKlaxton and Associates Law Offices.

"Hello."

"Hello."

The two walk towards the stairway exit and descend twenty-seven flights of 5 steps, landing, turn, 5 steps per floor. They do this in silence, twenty-seven times. The stairwell is rough concrete and caged fluorescent lights, in sharp contrast to the marble sheet that masks the opening to the mezzanine level. George thanks the security guard, exits to the street and looks up. He sees rows and rows and rows and rows of windows and windows and windows. Between the buildings, he sees a line of cloudy grey sky. George stands for a minute, breathes deeply as if for the first time, then puts his hands in his pant pockets and starts to walk home.

:)

Marcia is preparing for her first mid-afternoon nap since she was twenty-two and living in a shared house with three other sociology majors. She drank four paralyzers at the year end formal, made out with a law student and had to go home early. The next year she entered the workforce with an entry-level position at a Bay Street management consulting firm.

She knows she is probably in shock and that a bit of rest is in order. When she got home and let herself into her loft space, she realized she was still carrying the roses she had planned to give to Margaret for Secretary's Day. She opened the plastic wrapping, cut the stems at an angle and put them in water before going to get ready for bed.

Everything about this day seems strange. Checking out of the world, even for an afternoon, feels wrong somehow. You're not supposed to just get up and go home at one o'clock. In the end, it was Margaret who persuaded her. She said, "Marcia, as a representative of the HR department, what would you say to someone who had just seen what you'd seen? You'd tell them to go home. So go home." She'd held the bouquet throughout the entire conversation, not even thinking to give them to Margaret. Eventually Marcia conceded, although she took her laptop. In the cab, she laughed to herself at how easy it was to just walk out the door and go home.

"So this is what my apartment looks like when I'm not here", Marcia thinks as she lowers the blinds to her bedroom. She starts to undress, beginning with the blood-spattered skirt, her blouse, nylons and undergarments. Each of these items she drapes over the back of a white plastic and chrome chair.

She puts on her robe, goes to the ensuite bathroom and looks at herself in the mirror. Her eyes are rimmed red and her hair has gotten wild. She combs her hair methodically, brushes her teeth and returns to her bed, where she picks up the cordless and dials a number from the speed dial directory.

She waits.

"Hi mom. I know you're probably on a delivery, I just thought I'd call. I'm at home. I had a pretty strange day. Everything's fine, but I'm a little shook up. Could you give me a call when you get this? I hope things are good with you. I guess you'll be going to the cottage to open things up and put in the flowers pretty soon. Okay, then. Well. Love you. Bye."

She hangs up, puts the phone on her bedside table and gets under both sheet and duvet. She keeps the temperature at 68 degrees all year round. She likes it to be cold enough that her bed feels cozy and warm by contrast. By now it is 2:16. Marcia takes out two orange earplugs to drown out the sirens from the fire station two blocks down and inserts one into each ear. She places a black felt mask over her eyes to block out the light and rolls onto her side.

At first, she is lying, breathing, and immediately sees Frank's bloodied face. She was expecting this and shifts to thinking about the EVI (Employee Value Index), and the numbers from the past survey. They'd had to use a free pizza lunch to get everyone to fill out the survey, which had increased participation from a dismal 57% last year to a full 96% this year. The problem is that incentives are being used more and more. Incentive pay, bonuses, giveaways at the golf tournament, tickets to the latest imported Broadway musical, a chance to win a cruise for two. Really, the survey is all about listening to the needs of employees, but for some reason it's difficult to communicate this. People are just busy.

As her thoughts worry away, they begin to spiral inwards like water draining from a sink. Another level is aware that her breathing has started to slow and her face is heavier on the down pillow.

The duty sense that she had when she was there first was different than now. And there is a throbbing hum in the background. With 43% gone, how could she know when to stop? Then there's light above and her fingers are holding something woven and hard. She has to meet him later anyway and he said this time he'd come to her. Something is humming still, like a boiler in the basement and lights are flickering in front of her every few seconds now.

It's an elevator shaft. That makes sense, because the light is the other car way above and the other lights are the floors and that sound must be the engine or something way below. It's going up and going up feels good and the vibration in her feet feels good. And then it stops and the doors open and it's the hallway at work, so she goes down it to the door at the end. She doesn't even think, because she's got the surveys in the crook of one arm and she opens the door with the other and before she knows it, she's falling.

Marcia throws her arms back to break her fall, the surveys flying into the air around her. She sucks in air, sits straight up, throws open her eyes and stares at her bedroom wall.

She feels a sudden lurch of nausea in her lower abdomen. Marcia runs for the bathroom, lifts the light blue fuzzy padded toilet seat and leans her forearms on the bowl. Nothing comes. The seat falls and she uses one hand to hold it up, while the other holds back her hair.

The phone rings.

Marcia is sweating, but her nausea subsides enough for her to stand up. She flushes the empty bowl as a matter of course and walks back into the bedroom. The phone rings again. Her heart is pounding and she is still sweating, like inner temperature sweating. She looks at the thermostat on the wall. 68 degrees. The phone rings. She looks at her alarm clock. 2:28. Cold now, she gets back into bed and pulls the duvet up around her chest. The phone rings a half-ring which signals going to voicemail.

Marcia picks the phone up off her side table and listens. She pays five dollars a month for a call-screening option which allows her to listen to a message without being heard. She can choose to speak with the caller with the push of a button. She barely ever uses this function, but hasn't gotten around to calling the phone company, sitting on hold, then answering a bunch of questions about why she is discontinuing the service. Easier to pay the five dollars. She's actually been considering dispensing with the landline altogether, but she can't quite bring herself to do it.

"Hi honey. I'm back from duty. I was just down at Mrs. Whistler's. You know you can always call the Meals on Wheels office and they'll tell you where I'm at. I think you just called a few minutes ago. Anyway, I'm back now, so you can call if you get this message. I hope you're alright. It's not like you to call from home in the middle of the day like that. Okay, well, I'm here. I love you. Bye."

Marcia hangs up the phone, swings her legs over the side of bed and puts on her robe. As she walks through the loft space to the kitchen area, her eyes land on the clothes hanging over the back of the chair. She picks them up, rolls them into a ball and puts them in the garbage can she keeps under the kitchen sink. Then she gets a glass of anti-oxidant pomegranate and blueberry juice, takes her laptop from its case and sits down at the kitchen island to work. She feels fine. The afternoon light is shining directly through her eight foot south-facing cathedral windows. While she waits for the laptop to boot up, Marcia lifts her head and feels the sun fall on her face. She opens her eyes and sees a million particles of dust suspended in the light.

Chapter 4

Lewis, Francis James – Suddenly on April 27.
Mourned by wife Gloria, nine year old son Kevin and seven
year old daughter Kaitlyn. Beloved son of Hank and Helen
of Port Elgin and brother to Janice. Public service to be
held at Pineview Acres Funeral Home in Oakville. In lieu
of flowers, donations can be made to the Heart and Stroke
Foundation.

With Frank's death the machinery of tragedy and loss
springs to life: contracts with funeral parlor and interment
centre, letters to and from the widow and lawyer, life
insurance company and widow, life insurance company
and lawyer, lawyer and window manufacturer, Centre
Capital and lawyer, investment advisor with lawyer and
widow, HR and widow, HR and corporate security,
corporate security and IT – when printed, the paper
involved in the death of Frank Lewis would fill fifteen
cardboard filing boxes, all this information backed up and
stored in data warehousing facilities as far flung as Brazil
and India.

Each participant in the ripples caused by the event is
involved in this paper storm. In three separate locations,
three people are involved, in their own way with
understanding what happened and why: the detective, at
his desk, searching through the facts, the reports, the
diagrams, looking for links and patterns; Marcia, at her
kitchen table alternating between work and Facebook,
looking for solace, comfort, gentle platitudes of

tenderness; and finally, George, in the bathroom, reading Scientific Discovery.

Detective - Police Report
Transcript
Tuesday April 28th
Interview with Bernadette Longley
Personal Assistant to Francis James Lewis

"He had a routine. When he'd get a new team member, some kid out of college, he'd bring him into his office to give him a kick-off speech. It was this inspirational thing that he wrote a while back with a communications consultant. He's been doing it for years. He does it with all the new recruits. Here, I'll print you off a copy."

(file document)

The only constant in the financial world is change. In order to succeed, you're going to have to learn to embrace change. You need to learn to love change. It's no longer acceptable to keep up. If you're just keeping up, you're falling behind, because the market moves faster and faster. In today's market, you need to run as fast as you can just to stay in the same place. To get ahead, you need something extra. You need to be able to risk.

Risk-taking means taking responsibility and running with it. It means risking failure, because you can't wait to make sure before you decide whether or not to act. You need to learn when to act and when not to act, which means learning to trust your instinct. There's a saying that goes, "Risk-taking means leaping with the knowledge that you will either land on solid ground, or you will learn to fly." And if you don't, it means taking responsibility for your failure. You can't be afraid of failure. Fear is the enemy of risk. Fear is the enemy of success. Life doesn't give second chances. But it offers rich rewards for those brave enough to take the risk.

I'm going to show you what I mean. If I was to jump against this window, do you think it would break? We won't know if I don't try it, will we? I'll bet you $100 it doesn't break. If I win, I'll give it back to you when you take your first successful risk. If I lose?

"That's where he'd take out a hundred dollar bill, place it in the person's hand and then throw himself against the window. To show them what he meant by risk. I hated it. He swore up and down that the glass was shatterproof. That there was no way it could break. But, I always knew something would happen. All glass breaks doesn't it?"

"But it worked. His team hit their targets, every year. And every year they'd get the new strategy, asking them to do more with less, and every year, Frank's team would pull it off. He was a good man. My heart just breaks for that man's wife and kids."

Interviewer: (Inaudible)

"He had just called. He said that he had to pick up his dry-cleaning, that he was late for his next appointment. That if anyone called, to say that he was running behind and he'd be there shortly."

Interviewer: (inaudible)

"I don't know. It's just blocked off from 10:45 – 11:30. Maybe he was meeting a vendor. He didn't talk about it, but the last few weeks he's had a lot of meetings that I didn't book. I thought maybe he was being headhunted or something."

Interviewer: (inaudible)

End of Interview

Heath

Marcia – Internal Memo

Memo

To: All Centre Capital employees

Re: Workplace safety

Dear Colleagues,

All of us at Centre Capital are shocked and saddened by the tragic events of April 27th at our Toronto office. As many of you know, Frank Lewis, Vice-President of Network Operations died in a tragic accident. We at Centre Capital offer our thoughts and prayers to Frank's team, his friends and to the Lewis family.

The next few weeks will be difficult as we come to terms with what has happened and Centre Capital wishes to assure all of our family that we will be there to provide support through this process. Grief counseling will be available through our Human Resources Department and I encourage all of you to speak with your manager if you have questions or concerns.

Centre Capital wishes to assure all of you that our workplaces meet or exceed safety standards. Safety is all of our concern. We will do our part to ensure that tragedies like this never occur. But we need your help. Only you can make the safe decision.

As unsettling as these events have been, if there is one thing that unites all of us at Centre Capital, it's an unwavering focus on excellence and a commitment to deliver value to our customers. As professionals, as colleagues and as members of the Centre Capital team, we need to remember this commitment in the weeks to come. Our customers deserve nothing less.

Sincerely,

Bob Tillman

President and COO

Centre Capital Inc.

George - Scientific Discovery

A 27-year-old New Zealand university dropout named Peter Lynds says he has solved a mathematical riddle that has puzzled philosophers and scientists alike for over two thousand years — and in the process, he may have proven there is no such thing as a fixed moment in time. His recently published paper is making waves in academic circles and may in fact have solved a basic problem that has stymied the likes of Immanuel Kant, David Hume and Georg Wilheim Friedrich Hegel. The riddle in question is known as Zeno's paradox.

Several thousand years ago, in ancient Greece, a philosopher named Zeno sat thinking about time and math. And as he thought and thought, maybe sitting under an olive tree in the arid Greek summer, he became more and more convinced that he had uncovered a paradox. The word paradox in this context is taken to mean, "A phenomenon that exhibits some conflict with preconceived notions of what is reasonable or possible." In other words, a paradox is something that to the best of our knowledge is impossible. Zeno's Paradox can be described as follows:

A hare and a tortoise decide to race. It seems reasonable to suppose that the hare, who is observably quicker than the tortoise, will win the race handily. So sure is she of certain victory, that when the race begins, the hare decides to lie down for a quick nap before beginning. The tortoise, seeing his advantage, beetles off as quickly as he can. When the hare awakes from her nap an hour later, she sees that the tortoise has only managed to cover a mile. So, she gets up, scratches her ear and sets off to catch the tortoise. She covers that mile in a mere five minutes. However, in those five minutes, the tortoise has managed to move forward another fifty yards. Not a problem for the fleet-footed hare. She traverses those fifty yards in twenty seconds. However, in those twenty seconds, the tortoise has moved forward another yard. And in the time that it takes the hare to cover that yard, the tortoise has advanced yet again, and so on and so on. As long as time and space are infinitely divisible, the hare will never catch the tortoise.

The absurdity of this proposition must have made Zeno laugh when he first worked it out: a joke to tell his mates down at the Lyceum. But as he sat under the tree and went back over the story, a line must have appeared between his eyebrows. And as he thought it through a third time, the line must have turned in to a furrow. It wasn't possible. Of course the hare would easily pass the tortoise. And yet ...

Over the centuries, mathematicians, scientists and philosophers alike have scoffed at the simplicity of the problem. A variety of solutions were proposed: that nothing is infinitely divisible; that if you divide something enough times, it becomes zero; that if you add up enough miniature fractions, eventually you will have a whole, eventually you will have one. But none of these arguments have proved satisfactory and the paradox has persisted. The problem is that infinity is infinity, and the difference between one and zero is absolute. You can't add up a bunch of fractions to equal infinity. If you divide something a googol number of times, it is still a number. It never becomes nothing.

Enter Mr. Lynds. He argued that you can't isolate an object in motion at any instant in time. If you could, that object wouldn't be moving. It would be static. And nothing in the universe is static. The solution to the paradox is that time is indivisible. Time is movement. We measure time by placing it in a box, but it is the box we are referring to when we describe time, not time itself. It's like placing a dam in a river and trying to measure the water that passes over the dam. Time isn't the volume of the water, nor is it the dam. It is the movement of that water, the current of the river. Mr. Lynds' answer is elegant, simple, and almost obvious, but it turns much of our thinking about the way the world works on its ear. We constantly treat time as a measurable thing. Newtonian physics is built on this approach to time, and it has proven accurate time and time again (pardon the pun). We take snapshots to capture the moment. We have atomic clocks that keep time by the earth's radiation. We have machines that beep and draw a flat line the moment we die, a moment which by this definition, doesn't truly exist.

Perhaps we will look back on this discovery much the way we do with Einstein's discovery of the theory of relativity: a moment when an everyday Joe changed the way we see the world and our relation to it in a single, elegant, simple stroke.

Heath

This flurry of paper lasts three months before slowing to a trickle, then to nothing at all. For a period of time, it helps keep the memory of Frank alive for his wife, as she grows accustomed to widowhood. It provides something tangible, an anchor for the grief. For three months, these papers are a testament to the existence of a real human being, Francis James Lewis. Beyond this there is only silence and a rapidly fading mental picture in the memory of his family and friends.

As with everything, time marches on. Eventually, Frank's wife Gloria will remarry a decent man, similar to Frank in many ways. The children, Kevin and Kaitlyn will grow up with the story of their father's death as something that sets them apart from the other kids. The first night Kaitlyn talks about this terrible pain with anyone else will also be the night she loses her virginity. For many years to come, Frank's mother Helen will say, "It's a terrible thing to outlive a child."

For George and Marcia, there is none of the solace that comes with the official demands of paper. There are no cards of condolence for Marcia who witnessed the death of the man she was sleeping with. There are no survivor benefits for George, who was there when Frank disappeared. There is only the memory of breaking glass, the sound of the body hitting the pavement and the irresistible urge to imagine what all that air rushing past you really feels like.

Chapter 5

M arcia is nauseous and sweating again. It is
9:42pm, three days after Frank's death. This is her third
straight day of wakefulness. On the morning of Frank's
death Marcia woke up at 6:30. Since then, she has not
slept in 87 hours and 12 minutes. Her heart is pounding.
Each time she drifts to sleep, the nausea punches her in
the pit of the stomach, driving her insides into her throat.
She is red-eyed and beginning to be afraid. She is afraid
of her bed, afraid of her room. Mostly, she is afraid there
is something wrong with her.

Tonight she has been very careful. She ate a healthy
dinner and avoided snacking. She listened to John
Coltrane, the muted saxophone unlocking pockets of
stress in hidden hemispheres of her brain and releasing
the poisonous chemicals to be diluted and dispersed.
Around nine o'clock she started to casually get ready for
bed, pulling back her crisply made 400 thread-count
combed Egyptian cotton sheets. She drew a bath and lit
candles. She used relaxing lavender bubble bath and
drank chamomile tea. She did everything right. When
she laid her head on her down pillow she felt the familiar
tug that draws her thoughts down into sleep, into the
warmth below.

But at the moment when she's about to cross the line
into sleep, she feels something holding her back. Marcia
is already gone, she has already sunk below herself, but
this feeling is like a talon grip that pulls her back. "Let me
go", she wants to say, but no words come out. She tries to

see what holds her back, but there is only a presence, something at the edge of her bed. And now she's aware. Like swimming at night and realizing that there is nothing but inky blackness beneath you and now the water that was so warm is your enemy and your chest clutches the pouch of air in your lungs. She tries to move, but her limbs are locked and she can't scream and the only thing holding her is this talon like a hook lodged in her chest. Every ounce of herself is put into trying to move, trying to break this paralysis. And then it lets go of her and the falling back is worse than anything. It's the falling back that wakes her, spits her back into conscious, racing for the bathroom.

:)

For the third straight night, he is back in the office. It has been stripped bare since Frank's death. All the books, the furniture, everything is gone. The plastic sheet still covers the hole. It is flapping thunderously as George stands waiting. He knows he's supposed to be here. He's waiting for something. The plastic sheet is glowing and outside the wind is whining and howling. As George stares at the thick plastic sheet he sees a shadow start to take shape on the other side. At first, it is simply large and dark. The edges of it are indistinct, the glow of light bleeding into the darkness of shadow. But as it moves towards him, the black shape slowly becomes more solid, more like a man as it approaches. When it is almost directly on the other side of the sheet, the shadow stops, and an arm reaches forward. The arm pulls back the sheet and the shape steps into the room. He can't see the face, the light behind is blinding, but he hears it, he hears the whisper.
It says, "I see you George."
George wakes up.

:)

After flushing the bile, Marcia returns to her living room, sits cross-legged in her burgundy leather armchair.

She can feel panic rising in her, the night stretching
ahead. It is difficult not to feel frightened, alone in her
loft, hours from the logic that accompanies daylight. She
crosses the room, finds her handbag and finds the pack of
cigarettes stashed in the side. She flips open the lid,
fishes out the lighter. She counts the remaining
cigarettes: twelve. She pulls one out and lights it.

She immediately feels the control return. This
cigarette in her hand gives her a sense of stability, gives
her something to do. She exhales the smoke forcefully
and relaxes, lays her head against the back of the chair
and looks up into the exposed wooden joists.

When she has smoked the cigarette so low the ember
burns the end of the filter, she stubs it out and lights
another.

This is the beginning of her night.

:)

George is standing in front of the elevator banks that
service floors 40-58 of the office tower where he works. It
is 8:16am on Wednesday the 6th of May. He has been
standing here since 6:30.

The trickle of people arriving at work has increased to
a steady flow. Now, in addition to the young lawyers,
disheveled engineers and stately white-haired bankers
that accounted for the majority of the traffic between 6:30
and 8:00, there is the added volume of receptionists,
identifiable by their combination of skirts, nylons, socks
and running shoes. George tries to stand casually to the
far end of the elevator banks. He occasionally glances at
his watch, as if impatiently waiting for a friend or
colleague. He knows this is starting to wear thin: he has
been at the same spot for three days and is beginning to
recognize many of the people as they wait to go up to their
floors. And by the sidelong glances cast from behind
newspapers and raised from shoe-tips, George can tell
that they are beginning to recognize him as well.
Occasionally he sees a co-worker, and he slips around to
the other side of the elevator in an effort to avoid being
seen.

The first morning he didn't arrive so early. He had taken the week off work, as he had been advised to do, and showed up for work Monday morning at his regular 9 o'clock. But when the elevator doors had slid open and the people around him flowed into the empty car, George had stood rooted to his spot. "This one's too full. I'll wait for the next one." But when the next one had arrived, he let that one go, too. By 9:15, the crowd was started to thin and by 9:20 a car presented itself to George alone. He stepped towards the open doors and felt his chest tighten. He looked at the soft white lights from the suspended ceiling and the mahogany paneling on the side walls and felt his heart begin to pound. He stepped back and watched the doors slide closed. Taking out his phone, he decided to call up to Bernadette and let her know he had decided to work remotely.

But instead he watched The Discovery Channel all day.

Day Two was the same. In order to give himself some leeway, George showed up a little bit earlier and stood in front of the elevators. To distract himself, he played the game where he guessed which elevator would arrive first and entered his totals into the running account he kept on his Blackberry. Today he had only a 50% accuracy rating. Again and again he would be standing facing the elevator that displayed "Express Zone ▼", only to hear the soft ding of an elevator arriving behind him. This 35% drop in accuracy had so flustered George that he had decided to go home that day as well.

But today he was determined to go in. That was why he arrived at 6:30. It would give him plenty of time to take the elevator at his leisure without the added pressure of people all around. The last time he'd been here this early was the rollout of the Enterprise Portal. The week before its unveiling, George's entire team had put in round the clock hours. They'd all been given Centre Capital laser pointer pens as a token of gratitude for exceptional dedication and service. The batteries had run out after two weeks of terrorizing his cat with the red dot of the laser pointer. Three months later the cat slipped out the front door one morning on his way to work and never came home.

When he arrived today, there was no one about except a janitor with a large circular buffer polishing the marble floors. But again, George was seized with panic at the thought of closing himself in that metal box and inch by excruciating inch flying up to the fluorescent-lit floor of maze-like workspaces where he used to spend his days. He even went so far as to return to the stairwell he had used to exit the building nine days ago. He remembered that the corridor which led to the stairwell was hidden by a false marble panel that reached from floor to ceiling and was identifiable only by a small inset silver ring. George found the panel, opened it and walked down the corridor to the door that led to the stairwell. In front of the door was a red handle like a flag which read "Emergency Exit Only - Alarm Will Sound". He stands for a long time wondering if this is true, or if it is simply placed there as a deterrent. He hears Frank saying, "You'll never know until you try." A few weeks ago a home alarm company had knocked on the door of George's condo. They were asking if he would let them place one of their stickers on his door and windows, no cost, no obligation. It would act as a deterrent to thieves and the company would get to increase their presence in his neighborhood (which, according to police reports, was experiencing a high number of recent break-ins). George had said no. After the company representative had left, George wondered why he'd said no. He always says no. All of this goes through George's mind in an instant as he stands in front of the emergency exit door. After a moment, he turns, walks away from the door and returns to his post in front of the elevators.

And now it is 8:42 and there are swarms of people all around. Too many people. He imagines that elevator like a fat cell in a clogged artery and decides against it. This building has turned against George. He feels its sickness like a carcass rotting from the inside out and has to escape the smell. George goes up to ground level and dials Bernadette's number.

"Hi Bernie, it's George again. I'm pretty deep into things here and I'd like to keep going with this head of steam I've got and keep at it from home."

"George."

"If you see Peter, could you ask him to chair the project update call for me? I could dial-in from here, but I'm pretty behind on things and could use the time to catch up."

"George."

"He did it last week, so it shouldn't/"

"George, I saw you standing by the elevators this morning.

Silence.

"George?"

"Right. I thought I'd forgotten something and then realized/"

"Listen, George, I don't know what it would've been like being in that room. Everyone up here's pretty shaken up. I mean no one's getting a lot done, and we weren't even there."

George is standing staring at the cabbies standing outside their taxis, smoking and talking. He can't think of a single thing to say. The flow of people carrying laptop cases and boxes of files and backpacks and travel suitcases and courier bags opens about five feet in front of George and closes again about five feet past him. He stands stock still holding a small black square to his ear.

"George, do you remember that card I gave you? The card for that management firm? I talked to them last week and they've got someone on staff. She's a doctor with a background in psychology. I wasn't asking about you, it's for the whole team. We're going to a half-day grief and shock management clinic. I think it would be a really good idea if you gave her a call."

George reaches into the pocket of the shirt he is wearing. He pulls out two business cards. One is for "Dr. Elizabeth Schueller MD, MBA, BSc (Psych), Schueller Management Consultants." The other belongs to, "Detective Jerry Mauritz, 55 Division, To Serve and Protect."

"Or I can call and book an appointment for you if you like. George? I hope I'm not being too forward."

"No, no, of course not. I appreciate your concern. I'm looking at the card right now. I think you're right. Thank you."

"Oh, and George, I've already spoken with HR. I passed the expense through as some of Frank's training. So it's paid through until the end of the quarter."

"Thanks, Bernie."

"Oh, and I booked you off for two weeks, not one. So no one's expecting you back this week anyway."

"You did?"

"Yes, I did."

"Oh. Thank you."

"Okay, then. Call that number, George. I'll see you next week."

And she's gone. George is holding both cards in his hand, one for a detective, the other for a shrink. How had this happened? He looks down at the open neck of his shirt. It's the same shirt he wore the day Frank fell. He hadn't realized he was wearing the same shirt. This realization breaks George out of the dull glazed state he'd been in. Usually he rotates seven shirts and three pairs of pants with two blazers, depending on whether he'll be having external meetings with clients or vendors. By the time he reaches five dirty shirts and two pairs of used pants, he takes them to the drycleaners, which takes two days to get the less expensive rate. Fridays he wears jeans. In this manner, he continually rolls over his shirts, buying more when the cuffs start to fray, or the collar becomes too black to hide. This habit is deeply ingrained. George holds up the collar of the shirt he's wearing and sniffs. He thinks for a moment with head bowed, then puts Detective Mauritz' card back and dials the number for Schueller Management Consultants.

:)

The phone wakes her with a start. Her mouth is dry and her heart is hammering in her chest. The ring is a switchboard ring, one of those insistent double-buzzes:

her work phone, not her home phone. Marcia adjusts her headset and pushes the intercom button on her phone.

"Hi Margaret."

"Hi Marcia. Sorry to bother you, but I think it's your mom on line two."

"Okay, thanks." Marcia looks in the small mirror she keeps on her desk. She has a line on one side of her face where the cord from the headset pressed into her cheek. Her eyes have deep folds of purple around them. The rest of her appearance is perfectly put together. At 2:30 this morning, she did her ironing. At 4:00 she had a long hot shower. At 4:30 she gave herself a facial mask and before coming in she took the time to do her hair properly. But lack of sleep gnaws at her stomach and the corners of her eyes.

Marcia peels back the tinfoil of a roll of Clorets and pops one in her mouth. She breathes in deeply, stretches open her eyes and pushes line two.

"Hello?" There is too much energy in her voice.

"Hi honey, it's your mom. I'm sorry to bother you at work, dear, but I've been thinking about this sleep thing, and I'm worried about you."

"We need to get you set up on e-mail, mom."

"Oh, I've got e-mail. I just never think to use it. When you're as old as I am, you get used to doing things a certain way. When I think of someone, I just want to pick up the phone and call them. Anyway, I won't take up much of your time, because I know you're busy, but I came across something I think you should know about."

"What's that, mom?" Marcia is leaning back in her chair looking at a glossy print showing three people about to reach a mountain peak, with the word PERSEVERANCE written in bold font along the bottom.

"Well, I was visiting Mrs. Tyndall this morning. You wouldn't remember her, but she and her husband used to live across the street from us in the old house when you were growing up. Her husband, he's passed away now, but her husband got a job and they moved up north, but they came back when their first grandson was born. Anyway, her daughter Beth was there when I went in to visit Mrs. Tyndall this morning, and we got to talking. I hadn't seen her in years. Apparently she got married to Paul Griffin, you know Griffin Auto, when she was very young but recently they got divorced, which is such a shame. So Beth took the opportunity to go back to school to study Naturopathy of all things."

For once Marcia is grateful for her mother's story. She closes her eyes and listens to the sound of her voice.

"Well, we got to talking and I mentioned that you were having some trouble sleeping. She asked what kind of trouble, so I told her the story. You should have seen her face. I mean, it really is terrible, seeing someone die like that. I just can't imagine it. It breaks my heart to think what you must be going through."

Marcia's bowels cramp painfully and she winces, before cutting in. "What did she say Mom?"

"I'm sorry dear?"

"What did Beth say when you told her about my sleeping?"

"Oh! Well, this is where it gets interesting. She says that there are a number of things you can do to help with sleeping, but she thought that it sounded like you had something she called Post-Traumatic Stress Disorder. I wrote it down. And she said that the best thing for you would be take St. John's Wort for depression, Valerian Root for the sleeping and avoid bright light. Apparently, light triggers stress hormones and with what you're going through, you need to be very careful not to excite your body too much. She says it's all totally natural and safe."

"Mom, I don't think I have post-traumatic stress disorder. Soldiers coming home from Afghanistan get that. I just need a little time to process what happened. But thank you for thinking about me."

"When was the last time you slept?"

"I cat nap."

Silence, except for another painful rumble from Marcia's lower abdomen.

"I haven't slept properly since it happened."

"Well, anyway, I picked some of that stuff up. I happened to be near a health food store so I ducked in and picked up a bottle of each."

"You didn't have to do that, mom."

"Of course I did. I'm worried about you. And you won't worry about yourself, so someone's got to do it. Anyway, I thought I could swing by your work and drop it off. I know you're probably busy, but I thought maybe we could grab some lunch while I'm there."

"That sounds nice, mom, but really, I'm very busy. We're in the middle of a re-org and the responsibility for the entire high potential talent pool has been shuffled over to me. I have to go through every single training and career-development request for approval before the week's end."

"I know you're busy."

"I have to go."

"You're heading for the rocks, and the rocks are going to win. Take it from me, you don't want to go to war with your body. I know."

"I know you know. Thank you."

"I'm going to pop this stuff in the mail. Take care of yourself."

"I will. I love you."

"I love you, too."

Marcia pushes the release button and removes her headset. She rushes to the bathroom down the hall, which to her relief is empty. She finds a stall and unclenches a painful gurgle as she does. Her stomach has been increasingly upset with the lack of sleep, the body's response to pain, fear, trauma, so simple and predictable: vomit and diarrhea.

She returns to her office and sits at her desk, unable to decide what to do, all sense of direction gone these past few days. She is looking at the PERSEVERANCE print. Seven years ago her mother had been diagnosed with breast cancer. After the mastectomy they put her through a round of chemotherapy and radiation treatment. Her hair fell out and her face went gaunt and hollow. Her eyes were turned inwards, absorbed in fighting the pain and nausea. All the trappings of life had fallen away while she went inwards to wrestle with herself. In the end, she had won and grown full and round and chatty again. But the cancer had left a darkness that followed her like a shadow. There were moments when Marcia would look at her mother staring at the garden and she knew she was remembering that lost year. That was perseverance.

Marcia had never been quite so lonely as when her mother disappeared inside herself. The busy nature of her mother's love had always given her a protective coating that helped Marcia maintain her positive outlook on life. And when that was stripped away, she felt naked and exposed. Right now she is wishing she'd said, "Yes, mom, come up and let's go for lunch."

Silly. She gouges a tear out of her eye with her index finger and pulls down a stack of Request for Training proposals.

The first one is a request for communications training. *Individual is a director, only 35, high potential candidate for executive position in IT division. Engineer, strong lateral thinking skills, excellent ability to work independently, high standard of execution, positive feedback on his 360 evaluation. Recommended for communications training to increase ability to influence and impact, as well as raise individual and corporate profile.*

Marcia stops and thinks of the conversation she has just had with her mother. She's right. Part of Marcia's role in HR is to teach employees to adopt a high-level, proactive approach to their careers. She teaches them to take responsibility for themselves. And that means knowing what they need to succeed. Yes, that means delivering just in time solutions. It means doing more with less. But it also means knowing when to stop, addressing problems before they become insurmountable, seeing the rocks before you hit them.

"You're not well." Marcia picks up the picture-sized mirror that sits on her desk and looks into it. She is startled by the eye contact, almost embarrassed at the exposure that comes with looking into her own eyes. She looks old. As if draining the sleep from her body extracted some animating force that previously kept her skin taut. She smoothes her hair back, draws in a fortifying breath, smiles at herself and puts the mirror away. On her shelf she sees the folder for the executive management training firm they engage to provide communications training. She takes the folder down and opens it and reads:

Schueller Management Consultants provide a broad range of services to meet the executive needs of our clients. Our services include:
- Leadership Skills Development
- Speech and presentation writing and coaching
- Image and personal brand consulting
- Stress and time management
- Crisis coaching and grief management
- Negotiation skills
- In-house Psychologist and Medical Doctor

All of our services are conducted in a private one-on-one setting with the industry's top professionals.

The following page includes photographs and bios of the doctors, consultants, therapists and leadership gurus that make up the company. Schueller has helped train some of the country's top executives, transforming them into the graceful, intelligent, cultured individuals that bear the corporate brand proudly wherever they go. And they charge for it.

As Marcia moves to approve the request for communications training, her eye falls on the photograph of a handsome woman in her forties. She is smiling confidently out of the photograph at the viewer. She wears a black jacket with a red and blue scarf around her neck. Underneath her photo the caption reads, "Doctor Elizabeth Schueller, MD, MBA, BSc (Psych). Dr. Schueller provides clients with personalized medical and psychoanalytic therapy. With a specialization in stress management, Dr. Schueller helps executives be successful leaders at work and at home. Trained at Berkeley and Cambridge, Dr. Schueller helped establish the Sloan Institute for the Study of Sleep Disorders, before founding Schueller Management Consultants. She has worked with top executives across North America."

Marcia closes the brochure and puts it on top of the request for training. She pulls down the next one. A travel request for an industry conference in Mexico City. She closes it. Denied. Even when the application appears valid, Marcia routinely denies requests for travel to warmer climates. The investment rarely pays off.

Marcia stops and stares at the phone. After a few seconds she picks it up and dials. On the third ring she hears the familiar voice answer "Hello?"

"Hi Mom. On second thought I think I could probably spare some time for lunch if the offer's still open."

"Well that's just great. Do you want to meet at that little Italian sandwich place around one o'clock?"

"Yeah, that sounds great, Mom. I'll see you then."

Marcia returns the phone to its cradle lays her cheek down on her arm and closes her eyes.

Chapter 6

George is relieved to see the classic 1920s-style three-storey building. All the way there he was dreading showing up only to find yet another elevator. He'd already decided to skip the appointment rather than call up and have the doctor meet him on the ground floor. This building with its large foyer has a wide marble staircase that turns back on itself twice before reaching the top floor. The elevator, which most likely takes twice as long as the stairs, is a single narrow car with a folding metal gate that pulls back to allow access. George takes the stairs two at a time, his rubber-soled brogues squeaking loudly on the polished stone steps.

At the top floor the landing opens into a roomy reception and waiting area for Schueller Management Consultants. One side of the plushly carpeted area opens over the banister and looks down at the lobby below. The other shows a large reception desk backed by a huge wooden wall on which hangs an abstract painting. The painting, four feet high and six feet long, is composed of large swathes of peach and tan. The paint covers a canvas that has chicken wire attached to it, giving the whole painting a rough, architectural quality. There are two leather couches, four leather armchairs and an alabaster coffee table covered with such diverse reading materials as The Financial Times, The Economist, Harvard Business Review, Architectural Digest, Cottage Life, Golf Weekly and Psychology Today.

George hesitates before stepping on the carpet. He feels under-dressed in his khakis and windbreaker with the Cisco Systems logo on the arm. When he does enter to approach the reception desk, his feet feel cushioned as he walks. The receptionist is pleasant, professional, late forties with a slight Scottish accent that makes her seem friendlier than she really is.

"Hello. I'm here to see Dr. Schueller."

"Mr. Stevens?"

"Yes."

"Dr. Schueller will be with you shortly. Can I get you anything while you wait? Coffee, water? Are you hungry?"

"No, no, I'm fine thank you. I'll just have a seat."

When he sits in one of the armchairs, he sinks ever so slightly as the chair conforms to his body. The chair is one of the most comfortable he's ever sat in. George contemplates the painting behind the receptionist. He assumes it has been carefully selected for its gentle tones and fluid movement with contrasting texture. Beautiful, but troubled by the harsh angularity of the foreign material breaking the surface. Probably very useful as a sort of Rorschach test for the overwrought executive, for people feeling stressed and alienated from their lives. As if they're standing on the outside of life peering through the chain link fence. George can see right through that stuff. He's here to find out how to deal with his fear of elevators. And that's it. No examination of childhood, no dream analysis, no Rorschach tests.

Without thinking, George feels the spot on his arm where he got eight stitches as a child. He'd been climbing the backstop in the school ground to get a tennis ball when one of the school bullies had started to shake the fence. George fell, catching his arm on one of the sharp ends of the chain link fence. When he looked at his arm, there was no blood, but a crater where the fence had torn off a piece of his flesh. He remembers tugging on something that looked like an elastic band before realizing/

"George."

George snaps around.

"I'm Elizabeth Schueller. Liz. Please come in. Did Agnes offer you something to drink?

"Yes, thank you, no. I mean, she did offer and no I don't want anything. Thank you." George is slightly flustered, the buried schoolyard memory lingering, layering his experience as he moves back into the present.

"My office is right this way." Liz Schueller leads George behind the large wall that houses the painting and down a corridor of deep red wooden doors. Each door has a frosted pane of glass on either side and a plaque with the name of the office-holder on the door itself. At the final door on the left, Liz Schueller opens the door and extends her hand for George to precede her.

"Thank you.

"Please, sit anywhere."

The desk in this room springs from the wall into the room. Behind it there is a huge semi-circle window that starts at the floor and reaches well over six feet at its apex. This is one of the main features of the building seen from the outside. One wall, the wall with the desk, is covered with books, the other a deep blueberry-colored accent wall with soft halogen lighting. There are four more chairs like the ones in the lobby. Next to each chair is a small side table. Two of the tables have reading lamps, two of them have tissue boxes. George sits in a chair next to a table with a lamp. The natural light from the window behind the desk makes him blink several times. Liz Schueller sits in one of the chairs across from him and folds her hands in her lap.

"Hello", she says.

"Hello", George responds.

"Your assistant Bernadette called me a few weeks ago for an appointment. She said you'd been in the room with Frank when the accident occurred. First, let me tell you how very, very sorry I am about all of this. I knew Frank. We all did. He was an excellent client. But before we get into platitudes about Frank, let me say that that's not what I want to focus on."

"Platitudes?"

"I'm sure that's what you're getting everywhere else. No one knows what to say. But I assume you're here because you're looking for what you can't get everywhere else. Nobody understands what it's like to witness horror. They fixate on the event, not the repercussions. There's nothing lonelier than witnessing tragedy, because the only person you could conceivably share it with is dead."

She stops and registers the look on George's face. For his part, he is slightly light-headed. He's shut himself in since the accident, and hasn't actually spoken about it out loud since the day it happened.

"I'm sorry, you probably weren't expecting this. Therapists and consultants are just supposed to ask questions, listen and nod. Anyone can do that. I don't do that. I offer opinions and tell you what I think. That's why I cost so much. Who else in your life can you be absolutely sure is telling you the truth? That and the fact that I will dedicate all of my resources into getting you back in action. I'm not one of those people that like to draw things out. So. That's all the background I've got. Why don't you tell me why you're here."

George feels like he's been thrown a medicine ball when he wasn't expecting it.

"I'm scared of elevators."

"That's it?"

"Well, that's a big deal when you work on the fortieth floor of an office building."

"I'm not denying that."

"I had a panic attack. I had to be escorted by security to ground level. I haven't been able to go back up to work ever since. Three straight days I stood in front of the elevators and I couldn't get in."

"I see. You think it might have something to do with the fact you watched someone plummet forty stories to his death?"

"You said you offered something I can't get everywhere else. I can get made fun of anywhere else. Thank you, Doctor, I think this was a mistake."

George places both of his palms on the armrests on his chair and is beginning to push himself up.

"Sit down, George. Please. I'm not making fun of you. Well, I am, but not for the reason you think I am. I'm saying there's something else going on here."

He is still perched in a half-risen position.

"Like what?"

"I don't know. I just met you. Maybe you realized you're glad he's dead and that makes you feel guilty, makes you feel like maybe you did it. Maybe you keep dreaming about him. Maybe you were secret lovers. I don't know. It takes a lot to get an engineer into a psychiatrist's office."

Liz Schueller points at the small engineer's ring George wear around his pinkie finger. George settles back into his chair.

"Engineers tend to trust tangible things. That's why you wear the ring on your dominant hand, the hand you work with. Legend has it that the original rings came from the Quebec Bridge that collapsed in 1907. Wearing the iron ring on the hand that does your work serves as a reminder that lives depend on the work you do. You have a ceremony when you become an engineer and earn your ring. So do I. It's called the Hippocratic Oath. I know that what I do may not seem tangible to you. Dealing with sleep and dreams and the unconscious. But I am just as committed to saving the lives by building strong foundations as you are. I just work with different material."

"That's a very impressive knowledge of engineering tradition. But I build networks. Try to block spam."

"George. Why are you really here?"

George pauses. He draws in a shaky breath, grips the leather armrest hard.

"You were right. I keep dreaming about him. It's like he's coming back from the dead, like he's haunting me. Literally. I'm in his office and he walks into my dream, but it's not like we're in the same dream together. It's like I'm separate and I'm looking at his office through this two-way mirror, and he comes in through the window, but he's like this shadow or something, I can't see him properly. He walks up and looks through this two-way mirror like he's trying to hone in on me. And then he locks onto my eyes and says, 'I see you George.' And it's like the dream is just a dream, but he's outside of it, he's real and he can walk and talk in my dream world and he can really see me. It scares the living shit out of me. Pardon my language."

Dr. Schueller has been calmly listening to George speak. She leans in now, and speaks with clarity, each word inhabiting fully its place within the greater meaning of what she is saying.

"Okay, good, now we're getting somewhere. I'm going to ask you to do something. It might sound a little odd. I want you to keep a little book and a pencil next to your bed. I want you to do two things. One, when Frank appears in your dreams, I want you to write down what he says. Two, before you go to sleep at night, I want you to say something to yourself. I want you to say, 'Tonight when I dream, I am going to look at my feet.' Can you say that?"

"You're kidding, right?"

"'Tonight when I dream, I am going to look at my feet.' It is actually possible to be consciously active in our dreams, but it takes work. If he's walking around in your dreams, we need to get you walking around in your dreams too. It's interesting. In the dreams of small children, the dreamer isn't actually present in their dreams, there's no sense of self. As we grow and our relation to our self changes, that change is reflected in our interaction with our dreams. The fact that you describe your experience of dreams as that of a disengaged watcher who is confronted by the person you just witnessed die suggests a massive shift in your relation to self. Natural enough, but it can be exceptionally difficult to grasp this shift in our waking lives. How do you recognize that you no longer engage with the world in quite the same way? It's too subtle for our mind to grasp in concrete terms, so our dream mind tackles it."

"So, that's it? Look at my feet?"

"Eventually you should be able to move around, to talk in your dreams, just the same as Frank is now. The easiest thing is to look at your feet. We'll build up from there. Say it with me."

"Look, Doc/"

"You were expecting me to say it's all in your head, dreams aren't real, they're just the harmless expression of subliminal desires, tell me about your childhood, cry a bit and you're all better. Bullshit. You want to get better? Then you gotta go in there and figure out what he's trying to tell you."

There is a pause. During this last bit, Dr. Schueller has been speaking very quickly, almost aggressively. She is leaning slightly forward in her chair.

"You look stunned."

"It wasn't quite what I was expecting."

"What were you expecting?"

"I don't know. That it's all in my head, that dreams aren't real, just subliminal/"

"Well, this is what you got. Look, let's call this meeting a consultation. You think about what I've said and try what I ask. Then, if you feel like continuing, book a session and we'll see where we're at. How's that sound?"

"I'm sorry, Doc/"

"Liz."

"Liz. I didn't mean to be rude. At all. I feel very fortunate to be here and I'm sure what you're saying has value. It's just, I don't know, a bit of a cold shower."

"I know. Take a few days, see how it sits with you, then give me a call."

"Okay. Thank you."

George shows himself out of Doctor Liz Schueller's office. He walks down the corridor, past Agnes at reception, who calls out "See you soon Mr. Stevens", and down the first flight of steps. When he reaches the second floor landing, George sits down on the stairs and tries to catch his breath. He clasps his hands together to prevent them shaking and hangs his head to hide the fact that he has a pressing urge to giggle. He is shivering uncontrollably as if he had just emerged from swimming and is trying to warm himself. He already knows that he will be back to see Dr. Schueller.

Chapter 7

Sybil, Martha's mother, is still glamorous. She can't help it. She doesn't even mean to be. But she is tall and blond and can wear fur in the daytime without looking out of place. She takes up a whole corner of the little deli where she and Marcia are having lunch. Even when she lost twenty pounds and all her hair from the radiation treatments she was still glamorous. She'd gone to Little India and bought elaborately patterned scarves to wrap around her head.

Conversations with Marcia's mother are completely at odds with her appearance. Often she is discussing the benefits of bread machines or calling the guy in town about the sump pump at the cottage. Since whipping cancer, as she puts it, she spends most of her time volunteering or visiting with friends. She used to sell real estate, but doesn't anymore. She made enough off a few well-timed purchases during the boom in the 80s, that she can devote time, "to the things that really matter - people."

She is eating a bocconcini and tomato salad.

Marcia, next to her, is eating an eggplant parmigiana on a crusty Italian bun. She used to adore breaded veal sandwiches with sweet peppers and extra sauce until she saw a documentary on the meat industry. While she continues to eat meat, the image of baby cows being immobilized and force-fed to keep their flesh fat and tender was too much for her. Somehow eating baby anything crosses an ethical boundary she isn't willing to accept. She also buys free-run eggs, despite the cost. She read somewhere, "Be the change you want to see in the world." Gandhi, maybe.

Marcia and Sybil are just finishing their lunches. They've been talking about nothing, really. But there's a softness to Sybil's voice, as if hitting a consonant too hard might unsettle the patient. Conversations between the two are a combination of Sybil talking down to her daughter and looking up to her as the strong modern woman she's never been. Today, Marcia is simply happy to be wrapped in the torrent of words, stories and relayed episodes of Dr. Phil that accompany any visit with her mother.

When both women are finished their lunches, Sybil stacks the styrofoam plates on top of each other and sweeps the counter of crumbs. She places her large black handbag onto the counter and pulls out a small paper bag, neatly folded over at the top. Marcia is surprised at the crispness of the bag as it emerges from that giant, cluttered purse that accompanies her mother wherever she goes. It's amazing anything could escape uncrumpled. Her mother places the bag on the counter and slides it over to her the way they complete a drug transaction in the movies.

"I know you think you're fine, honey, and you would know better than I would. I don't know how you do what you do. But I do know sometimes we all need a little help."

"You didn't have to do that, mom. And I looked it up on the internet. St. John's Wort is for depression."

"You don't think you're depressed?"

"No, I'm not depressed. Why would I be depressed?"

"You know your father used to do the same thing. Something would happen and he'd just go to work. Sometimes he'd work seventy hours in a week. But if you asked him what was wrong, he'd just say that he was busy at work and couldn't afford to slow down. If you pushed him he'd fly into a rage."

"He's better now."

"So you say."

"I don't want to talk about Dad."

"I know. I know. I'm just using it as an example. Maybe if he'd been able to talk about it more things could have been different. I don't think he even recognized it when something was wrong. It was always outside him, never himself, you know what I mean? Anyway, I just think, I wonder, do you have someone you can talk to? A friend, are you seeing someone?"

"I'm fine."

"It's a terrible thing to be lonely. I know, in the end we're all alone, but in the meantime a little company can go a long way."

Marcia is staring out the glass window of the deli, between the letters that announce the perennial specials of "Best Veal Sandwich in Town and Pasta Salads". Her father lives in a giant sprawling house in the suburbs with his second wife. His second wife is beautiful, but not as smart as Sybil. The house is huge and modern, but without the character of the family house Marcia grew up in. It's as if he hit 40 and decided that his life was a little too bright for him, too much glare. So he rebuilt it in a muted fashion. The same palette, but in pastels. He left before she got cancer. At least they can't pin that on him.

"Okay, mom. I know you're worried about me. Honestly? I'm a little worried, too. But I am treating this seriously. I'm taking care of myself. And I appreciate you looking out for me."

"It's just that sometimes taking care of yourself means knowing when you need someone else to do it for you. You can always come home, you know. It would be fun. Make popcorn, watch some movies. Ever since the big M, I don't sleep much myself!"

"Mom!"

"Well, it's true. You just wait."

"Alright, I'll think about it. Thanks. And thanks for lunch. You didn't have to do that."

Sybil reaches across the table, holds Marcia's head gently between her hands and looks her in the eyes.

"I'm still your mother. You call if you need anything."

She gives her a solid, full kiss on the cheek, rubs the lipstick off and smiles at her daughter.

"I will. I promise."

Marcia leaves the deli while her mother is gathering up her things and putting on her layers. She's holding the delicate paper bag. As she walks down the dirty backstreet where the deli is located, she opens the bag and peers in. And laughs. Nestled in the bag next to the bottles of Valerian Root and St. John's Wort is a tiny airplane bottle of brandy and a condom.

She crumples the bag closed and looks up. As she does, Marcia feels a prickling sensation behind her eyes and hears a roaring like the surf coming in. For a second, her sense of horizon is lost. She feels nauseous without the vantage of up or down. Marcia shoots out her hand and feels the rough peeling paint on the concrete exterior of the parking garage she is standing next to. It steadies her enough that the roar begins to subside in a series of fading throbs. Until she is, again, standing on a side-street, clutching a brown paper bag. She waits to make sure the attack is gone. Then goes back to the office.

:)

It is now 14 days after the fall, two since he sat across from Doctor Elizabeth Schueller. He has been in his apartment continuously since that meeting. Turning what she said over and over in his mind like some kind of computer-generated 3-D diagram. And watching tv. And ordering in. And surfing the net endlessly, wandering from online poker games to porn sites to forums on quantum mechanics to more porn.

George is restless and stiff from sitting and hunching into his little apartment. At this moment he is watching a classic BBC-produced series called Cosmos. He is bleary-eyed from the endless visual stimulation. It's the science shows that bring him rest: engineering feats of the ancients and the birth and death of distant stars with the white dwarfs and the pulsars and the supernovas. This is so much bigger, so much more vast than anything his little apartment could ever contain, that he is soothed by the lack of need for a response from him. The stars will continue to burn and be snuffed out and the ancients will continue to sleep with their secrets buried in their tombs.

It is all so endless and undisturbed and will remain that way regardless of what he decides or doesn't decide to do.

When the 1980s blue and pink graphics role the credits, George shuts off the TV, satellite and stereo, stands up, stretches his back and shuffles down the parquet hallway to the bathroom. He brushes his teeth and pees. He never looks in the mirror. He's not scared of what he will see, he's just not in the habit of examining his appearance. He shaves in the shower. He will sometimes go several days without looking in the mirror and even then it will only be because he can feel an obviously errant tuft of hair at the back.

When he shuts off the bathroom light, he is caught in darkness for a moment. He is standing in the hallway and starts to walk, his index finger tracking the wall as he moves towards his bedroom. About midway, he hears something, something from somewhere under his feet or coming from another part of the building through a heating duct. It's very faint, but regular, like the sound of a slowed-down clock or the lub-dup of a distant heartbeat. As he listens it slows and flattens out, now more like water dripping into a plastic garbage can. There's a knock at the door. Except it's the sharp rap of a brass knocker, not knuckle on wood. George looks at his watch. 11:08. Late for a visitor. And he rarely has visitors.

George walks down the hall to the vestibule, switches on the light and opens the door. Standing in front of him is Frank, dressed casually in jeans and a loosely knit cotton sweater.

"I have a message for you."

Still silent, hand clutching the doorknob.

"You're supposed to look at your feet."

"Thank you." George looks down at his feet. He realizes his foot has been bothering him all night, a sharp pain right between the ball of his big toe and the pad of his foot. He lifts his foot up, slides off the slipper and sees something drop to the ground in front of him. He bends down and picks up a half-inch flathead screw. He picks it up between his finger and thumb and stands to show Frank the screw, but Frank is gone. George steps into the hall and looks each way, but the corridor is long and empty. When he steps back inside, George realizes that the sound has also stopped.

George opens his eyes and sits up in bed. He swings his legs over the edge and goes to the kitchen counter where he keeps his phone. Next to the phone is a pad of paper and a pen. He picks up the pen and writes. "Friday night. Saw Frank again. He told me to look at my feet. When I look up he's gone." He picks up the pen and paper and walks back to bed. In bed he places the pen and paper on the nightstand next to his alarm clock which shows 11:14. He rolls over, places a pillow between his knees and goes back to sleep.

:)

She's squished in between the examining table and the wall on the only chair in the room. If she looks at the wall directly to her left, she sees a plastic diagram of a male human torso which is split down the middle to show both the inside and the outside. It is slightly raised to show depth, like the mountains on a globe of the world. If she looks directly to her right, she is staring at the right stirrup of the examining table, which is thoughtfully covered with a hand-knit pink and yellow bootie. So she stares straight ahead at a government-issued poster broadcasting the dangers of smoking. The picture is of a mouth, throat, pair of lungs and a heart. Swirling smoke is shown entering the mouth and filling the lungs. Bullet points with phrases like "Increased risk of heart attack" and "Emphysema" are linked to spots on the smoke's trajectory by little lines.

The picture makes her crave a cigarette. She opens her handbag under the pretense of finding her Blackberry and returning some e-mails, but really she wants to touch the slender pack of ultra-lights she carries with her.

Which is when he enters. Predictably.

"Still smoking, eh?"

Marcia closes her handbag quickly.

"Trying to quit."

"That could be part of the problem, you know. Nicotine's a stimulant."

"I know." Marcia hates her doctor. She always has, although, she's never thought to change doctors. There's nothing wrong with this one, it's the feeling of being in a confessional that eats at her. "Forgive me, doctor, for I have sinned. It's been 6 months since my last check-up."

"Well, thank you for coming in."

"They wouldn't give me the results over the phone."

"The tests are back, and the news is positive. There doesn't appear to be anything out of the ordinary. Your blood pressure's a bit high, but that's to be expected given the smoking. And if in fact you aren't sleeping, that could be a contributing factor."

"What do you mean 'if you aren't sleeping'? You think I'm lying?"

"Well, here it is, Marcia. Over 75% of people who report sleep disorders are in fact sleeping. People who swear up and down that they haven't slept a wink, in fact routinely sleep anywhere from 4 to 7 hours. It's their perception that they haven't slept, maybe because the quality of their sleep has changed, or the nature of their dreams. Maybe they wake up frequently. What I'm saying is that with all your tests reading normal, I really don't have much to go on here."

"Except what I told you. And the fainting spell."

"Ah yes, the fainting spell. You say you didn't actually faint, is that right?"

"No, but almost."

"Marcia, you mentioned an event a few weeks ago. An accident."

"You think it's psychological."

"It could be. You haven't been taking any anti-depressants have you?"

"No. My mother gave me some St. John's Wort, but I haven't taken any yet."

"Throw it out. And anything else that's unregulated or untested and potentially unsafe. You've been in a state of shock. But your body is fine. You're young and you're strong. I'm going to prescribe a sleep medication. You should take one dose before bed for the next two weeks. After that it loses its effectiveness. I think if we can get you over that hump of falling into deep sleep, you should be fine. A couple good night sleeps and you should be right as rain. Just don't mix it with alcohol. And you might want to think about some counseling. Anxiety is the enemy of a good night's sleep. And in the meantime, you might want to think about quitting smoking. At least avoid having a cigarette in the last few hours before going to bed. If the problem persists come back and see me in two weeks."

The Doctor hands Marcia a piece of paper, smiles a thin-lipped smile and leaves the examination room. Marcia looks down at the square of paper in her hand. Triazolam. Marcia looks at her watch. After sitting for seventeen minutes caught between the eviscerated plastic corpse and the cutesy pink and yellow leg-spreader, Marcia was able to see her doctor for two and a half minutes. Then given a drug that she's never heard of with absolutely no explanation. No description of side-effects, no concern about healthcare philosophy, no room for questions.

She stands and smoothes her hair. She has her hair back today, and re-does the ponytail to quell the anger she feels inside. It's like this every time she comes here. Marcia leaves the examination room. Attached to the clinic where her doctor has his office is a pharmacy that dispenses the prescriptions. She enters the dingling door and walks to the counter.

"Hi, my doctor gave me this prescription?" Her voice rises slightly as if the statement was a question. She pays for the drug and walks into the street.

:)

George is standing in his parents' basement, next to his father. His father is slightly shorter than him. He has lost most of his hair except for the sides and a small patch in front. Whenever he sees his father, George is grateful for his full head of hair. They are in the family room, the walls lined with wood paneling, a beer in hand. George's father had a small wet bar put in years ago, for hosting parties, although they haven't had a real party since the 70s. But the real attraction of the basement is a full wall of vinyl records and a five foot long wooden stereo cabinet hi-fi system. The wall of records is a custom-built unit designed specifically for holding his father's record collection, a collection George can remember poring over as a child: Janis Joplin's greatest hits, with her round sunglasses leaning over the handles of a motorcycle; Pink Floyd The Wall, with the terrifying pink faces of nightmare teachers and marching hammers; Nana Mouskouri, with those inexplicable glasses.

Upstairs, his mother is doing the dishes, while his father is showing him his newest acquisition. "Original pressing of Iron Butterfly. Very rare. Seventeen minutes of In-a-gadda-da-vida. You know, that was supposed to be In the Garden of Eden, but he was too drunk to say it."

"Yeah, you told me that story."

His parents weren't hippies. His dad was in engineering school while others were marching and sitting-in and making love. He liked structure too much. The chaos was uniformly unappealing to a man like George's father. But he loved the music. He started collecting the music and listening to it in the basement, over and over, as if listening for some secret hidden message buried between the grooves of vinyl. His collection is into the thousands and probably worth a lot of money by now. George can remember as a kid putting on huge earphones with squishy soft black rings that covered half his head and listening to CCR and The Animals over and over. It was a point of contact between the father and the son.

"Of course, you can get anything you want on eBay now. I don't though. Misses the whole point as far as I'm concerned. Half of it's in the hunt, finding some gem that's been buried in someone's garage for thirty years. Found this one at the old Records on Wheels, you remember that place?"

"Sure." Growing up, they'd spent almost every other Saturday in that tiny record shop. He and his dad in the record shop while his mother and sister Emily would try new recipes clipped from magazines and occasionally go into town to shop for clothes. He rarely sees Emily now, she moved to Silicone Valley years ago and only comes back at Christmas.

George runs his fingers along the spines of the records. He's run his fingers over these same records over the course of three decades, now, the feeling the same, the sound instantly conjuring up his younger self.

"I heard about that friend of yours. Frank."

George stiffens slightly. He'd thought it strange his father had invited him to the basement for a beer. They don't have that kind of relationship.

"Oh yeah?"

"Crazy way to die, eh? And two kids, too."

"Yeah." George pulls out a record: Neil Young and Crazy Horse, Everybody Knows This Is Nowhere. Neil, plaid shirt, dog at his feet, leaning against a tree. He flips it over, looks at the songs, remembers the opening chords, the driving rhythm, mouths the words, "I wanna live with a Cinnamon Girl."

"I remember you used to play hockey with him."

George is trying to remember the middle lyrics. "A dreamer of pictures I run in the night, something or other moonlight."

"That boy could skate. And score. But boy he was fast! Give him the puck and he was gone. You remember that?"

It's bugging him, that he can't remember the middle part.

"Hockey was never your thing was it? I mean, you could skate okay, you just couldn't stop or turn so well!"

"Yeah, I remember Dad."

"Anyway, your mother and I saw in the paper that he'd died, and how he died, and well, I guess we just wanted to see if you're alright."

George slips the album back into place on the shelf and turns to look at his Dad.

"Yeah, I'm fine, thanks Dad. We kind of went our own ways. I mean, we worked in the same building but I barely ever saw the guy. He's just a little slick for my taste, you know? Anyway, yeah, I feel bad for his wife and kids, but I can't say it's really affected me much."

"Okay. Just checking. We don't see you so much, and your mother worries, so we thought we'd just check. Speaking of which, I think your mom made one of her rhubarb and strawberry pies. You interested?"

And that's it, both men relieved to let it slip away.

:)

On the commuter train back from his parents' house that night, he passes a patch of beach along the lake that hasn't yet been swallowed up by houses, where he and Frank and some of the other kids used to come and play. There was a dirt path that used to run down the bank to the beach where they built a ramp to jump their bikes. Frank broke his arm going over it. Their parents had made them promise they wouldn't hang out by the water, so they'd both had to pretend Frank had broken it falling off his bike at school. After Frank broke his arm, George stopped going to the beach as much. He never did try the jump they built together.

Now, as the train whips past, the beach is deserted. A plastic bag is picked up in the rush of air from the passing train and thrown into the air. It floats for a long time, before finally settling onto the surface of the water. George leans his head against the window of the car and closes his eyes.

:)

The first night, Marcia takes the Triazolam at 8:15. She lies down, curls up and falls asleep at 8:55. She wakes up to the sound of her alarm at 7:30. She remembers no dreams. The euphoria of having slept through the night carries her through until after lunch, after which point the weight of the last two weeks of sleeplessness comes crashing down. She recognizes that it will take some time for her body to recover and returns home in good spirits.

After a light meal of micro-waved frozen organic pasta and vegetables, Marcia lies down at 7:30. This time she is asleep by 7:45 and sleeps through until her alarm sounds the next morning at 7:30. She does not dream and does not feel refreshed. All day she feels like she's trying to push her way through a rubber sheet. But at the end of the day she's still looking forward to seeing her bed.

On the evening that Marcia is preparing for her third night of drug-induced sleep, she decides to revert to her regular routine, believing that her body will follow suit. She watches two re-runs of Law & Order, reads an article on workplace morale and shuts off her light at 10:35. She is asleep within the space of five minutes. She wakes up at 7:30 to the sound of her alarm. She feels more exhausted than ever. She feels disoriented. The absence of dreams makes each morning feel more like emerging from a coma than waking from a refreshing night's sleep. At work, during a scheduled 2:00 presentation on projected call centre employee attrition rates for the coming three years, Marcia falls asleep. Sound asleep. At 2:20, after having been asleep for 10 minutes, Marcia sucks in her breath sharply. She stares about the room wide-eyed with no recognition of place. The presenter has stopped speaking and is looking at Marcia, hesitating before deciding whether to be annoyed or concerned. Marcia excuses herself. She goes home at 3:00, unable to accomplish anything further at work.

At 3:20, Marcia takes a dose of her medication and goes to bed. When she wakes, it is dusk. She tries to move, but can't. There is something at the foot of her bed that is disturbing. She can't see, but she can feel it. She goes to turn on the light, but can't move her arms. She tries to ask, "Who's there?", but can't open her mouth. Someone is there, at the foot of her bed and she can't move or make a sound. Now she's trying to scream. The tendons in her neck stand out with the effort. She can feel that something is about to happen. She makes one more wrenching effort and sits straight up in bed, every muscle taut. The room is empty. She looks out the window and can see the bellies of circling seagulls lit from below as the sun sinks along the horizon.

Marcia gets out of bed and walks into her bathroom. She takes out the remaining Triazolam and drops the little pills into her toilet. She watches them as they circle the bowl and are sucked down. Looking in the mirror, Marcia feels a little more alone and a little more scared than she did before she started the medication. She goes back to her bed, picks up the phone and pushes the button that will dial her mother's number. She waits.

"Hi mom. Haven't talked in a while, just checking in. Very funny, by the way. So far I've only used the brandy, but here's hoping. Talk to you soon. Bye."

Marcia hangs up the phone, pads out to the living room and turns on the TV. The night is extraordinarily long. After two hours of late night talk shows, she is feeling cramped and cagey. It's too late to go for a walk, so she takes out her yoga mat. Her muscles seem to inflate as she draws in breath, focuses inwards and brings her body slowly into the present. Each muscle is dragged out of its torpor and after 35 minutes, she feels like she's had a steam bath, or been in an oxygen chamber. She feels fully awake, in a way she hasn't since she started taking the medication. It is now 2:07 am. She decides to bake. Her mother sent her a recipe for Morning Glory muffins months ago that look healthy and delicious. There's barely any sugar, the grated carrots, zucchini and raisins providing natural sweetener. This takes her until 3:18, after washing up. Marcia looks about the loft. She normally doesn't have this kind of time. She goes to her one book shelf. It has very few books: the large photo version of Into Thin Air, with its glorious crisp shots of Everest and harrowing details of what happens when people are killed by the wild; books from university sociology courses; The Girl With the Dragon Tattoo; a few classics. She chooses Love in the Time of Cholera, a gift from an old boyfriend, and settles into her armchair, wraps a fluffy red wool blanket around her waist and starts to read.

Eighteen minutes later, her eyes snap open and she pauses halfway out of the armchair, unsure if she's going to be sick or if it will pass. She focuses on the Ikea throw rug in front of the television stand and the nausea passes. 3:56. She goes to the television, takes out Titanic and watches the entire movie. She doesn't re-enter her bedroom until 7:00 the next morning when she goes to get dressed.

The following nights Marcia is unable to fall asleep at all. Her waking life becomes a permanent state of sleep latency. She is becoming terrified of her bedroom. Her nerves are shot. She can't tell anyone. She can't talk about Frank. She feels cold all the time. On the third day after stopping her medication, Marcia is standing at a street corner on her way home from work. She sees a black and white shih tzu with pink ribbons at her feet. She reaches down to pet it, but recoils when the dog pulls back its lips and snarls.

"Lady, you alright?" she hears behind her.

She looks up to answer the question and sees a young man with a mohawk and dirty green combat pants. "Fine. It didn't get me."

"What didn't get you?"

She looks down. There's no dog. Up and down the street. No dog. "Nothing. I'm fine. Thank you." The light turns green and Marcia joins the rush of people as they cross the street.

When she gets a block away, Marcia ducks into a back alley and presses her back against the building. She opens her handbag and pulls out a cigarette which she shakily lights. She exhales. Hallucinating small dogs is a concern. Marcia takes two more drags, then crushes the cigarette underfoot and heads back to her office.

It is two weeks and two days since Frank died.

Chapter 8

"When I opened the door it was Frank. He said he had a message: that I was supposed to look at my shoes. When I looked up, he was gone."

"Anything else?"

"I can't remember. No. Yeah, there was a sound. Like a metronome, but really deep."

Elizabeth Schueller is sitting in a chair to the right of George. It is angled slightly towards George, but they are definitely sitting next to each other, not across from each other, as before. There is a side table between the two of them with a tissue box and two glasses of water on it. When they speak, they each have the choice of looking across at each other or staring out at the pigeon-shit drenched façade of the building across the street. Mostly, the speaker stares out while the listener watches the other's face. It is comfortable this way and George appreciates the privacy it gives him.

"That's a great start, George. And I'm glad you're back. I was hoping you'd come back, actually. I know coming to me is a big deal to you and I hope I didn't come across like an asshole last time, but it's pretty important to me that you know where I'm coming from."

Her bluntness runs contrary to everything that the office communicates. He had expected a professional veneer to cover their sessions, but again he is surprised to find himself knocked off-kilter by her directness. He expected to be spoken to like a client, or a patient.

Instead, she speaks to him as George Stevens. It's unsettling.

"You don't write things down?" Dr. Schueller sits without pen or paper, arms relaxed on the chair.

"I remember. Usually I jot a few things down after you leave. Wouldn't you rather I actually listen to you?"

"You're the strangest doctor I've ever met." George is unable to suppress his smile, like the grin he gets when he smokes pot.

"Thank you." Dr. Schueller smiles back, her eyes sparkling with pleasure. She is dressed crisply, a black business suit with a silk tan chemise cutting across the blazer's diving neck. She is unadorned, except for a simple gold band on her ring finger.

"The reason that I ask if there's anything else is that usually things are in dreams for a reason. And it's not complicated. You don't need me to interpret your dreams. The fact that Frank was telling you to look at your feet when I specifically asked you to say to yourself, 'Tonight when I dream, I'm going to look at my feet' is pretty obvious in its significance. You're getting Frank to tell you something that you can't or don't want to tell yourself. The metronome. What does a metronome sound like? A heartbeat, right? Only deeper and far away, like the tell-tale heart, right? It's usually pretty obvious stuff. You can do it yourself. But that's not what I'm most interested in. In our first session you told me the problem is elevators. Maybe you just don't want to go to work. Do you like what you do?"

George stares straight out the window. "I hate it. I mean, I hate it. Not the work, not the programming, that's fine. But it's, I dunno. Sometimes, I just stop and think, 'This is my life.' You know, I'm sorry, I can't call you Liz. It's too weird. I wouldn't be talking about any of this stuff if you weren't a doctor, so it feels stupid not to call you Doctor."

"Call me Doctor Liz. Call me whatever you want, just call me." George, who has been staring out the window, turns and looks at Dr. Schueller. "Sorry, I'm a Dean Martin fan."

"Are you really married?" It is Dr. Schueller's turn to break eye contact and turn to the window.

"No."

George smiles and continues to look at the profile of Dr. Schueller's cheek. There is a small mole, where the skin is darker. The hairs that grow out of it, dark and wiry, have all been plucked. "You're right. I hate where I work. There's this guy that sits next to me. He eats about a half pack of Rolaids a day. Always on a diet. Golfs, plays squash down at the racket club, doesn't drink coffee. But he's always got indigestion. And when he presents, he's got this thing he does with his shirt sleeves, always pulling the cuffs down. I'm sure he doesn't know he's doing it. And it's because he really cares. He wants to succeed and this is the life he's got, so he takes everything so seriously. The only way to survive is to permanently disconnect yourself, but that's no way to live."

"Why do you do it?"

"The money's good."

He's starting to enjoy this conversation. He's feeling drawn out and engaged by this person.

"Seriously."

"It's easy. I'm good at it. They leave me alone because I'm fast and I don't have a family. They like people without families. For certain stuff. And I like programming. It's engaging. I mean, when you're doing it, that's all you're thinking about. The possibilities you are grappling with are absolutely endless but the objective is set and the rules are clear. The parameters with which you define those possibilities are a choice between binary opposites. Simple as that, 1 or 0, yes or no. Which is perfect. It's beautiful. It gives you a form of control over the endlessness of the universe." George pauses, suddenly self-conscious. "Geek-talk, but you asked."

"There's a spirituality at work there. There always is. We call them core beliefs, values, but there's always some kind of God squatting at the bottom of the pile, waiting to be uncovered. So the question is, 'What made you lose your faith?'"

Dr. Schueller's tone remains even throughout this, as if the conversation hadn't just taken an abrupt turn. As if just stating the obvious. There is a moment while George decides what to do with it.

"I'm not disregarding what you're saying. I'm not. A couple of weeks ago I would have laughed in your face. But I'm not. But this isn't the kind of conversation I feel equipped to have. I don't understand what you're saying."

"That's okay. There's no point in telling you things you already know. I want to challenge you to think. Between our sessions, I want your brain to keep working away at what we talk about. Particularly when you sleep. I think it's enormously positive that you were able to follow instructions into your dream life. I'd like to build from there. The next thing I'd like you to do is to look at your watch. When you're dreaming, I want you to be aware that you are dreaming and tell yourself to look at your watch."

"Sure, okay."

"We're good?"

"We're good."

"Let me walk you out." Dr. Schueller and George both stand up. There is a moment of awkwardness, before Dr. Schueller holds her arm towards the door, inviting him to pass in front of her on the way out. They walk side by side down the hall in silence, their hands a fraction of an inch apart. As they emerge from the hallway to stand next to the half-wall that backs the reception desk, Dr. Schueller stops and extends her hand. "Thank you, George. You can book your next session with Agnes." Dr. Schueller makes direct and prolonged eye contact with George as they shake hands. Then slices the contact with a scalpel and walks towards the woman seated with her back to them.

George's eyes follow Dr. Schueller as she walks to the woman, stops, inclines her head slightly and asks, "Marcia?"

The woman turns her head slowly, blinks, smiles and says, "Yes." She stands, again slowly, and turns her whole body towards the doctor. She is slightly shorter than the doctor, around five foot five inches, George would guess. Her light reddish-brown hair, auburn the package probably calls it, is pulled back, the ponytail ending just past her shoulders. She is thin, almost drawn. But very pretty. Young, but with the beginnings of crow's feet around her eyes, between 30 and 35, George would have to guess. "Dr. Schueller?"

"Please, call me Liz."

"Liz."

"Would you like to come with me? My office is down the hall. Did Agnes offer you a water, coffee?"

"I'm off caffeine. Doctor's orders!" A nervous laugh. The two woman are approaching George and moving past, and there is something hyper-real about the experience. Like how light shifts from blue to red as stars in orbit approach then pass, or how the Doppler Effect distorts sound as an object hurtles towards you then recedes. Sound slows down to a deep bass as the women approach. Dr. Schueller turns her head and smiles at George. She is saying something but he can't make out the words. He is staring at the other woman, staring at the side of her face, sliding along her skin as she turns her head and makes eye contact with George before turning down the hallway with Doctor Schueller. As they move away, the bass sound speeds up, back to normal, and George is left standing, his head throbbing, his eyes glued to the space the women just vacated.

"Mr. Stevens?" Agnes' upbeat Scottish voice snaps time like a rubber band and George turns to the woman behind the desk. "Would you like to book your next appointment with me?"

"Who was that?"

"I'm sorry, Mr. Stevens/"

"Of course you can't. Sorry, stupid of me. She just looks very familiar. Yes, I'd love to book an appointment. Actually, could I trouble you for some water? I, I don't know, I just feel a little, I could just use some water if that's okay."

George is rubbing his face, all of a sudden feeling disoriented and unsteady, the same feeling he had just before the elevator doors closed on his first panic attack. He'd seen something just before the doors closed, something that had caused his heart to race, just like now.

"Of course, Mr. Stevens, I'll just be a moment." Agnes removes her headset and turns down the hall the opposite direction from Dr. Schueller's office.

The moment she's gone, George leans slightly over the desk and turns his head to read the large appointment book on the reception desk. He finds his name under the column marked ES. The slot directly below his name reads Marcia Winters.

Marcia Winters. He flips forward in the book to see if there are any more bookings under that name. He has fully extended himself to read the book to the point where his shirt is sliding out from his pants.

"Mr. Stevens?"

George leaps back from the polished wood counter.

"I'm sorry! I didn't hear you coming. I'm a little jumpy. I can't remember if we booked another appointment or not. I was just looking, I probably shouldn't have done that, I should have waited for you to come back and then just ask you/"

The lie comes quickly but smoothly.

"We didn't get to booking you an appointment, you asked for water. Here you go."

"Thank you."

George takes a sip from the water.

"How's Thursday? Dr. Schueller has an opening between 2:00 and 2:30."

And swallows.

"Yes, thank you."

"I'm going to write it down on a card for you."

George breathes in and moves to close it off with an apology.

"Thank you Agnes. You're very kind. I hope I didn't do anything wrong."

"You haven't done anything wrong, George. We'll see you on Thursday."

George hurries out of the office, head down, cheeks flushed.

:)

"This is such a pleasure. It seems strange that we've had such an ongoing relationship and never actually met face to face."

Dr. Schueller is holding open the door to her office.

"Thank you, Liz. Well, we've never had reason to look elsewhere. Your firm has consistently produced excellent results. Everyone we send to you has nothing but the highest praise for the work you do."

"That's always great to hear. And it must be true, or you wouldn't be here yourself, would you? Please, have a seat." Dr. Schueller indicates one of the four chairs facing the window. She sits behind her desk and opens a notebook. There is silence while she writes in the book, before looking up at Marcia and smiling. "Now. What is it you've come to see me about?"

"I'm not sleeping."

"How long?"

"Three weeks."

"Any idea why?"

"It happened around the same time I witnessed a man fall to his death. I was on the street at the time."

"Of course. He was a client. I think the whole Bay Street community has been greatly saddened by the event. If I'm not mistaken, he was referred to us by you."

Marcia shifts in her seat. "Yes, I knew him."

"Did you realize it at the time? Did you see his face? Or did you make the connection afterwards?"

"I saw his face."

"I'm sorry. That must have been very hard. Did you know him well?"

"He was a high-potential leader. We were working to increase his visibility both in the company and out."

"I see."

"Your website says you also specialize in sleep disorders."

"I do."

"Every night when I got to sleep, I wake up nauseous ten minutes in. I feel like I have to throw up. I never do, but the nausea is overwhelming."

"Every time or just occasionally?"

"Every time. Except when I was on some medication my doctor prescribed, but that just seemed to make things worse."

"Medication?"

"Sleep medication."

"Do you remember the name of the drug?"

"No. Something with a T. I flushed it."

"So you haven't actually slept more than ten minutes without the assistance of medication for 3 weeks?"

"That's right. And I had a fainting spell a few a days ago. Before I came here I thought I saw a dog, but when I looked again it was gone."

"Anything else?"

"I'm cold all the time."

"Anything else?"

"Apart from being tired?"

Dr. Schueller laughs a full-throated laugh. "A sense of humour is a good sign." Dr. Schueller has been writing the entire conversation down. She looks up at every pause and for every question she asks. At this point in the conversation, she puts down her pen and looks at Marcia.

"I'm glad you've come. I think I can help. I've worked very hard in my career to gain expertise in a number of interrelated fields. I've studied medicine and psychology, with a focus on stress-inducers and their effect on sleep patterns. Have you exhausted all your other options?"

"I tried sleep medication, relaxation, cutting out caffeine, not smoking after five o'clock."

"Exercise? Sex?"

"Exercise. I've been to the gym every second day."

"Are you interested in examining your sleep patterns? It would involve coming down to the sleep lab for a night, maybe two. And, of course cost."

"I have my training budget for the past two years."

With confirmation of budget, they are out of the gates.

"We take sleep for granted. It's something that is given to us at birth. It can be bewildering when it is taken away. We realize how much everything in our lives is built on the foundation that it provides. We rely on it for our physical, our mental, our emotional and even our spiritual well-being. What is scary about it is that we feel we have absolutely no control over it. In some sense, that's true. But we now know a lot more about sleep and how it interacts with our conscious selves. I'd like to start work sooner rather than later. If it's convenient, I'd like you to come in to the lab, tonight if possible."

"Yes I'd like that. I want to feel like I'm doing something."

"I understand. I appreciate you coming to see me. Agnes out front can help you with the details about the lab."

"Thank you Liz."

"I'm sorry for the circumstances, but it's a pleasure to be of assistance to someone who has supported our work so fully over the years. Say hello to Carol if you see her."

"Of course. Thank you."

Marcia stands and the women shake hands, as if an agreement has been reached, the meeting a negotiation of terms completed, the outcome decided upon, service levels set. All that is needed now is execution. They smile at each other, Marcia turns and leaves the office on her own, down the hall and out. The meeting lasts ten minutes from start to finish, for which Schueller Management Consultants will invoice Centre Capital $1000 under the heading Initial Consultation. Carol is Marcia's boss. Head of HR, personally responsible for the career needs of 500 executives and over 20,000 employees. Potential clients, in need of career counseling, grief management, sleep therapy. Frank Lewis falling out of a window might mean a significant amount of work. All of it channeled through Marcia Winters.

With Marcia gone, Dr. Elizabeth Schueller closes the door to her office and walks to the leather chair behind her oak desk. She turns her chair to face the semi-circle window that frames her desk and leans back, fingers locked behind her head. The window is why she took this office: it gives her a funnel for her thoughts.

The Schueller office is close enough to downtown to serve its corporate clientele and far enough away to see the cluster of office towers plastered against the grey skyline. As she stares out the window, she imagines seeing a body burst from the straight line that is the building closest to her. She thinks of these two clients that have been in her office, filling it with the weight of witnessing that fall. One at the top of the trajectory, one at the bottom, and in between, this body falling. As she imagines it, it takes five seconds for the body to make the journey. Five seconds that separate George Stevens and Marcia Winters.

:)

George is sitting on the landing where he sat after his first session with Dr. Schueller. Next to him is the empty water glass Agnes gave him. It's been next to him for the last ten minutes, but he's too embarrassed to take it back. He is waiting for Marcia Winters to emerge from her meeting with Dr. Schueller. He's spent the last half hour vacillating between wanting to talk to her and simply wanting to see her again. He doesn't want to come off as some kind of creep, some kind of predator who lies in waiting for women at their weakest. He's plagued by doubts. He can't even be sure that it's the same person. At best the magnification on those binoculars is 50X, which is good for certain types of viewing, but he has to be sure. And then, what does he think he's going to say? The most troubling part is that he can't even he 100% sure of his own motivation. There is no question she is an attractive woman. He can't picture her without remembering the arc of her throat and the curve of her body framed in the giant office window.

It's the light, dusty sound of nylons moving against each other that snaps George out of his internal argument. They are black, disappear at the knees under a knit wool skirt. Then the heels clacking in a double-hop gait as she passes him and continues down the marble stairs. He stands quickly, knocking over the water glass sitting next him. She is about five steps past him when she hears the echoing sound of glass on stone and turns her head to find its source. They don't quite make eye contact, as he is stooping to catch the glass before it rolls to the first step. For her it is a non-event, immediately forgotten. For him, a lost opportunity to be agonized over in the coming days. She continues down the stairs, crossing the atrium of the building until she is about to exit through the revolving door, when she suddenly stops and breathes out. Her shoulders drop. Even from where George is standing, he can see her face slacken, the muscles losing their tension. Then she straightens herself, smoothes back her hair and pushes through the door and out.

George is standing on the landing of the marble staircase, holding the water glass in both hands. Reality sneaks back with a sensation like pins and needles and George becomes aware of himself. For a moment he thinks about returning the glass, making some kind of joke about his forgetfulness, maybe trying to sneak another look at the appointment book.

He slides the glass into the oversized pocket of his windbreaker and exits the building, out into the overcast afternoon.

Chapter 9

Things settle on George's kitchen table like silt. The table is where George throws things when he walks in the door – keys, bills, flyers, flimsy grey plastic bags containing cream, cans of soup, bread, bananas. If they aren't moved within 24 hours, they tend to sit for weeks. He eats his meals sitting on the leather couch that dominates the living room. Hot bowls stick slightly to the material when he picks them up. The coffee table holds things in active use: remote controls, half-empty glasses of juice.

George opens the door to his apartment, throws his keys on the table, takes the empty water glass from his pocket and places it on the table. He removes his jacket and hangs it on the back of the lone chair that sits at the table. He stands for a moment, considering. Then picks up the laptop sitting on the table, crosses to the couch and sits down heavily. He places the laptop on the coffee table and opens it. As soon as he boots up the laptop, it begins scanning for a network connection. In this densely populated downtown area it finds several, but identifies its companion, the female counterpart to its searching male address.

A username and password and he sees his personalized homepage in the Centre Capital intranet. A ticker runs the Centre Capital stock price across the bottom of the page. A photo of Bob Tillman, President and CEO of Centre Capital dominates the upper right side of the page, followed by a message of hope and a passionate call to arms for all employees to join together in making Centre Capital the market leader going forward.

He isn't sure what he's looking for. George enters the company directory, types in Marcia Winters. And there she is. Marcia Winters, Director of Learning and Development, Human Resources. Her office is located across the street from his. Twentieth floor. E-mail: Mwinters@centrecapital.com. Phone number. Assistant Margaret at extension 5472. Access to Outlook. But that's it. No picture, no bio, nothing to give him context, a story to attach to that name. He Googles the name, but there's no photo on the LinkedIn or Facebooks profiles, which seems odd until he remembers the HR presentation he'd attended about Managing Your Personal Brand Through Your Online Presence. The speaker told a few horror stories of people's photos being used against them at job interviews and identity thefts and had encouraged everyone to use the strictest of privacy settings. He scrolls through twenty screens of Winters family reunions, Appalachian society membership lists and blogs containing the two names buried somewhere deep within the pages before finally giving up.

He copies the information from her file into a separate folder and exits the company directory. It's what he was looking for, but now he's not sure what to do with it. Maybe he hadn't expected it to be so easy. Or fast. His laptop is humming away. The afternoon sits in front of him and he can't watch any more TV. He decides to check e-mail. He enters his information. And waits. He hasn't checked his messages in two weeks. He's never gone this long without checking messages. George's heart starts to race as he sees the number of new messages flashing at the bottom of the screen. When it finishes, George is faced with well over a thousand new messages. He scrolls through them in wonder. Some from friends and colleagues with subject lines like "Condolences" or "Concern". One from a high school friend with the subject line "I heard the news". Many, many of them are marked FYI with a list of recipients up to 30 names long. Some have little red exclamation marks next to them. There's even one from Bob Tillman, president and COO of Centre

Capital which appears to be addressed to him individually. He clicks on it.

Dear George,

Please accept my personal condolences on the loss of your friend and leader, Frank Lewis. All of us are deeply distraught and offer our thoughts and prayers to friends and family.

Sincerely,

Bob Tillman

Followed by a scanned hand-written signature. "Well, that's nice", George thinks. He considers saving the e-mail, then clicks Delete and continues to scroll. On and on they come as he holds the arrow on the down button.

He scrolls to the top, chooses Select All from the Edit drop down list. All the messages turn blue. His finger is on the Delete button, when he notices the address on the first message – Flewis@centrecapital.com. A message from Frank. Unread. He clicks on it. There's no message, only a hyperlink:

http://darwinawards.com/darwin/darwin1994-02.html. He clicks the link. At the top of the page is the tagline "Named in honour of Charles Darwin, father of evolution, Darwin Awards commemorate those who improve our gene pool by removing themselves from it." The Darwins. Every year his friends circulate the list of the latest, greatest stupid ways that people die. They have a good laugh.

He's about to close the window when he notices the date. 1984. This isn't the latest. It's a specific page, dug out of the Darwin Award archives. He scrolls down and starts to read the page.

Olympic Freefall Offers Exciting Physics Lesson

(5 July 1984, Chicago) Near the top of one of the Windy City's mighty skyscrapers, a twenty-nine-year-old attorney named Reginald was locked in a heated dispute with one of his colleagues. "They were arguing about the Olympics," remarked the firm's controller. Determined to settle the aspect under discussion, the two friends decided to have a race down a long hallway on the thirty-ninth floor of the building.

On the way down the hall, Reginald, who was not wearing his contacts due to a scratched cornea, lost his perspective and crashed through a plate-glass window. He fell thirty-eight stories (the building had no 13th floor) before striking the pavement, at which point his velocity was zero. A moment before he terminated his 6-second freefall, however, his velocity was approximately 94 miles per hour in a vertical direction. The abrupt velocity change proved too much for Reginald to withstand, and he promptly died.

The building was constructed in the 1950s and they installed a new and remarkable window system designed to eliminate the need for outdoor window washers. Each window was framed by rubber tubing and mounted in the frames with metal pins top and bottom center, a sort of bisected bicycle tube on a pivot. To clean the outside of the window, one simply deflated this tube and swiveled the entire window around to clean the pane. The tube was then re-inflated to hold it in place. This system worked well for many years, withstanding the traditional gusty wind this lakefront location experiences. Unfortunately, rubber is organic and eventually deteriorates. Many of the windows became loose as a result. So what may have happened was that the window simple gave way and swiveled when the man hit it, ejecting him from the building like a revolving door. This information was kept quiet -- after all, the building was owned by an insurance company."

By now, George's heart is pounding. The story is too strangely similar. He switches programs, back to the e-mail. Right clicks and checks the Properties box on the e-mail. Sent: 27/04/12 10:36 am. Received: 27/04/12 10:36 am. April 27th. The day Frank died. 10:36 am. Frank wasn't even in his office. He was getting coffee. George was in Frank's office at 10:36.

Some kind of server delay probably. Messages can disappear for days; resurface as if nothing had happened. He ought to know, he helped build the infrastructure. The whole portal project was rushed because Frank committed to a roll-out date without actually consulting the people who were building the platform. They met the date, but there were still a ton of glitches. Things George had meant to go back and fix. Things he probably would have fixed if there had been some kind of acknowledgement of what went in to that project: a thank you, maybe a vacation, a team-building exercise in Vegas, something. But no. So fuck it, the glitches were left where they were. The odd message fell into a black hole, but it always reappeared.

But why would Frank send him an e-mail that almost perfectly described the manner in which he was about to die?

George clicks on the X at the top right corner of his e-mail program. Clicks on the start menu and chooses Shut Down. He closes the lid on his laptop and sighs through his nose. He crosses the room, picks up the phone and dials the number of the person he sometimes buys weed from. Waits.

"Yeah?"

"Hey James, it's George. You around?"

"For the next little bit."

"You mind if I swing by?"

"Yeah, man, come on by, I'm here."

George hangs up, picks up his keys and exits the apartment.

:)

The question is pizza or tea. The last time he did mushrooms was twelve years ago. He and a couple of the coders working out the Y2K debacle. They bought a quarter, crushed them up on top of the pizza they ordered and played four-person Quake until four in the morning. And giggled until; they couldn't breathe, tears running down their cheeks, stomach muscles aching. This time, James threw him a free gram with the ounce of weed he bought. He said a buddy had just driven across the country. Said he brought back pillowcases full of mushrooms that he picked off a soccer field in Victoria. Said they were good. So was the weed. Red-veined buds, thick with resin. George isn't a heavy toker. But when he does, he has a habit of smoking one joint after another, until his brain feels thick and clogged.

Too much effort on both counts. George sticks the styrofoam container of left over chow mein into the microwave and goes to roll a joint. He sits at the coffee table, takes a CD cover for a very old Pearl Jam album and starts to cut up one of the buds. He rolls the joint, ZigZag white, tears a thin strip off the pack and uses the toothpick from his Swiss Army knife to put the filter in place. Then tucks the extra paper in around the makeshift filter, places the whole joint on his tongue and pulls it slowly out of his mouth.

He is trying not to think about the e-mail, but his mind keeps drifting back. The Darwins.

The microwave dings. He walks to the kitchen with its cheap white melamine cupboards and fluorescent lights. George pours a glass of orange juice from the near empty fridge, opens the microwave, grabs a fork and takes the chow mein back to the coffee table. There he takes the small bag of dried brown mushrooms and dumps the contents into the noodles. He mixes it up, picks up the remote, turns on the TV and starts to eat. It's on the Discovery channel as usual, a program about solar eclipses. George stops chewing and puts the chow mein down. Science always makes him want to smoke pot. He lights the joint and inhales deeply. For a second he thinks he's going to start coughing convulsively, but he forces himself to relax, exhales, takes a sip of his orange juice and the feeling passes. He smokes half the joint and stubs it out for later.

"The average total eclipse lasts only seven and a half minutes. But the impact of this gravitational alignment is much more far-reaching. Not only are the tides affected, there is some indication time itself might be affected, or at least clock rates which may or may not be the same thing. While general relativity predicts this effect, actual changes in time have been difficult to measure, in part because of the range of instruments used to measure it. A Foucault's pendulum or a cesium atomic clock may respond very differently to the change in gravity being exerted upon it.

Which does open up the question, "What exactly is it that we are measuring when we use a clock to measure time?"

George changes to the Sports Channel: golf. The other sports channel: darts. He watches long enough to take another large bite of the chow mein. The '70s and '80s classic channel: Dukes of Hazzard. The Toons Channel: Pinky and the Brain. George puts the remote down. He puts the remote down, more because he thinks this animated program is what he should like when he's high than out of any actual desire to watch the program. After a minute, the high pitch squeaky voice starts to scratch at the top of his skull. He isn't able to focus on anything else, just that chipmunk voice eeking away about taking over the world. He changes the channel. National Geographic: four large vultures perch on the carcass of a wildebeest, while one lion prowls in the background and one feeds from the animal's haunch. All the regular channels only have daytime programming. Talk shows. Celebrity interviews. How to lose weight. Soap operas. Cooking shows. He pushes the mute button and starts to surf rapidly between channels. When he reaches the simulated fireplace channel, he turns the TV off in disgust. He lights the remaining half of the joint left in the ashtray and smokes it while he stares at his off-white walls. There is nothing on his walls, not even a poster.

Eventually, George turns the TV on again and flips back to the Discovery Channel. He looks at his watch. He spent 15 minutes flipping between channels, only to realize that where he started was where he wanted to be in the first place. Except that in the course of flipping, the program he was originally watching is now over. Now there is an over-enthusiastic British scientist with a comb-over sitting on a rock by the ocean talking about the evolution of physics in the twentieth century.

"In 1925 Louis de Broglie postulated that matter should possess both particle and wavelike properties. This has become known as the particle/wave duality. Imagine you are standing by the water's edge. You drop two stones in the water. You hear them hit the water at the same time. And out from the middle the ripples spread in little waves, made up of crests and troughs. And where the waves meet, the crests that hit other crests get bigger and the troughs that hit other troughs get deeper and where a crest hits a trough, they cancel each other out."

George's mouth is been hanging slightly open. From the moment the narrator asked his audience to, "Imagine ...", George has done so, fully and completely. There is a basic '80s computer animation showing two waves moving agonizingly slowly towards each other. Where the big curvy lines meet on the same side, the curves get bigger and where a curve on the top meets a curve on the bottom, they turn into a flat line.

"For years scientists had been trying to figure out whether light was a particle or a wave. Eventually, they were able to isolate a single photon, a particle of light. To decide the matter, no pun intended, they conducted an experiment. They placed a screen with two slits cut in it a few feet from a wall and then they shot a single photon at it."

Again, the animation of two lines, followed by a dot that bursts with a cartoon explosion and starts to fly towards them.

"And what they expected to see was two slits of light on the wall behind the screen."

Animation showing two slits of light.

"But instead what they saw was bars and bars of light of varying strength."

A giant X through the two bars of light.

"Bright light at the centre and then dark and then another slightly dimmer bar of light and then dark and then another dimmer bar of light and so on, radiating out from the original bar. Just like the ripples from the two stones dropped in water."

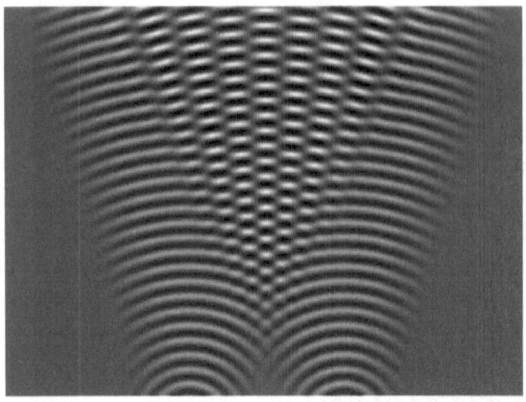

Back to the animation of the waves colliding. Then back to the bands of light again.

"Which means that light was acting like a wave, when they'd only shot a particle. Here you had a particle of light acting as a wave."

And then back to the man with the comb-over, inexplicably delivering this monologue from what George can only guess are the shores of the Atlantic. Perhaps the hometown of Louis de Broglie, the location of this monumental leap forward in human understanding. The man is particularly excited now, gesturing emphatically with his hands as he makes this final point.

"And then they saw this behavior in electrons, too. In fact, when they got down to it, they started seeing an awful lot of this pattern, this total and complete paradox. That the most basic things of the universe can be two things at once. This is the heart of quantum physics."

Theme music, and commercial. Until now, George has been leaning forward, towards the TV, but now with the commercial, he relaxes back into the leather couch. He remembers the particle/wave duality from high school, but like everything else his attitude had been, "Yeah, so what?" He was only now, in his thirties, starting to regain a sense of wonder about the world. He wonders how he'd missed something so central, so awe-inspiring as this basic paradox. This basic flaw in the human mind. George starts to laugh. The whole notion of this photon, this tiny little thing, if it can even be called that, this little event in the universe, causing so much confusion. "I'm a particle! No, I'm a wave!" George doubles over with laughter. He is in love with this little British man with his humility in the face of the universe.

Like from a speaker in the upper corner of the room, up and to the right, George hears Dr. Schueller's voice. "There's always some God squatting at the bottom of the pile." He thinks of this little Buddha-like scientist and starts to giggle anew. He is laughing so hard, he is becoming short of breath. His sides are starting to hurt, his cheeks ache. He hasn't laughed this hard since he was five and his friend Francis fell off his bike and flew headlong into a rhubarb patch at the end of the lane they were racing down, no that's not right, where did that memory come from? George stands up and has to steady himself. Takes a sip from his orange juice. He is suddenly very high.

He walks to his window and looks out. It is windy and the branches on the tree outside are swaying in the gusts. As George watches, it seems to him that the swaying of the branches is following a pattern. Three small gusts followed by a third strong gust that pushes the branch in then releases it. He has the feeling of watching a nature screensaver. The thought is disturbing and he stands watching the branches until the pattern is broken. Eventually there is a single sustained gust, before the wind lets up for a moment, allowing the branches to drop. George takes this lull as an opportunity to break away from the window.

He goes to the kitchen for some microwave popcorn. As he pushes the popcorn button on the microwave, he notices a slight trailer-effect as his hand moves in front of his eyes. Purplish. He passes his hand in front of his eyes again and sees the container of the shape of his hand dissolve and stretch out in the air behind, like a paintbrush of watercolours being dragged through water. "Our skin contains us because time allows it to", he thinks. "If our bodies were to fall out of sync with the world, we might dissolve, lose our solid shape. Time would pass us by." The popcorn is popping vigorously now. He looks into the microwave to watch the bag expand from the inside. When it is done, he removes the bag, grasps the opposite corners of the bag to open it, and drops the contents into a stainless steel bowl.

A crack of thunder sounds directly above George's apartment. It is so loud and unexpected that George jumps, showering popcorn over the kitchen table and floor. This makes George laugh. He puts the bowl down and picks up the popped kernels. Half go back into the bowl, half into his mouth. The sound of torrential rain has followed the thunder and is punctuated by low rumblings. George crosses back to the window to watch the rain slice through the darkened air. He draws his wheeled office chair to the window, places the bowl of popcorn on his work table and settles in to watch the storm.

The black clouds have given the late afternoon air a thick grainy feel. The rain falls as if propelled by something stronger than gravity. The darkness outside and the light from inside the apartment bounce George's face back at him in the window, making it hard to see past his own reflection. He stands, turns out the lights in his apartment and returns to the chair. Now when he looks out, he sees nothing but storm. He closes his eyes for a moment to listen to the rain, seek out a rhythm. From the periphery of the darkness, he sees Marcia Winters, outlined in the office window, walking towards him at the Schueller offices, sliding past in space. She stops, rotates, frozen. He moves in, can see the surface of her skin, can see the short wisps of hair that escape the clip, can almost taste the skin at the top of her neck by where her ear/

George snaps his eyes open. A horizontal line of lightning lights up a cloud off to the east, followed by a crack of thunder. George grabs a handful of popcorn, stuffs it in his mouth, chews. He's wishing he wasn't so high. But there's no point fighting it. He goes to the stereo, puts on an old Wilco album and returns to the window. With the lights off and the music swelling, George's mind rushes out to meet the storm.

:)

Frank is walking down a long hallway. The walls are smooth wood panel wainscoting below, with white stucco above. At intervals of twenty feet there are frosted glass light shades on alternating sides of the hallway. They aren't lit. Between each light shade, there are wooden doors with brass elephant knockers. None of the doors have numbers. At the end of the hallway, there is a light. The light is coming from a hole that is covered by thick plastic like the kind used for home renovations to prevent the spread of drywall dust. Behind him is nothing.

Frank walks to the light. The closer he comes to the plastic sheet, the brighter the light grows. It is glowing around the outline of a figure, a body. He knows that he must speak to the person on the other side. As he reaches out his hand to draw back the plastic, he speaks to the silhouette. "I see you", he says. There is a sound like screaming wind, he feels himself sucked back in space, all light is extinguished.

First there is only the sound of his heart. Then the breathing. He blinks. He is still standing. There is a faint light. He is in the hallway again. Behind him is still nothing. He starts to walk down the hallway. The light grows stronger and he can hear the sound of the plastic sheet flapping in the wind.

Frank stops. This time he turns to one of the doors lining the hallway. He reaches out, lifts the brass elephant head and raps the trunk three times on the door. There is a pause. He hears fumbling, followed by the door opening. He sees a face he recognizes, like someone from public school years ago. Frank opens his mouth to speak and it is filled with words he's never thought or heard before. "I have a message for you. You're supposed to look at your feet." The man in front of him looks slowly down at his feet.

Frank panics. He turns to run. Standing behind him is the same man. At his feet, long fingers of mist drift along the floor. More words fill Frank's mouth. "I'm sorry to trouble you, but would you happen to have the time?"

The man looks slowly down at his watch, as if the act requires physical exertion. "Yes, it's 10:56."

"Thank you." Frank takes three steps, then stops. He can hear a soft sound repeating itself from somewhere. He walks slowly down the hallway, one ear cocked. When he arrives at the door the sound seems to be coming from, he opens it and steps across the threshold. He shuts it behind him. There is no light, but the sound is louder. It's the sound of dripping water, but softer and warmer than a leaky faucet. Like a humid cave. He leans his back against the door and slides down. Frank closes his eyes and starts to count the drips.

"Eight hundred and seventy-five. Eight hundred and seventy-six. Eight hundred and seventy-seven. Eight hundred and seventy-eight."

When he reaches nine hundred, he starts again at one, followed by two, followed by three. Eventually he drifts off to sleep. When he awakes, he is back in his office.

:)

Ahead of him, he can see a thundercloud. Flat and dark on the bottom, it boils up and explodes dense and white into the sky. Beneath him the ocean is calm, waves bumping up against each other as if unsure which direction to go. The sun has set behind him, but the inside of the cloud glows orange with the last of the light. His arms are outstretched and he is flying very quickly towards the cloud, his khaki pants flapping softly against his legs. Even in this dreaming state, he is aware of the silliness of holding out his arms, like a parody of some comic-book hero. But the gentle wind and the humidity are on his face and it feels right. The cloud is roiling and unfolding the closer he gets, growing ever-larger by the second. He can see and hear the rain now. There's no lightning, no sense of danger, just the awe of the immensity of this intangible thing before him and a desire to join with the light glowing inside. He approaches until the cloud is all he can see. It takes on texture as he approaches. The air is humming with electricity, his skin feels charged and warm. Everything about this feels good.

And in a moment he is inside the cloud. There is no sense of direction here, no up or down, only a diffuse light that removes any possibility of fear. He is slowly floating forward now. It is difficult to see, difficult to separate himself from the mist. It is as if he, too, is charged and humid and glowing. "This is like the beginning of all things", he thinks. Ahead, he sees a thinning of the mist. He is moving forward, as if being pulled through the cloud and as it clears he begins to see hard shapes, straight lines. The feeling of flight, the moment of exhilaration that came with entering the cloud is dissipating, leaving a feeling of longing, a desire to go back. Now he sees a hallway and a prickling anxiety creeps into his consciousness, a nagging feeling that he is supposed to remember something. There are wisps and tendrils of cloud curling along the carpet. He walks to a door and opens it. He sees a man in front of him and suddenly remembers what he came for.

The man in front of him says, "I'm sorry to trouble you, but would you happen to have the time?"

The flying man in the khaki pants looks slowly down at his watch, as if the act requires physical exertion. "Yes, it's 10:56."

"Thank you" says the other man and turns to walk down the hallway.

The man in khaki pants turns away, opens the door to his apartment, walks down the hallway and crawls back into bed. He is pleased with himself, that he remembered to deliver the message to Frank. Until then, he'd felt uneasy, nervous he'd forget. It's a difficult hand-off, between worlds. He isn't used to the specificity required when interacting with the other side. It demands results, concrete actions, deliverables. But now that he has fulfilled his duty, he feels calm and relaxed. He settles back into his bed and looks at up at the walls of his room that are ringed with all his various collections, from Star Wars figurines to O-Pee-Chee hockey cards. He smiles to himself, flips to his side, stuffs a pillow between his knees and falls deeply asleep.

:)

George opens his eyes. He looks to his right at his alarm clock. 10:56. His tongue and teeth feel coated with peach fuzz. He rolls out of bed and pads to the kitchen, takes out the orange juice and drinks a glass. The apartment is a display of his evening. The empty chow mein container on the table, bottles of beer perched around the apartment – two by his computer monitor, one by the window and four sitting on the coffee table next to the remote control which is next to the open baggie of weed, next to the shredded pack of ZigZag whites. And his still soaking wet jeans and t-shirt hanging over the back of a kitchen chair, a towel bunched on the floor underneath them. In the middle of the storm, George went out to sit in a parkette a block away. He sat and felt the fury of the rain. He sat until the rain turned to mist, then disappeared. He watched as the black clouds left and the air brightened around him. Waited until he heard a robin venture a chirrup, then went home. He started to come down from the mushrooms around midnight, but managed to prop up the high with joints until almost 2:00.

Seeing his apartment this way gives George a jolt of nausea that feels like guilt. He moves to the bathroom, head held still, takes two Tylenol and then brushes his teeth. And brushes. And then showers until he feels like the residue of last night is finally washed away. He hopes no one saw him sitting in the rain. But he's still glad he did it.

George begins to tidy the remains, empties into their case, weed and papers into the ceramic buddha belly, dishes in the sink. It's while wiping the coffee table that he notices the laptop and remembers the e-mail from Frank's desktop. The Darwin link. And the surge of nausea hits again. Something about the computer, something his mind is hiding from him beneath the coat of muck left by the drugs. He flips the lid of the laptop and turns it on. While it's booting up, George makes coffee and pours himself a bowl of Cheerios. He eats the Cheerios at the counter, waiting for the coffee to brew, trying to remember last night. But everything seemed so clear, so clean last night. He knows that for the first time he had the feeling that things made sense. He remembers the feeling but can't remember why.

The coffee pot pops and sputters to the end of its brew cycle. George mixes it with two fingers of cream and two heaping tablespoons of sugar before returning to the computer screen. He logs on, types his password. When the logon box disappears, it's the first thing he sees: a folder sitting square in the centre of his screen, underneath which reads MWINTERS. Next to it is another identical file which reads GSTEVENS under it. Next to that, one that read FLEWIS. George stares at the screen for a moment, his mind racing, panic flickering away in his chest.

"Holy shit."

He stands and walks to the window. Brushes his hair back from his forehead. Goes back to the laptop and moves the cursor over top of the GSTEVENS file, then double-clicks it. Another box pops up and he scrolls back through dozens of files. Performance reviews dating back eight years, an employment profile, security checks, credit checks, copies of memos. He closes the dialogue box again and stands up, crosses back to the window.

"I'm such an idiot."

He remembers it all quite clearly now. He was thinking about that woman again. It was around midnight that he remembered the backdoor. It had been there for months. He'd eventually meant to go back and close it up, but at the end of the portal project, he'd left the system admin permissions in place. At first this was because it wasn't really ready for the launch date Frank had agreed to. He'd left the backdoor open so that he could go back and tweak things after the system went live. He remembers the team meeting when Frank dropped the bomb, "This baby's like an airplane. We're in mid-flight and we have to change the engine. Stopping is not an option. We've got four months to put this system-wide enterprise portal in place. I know we can do it, but it's going to take teamwork and commitment. I need your buy-in." He held his fists out and shook them for emphasis on this last statement, his eyes gleaming with clarity and focus. When they'd prioritized the key actionables going forward and aligned their priorities to maximize synergies, George had been charged with creating the overall structure, which was then filled with content by his colleagues. "Do I have everyone's buy-in?"

"Fuck you, Frank." Of course that part was muttered under his breath. He had nodded mutely like the rest of the team.

"I need to hear it. We've got to pull together as a team. Do I have your buy-in?"

"Yeah!" Most of the team was genuinely enthusiastic. They liked Frank's style. He made them feel cool, a part of something.

Fuck you, Frank.

He knew Frank's game. He talked teamwork, but only when he could be the star quarterback. He was all about taking, never giving anything back. So George cut a few corners. Left open a door that gave him personal access to the entire company directory. Sure it was wrong. But he never thought he'd use it, it was just a game he played. Until last night, when he tunneled into the most restricted area of HR records. Directory after directory of information on people. Photographs, video clips, personal histories, police reports, everything imaginable. And right along with the others, MWINTERS, GSTEVENS and FLEWIS. He made copies of the folders without even opening them.

It seemed so clear last night. He was taking back his life. This job took his life from him and it was wrapped up in these three files. So he took them back. Somehow he knew that these three files held the answer to why he couldn't step into an elevator, why he was locked up in his apartment getting high, why he was seeing a corporate shrink, why he couldn't get that woman out of his head.

George walks back to the laptop and in succession opens each of the three folders. He right clicks and opens each of the files marked Employee Profile, each followed by a different six digit number. They all have a picture. His is the same picture as the one on his employee ID card. Flat, dulled, almost difficult to recognize. A picture that could belong to any number of network architects in any number of companies. Marcia's is unflattering. Her hair is shorter, plain-looking. She is staring straight ahead, as if unsure when the picture is going to be taken. Frank's is of a higher quality. When employees gain VP status at Centre Capital, their picture and bio are printed in the business section of the paper and a professional photographer is hired for the headshot. This is the photo in Frank's file, relaxed and smiling.

George arranges the files so that the three pictures fill the top half of his screen. He then goes to the kitchen to make some toast. He pours another cup of coffee, spreads peanut butter on the toast and returns to his computer. He takes a bite of the toast, takes a sip of the coffee, then opens up the first file in the folder marked GSTEVENS and begins to read.

PERFORMANCE PLANNING AND REVIEW SUMMARY

The following objectives reflect Centre Capital's commitment to the Balanced Scorecard as an accurate means of reflecting an employee's impact on a range of key stakeholders. This approach balances employee, company and customer satisfaction.

I. OBJECTIVES AND ACCOMPLISHMENTS

Objectives will relate to one or more of the following Corporate Strategic Goals:

• FINANCIAL PERFORMANCE (profitability, business growth, asset quality, management control);

• CUSTOMER SATISFACTION (external and/or internal);

• EMPLOYEE EFFECTIVENESS (team leader's impact on the team's commitment, competence and cost effectiveness), and/or;

• ALIGNMENT TO CENTRE CAPITAL CORPORATE BRAND

George's eyes begin to hurt and he can already feel himself getting irritated. The review period is from several years ago. He remembers his first project: a firewall to block the budding strains of viruses. It was exciting work. Like a video game, with the feeling that they were out there prowling around and he and his team had to build the defenses before the clock ran out. Back then it was that simple, like an interactive form of Space Invaders.

Under Managerial Leadership Capabilities, a 1 means Exceeds requirements, 2 means Meets requirements and a 3 means Needs improvement to meet requirement in this area. George is surprised to see that in this review he consistently scored 1s and 2s. Included in his substantial list of 1s are: Organizing, Planning and Resourcing; Teamwork and Cooperation; Direction/Accountability Clarity; Change Leadership; Relationship Building; Acquiring, Allocating and Balancing Resources; Performance Management and Integrity. This last one gives George a surge of pride in spite of himself. Eight 1s out of a possible twenty-one. In the final section marked Managerial Leadership Capabilities Improvement and Development Plans his evaluator has written:

Possesses strong technical ability. Demonstrates an aptitude for collaborative problem-solving and trouble-shooting. Needs to develop high-level thinking and increase ability to influence and impact. With development in above areas, could present high potential for leadership role.

He's surprised to read this. It was his first boss, Jim Townsend. He remembers Jim telling him something along these lines, but George hadn't believed him. He figured it was what he said to all his employees and had ignored it.

George closes the file and returns to the directory. He skips down to a review from three years ago. There's a perverse pleasure in reading through these files. It provides a glimpse into how the rest of the world sees him. It reminds George of the first time he Googled himself. It didn't turn up much. A few links to Centre Capital pages, a few mentions in RFPs and a score of links inviting him to contact high school classmates.

This second review contains a similar number of 1s in the technical areas, but also several 3s in the Personal Effectiveness and Emotional Intelligence sections. George can't help but snort. Specifically a 3 for Listening, Understanding and Responding; Courage & Self Confidence and Self-Awareness and Feedback. The final section reads:

Excellent technical skills. Difficulty accepting change and assuming mantle of leadership. Needs to increase personal commitment to the overall success of the team. Needs empowerment to take more risks.

George's jaw clenches on this last word: risks. Under evaluator/coach is Frank Lewis, Vice-President Network Operations.

"See where risk-taking got you, you fucking moron."

He closes the GSTEVENS directory and opens FLEWIS. Last year's review.

Ten out of a possible twenty-one 1s.

Demonstrates excellent leadership skills. Strength in Strategic Business Visioning and Planning, with superior team motivational skills. In line for advancement. Recommend continued development in communications area to increase public profile.

Communications training. It's so obvious. That speech. Something he made up with a communications consultant. George starts to laugh. That's what killed him. A communications consultant and a speech about risk-taking.

George stands up and walks to the window. He stares out at the parkette where he sat last night. He knows he's on the edge of something. He shakes his finger in the air, taps the window lightly. He crosses back to the couch, sits down, takes a sip of coffee and opens the file for Marcia Winters. He's sorting through her personal files, archived files, e-mail threads, quarterly activity reports. There are three times as many documents in Marcia's folder as in either Frank's or George's. She's clearly fastidious about the submission of the documentation. He finds what he's looking for in a folder marked Outlook. In it are hundreds of archived agendas. And in each is the password allowing access to her calendar. George jots it down, exits and logs on to the intranet. Finds her calendar and types in the password, allowing him to input, but not delete. He flips back to two days ago to when he saw her at Dr. Schueller's. There's a two hour slot marked with an SMC. Schueller Management Consultants. He flips ahead again, looking for the same thing. Nothing. Just meetings. He flips back to the morning Frank died. April 27th. A tag at the top reminding her it's Secretary's Day. Between 10:30 and 12:00 there is nothing, simply a colored square signaling Unavailable. He considers going into her personal files and finding her home address, her license plate, but decides against it. Too creepy. He decides to take the obvious route. He books a meeting. Surprisingly, there's a slot open tomorrow morning at 9:00 am. He types in his own name, George Stevens. Underneath he writes re: Program to Develop Leadership Capabilities. He leaves his cell number.

George closes the laptop. He breathes out. He's not sure if what he's doing is right or wrong. But he knows now that he wants something more than what he's got. And it doesn't seem likely that anyone's going to walk up and give it to him. So it's time to start taking a few risks.

Chapter 10

The storm passed over an hour ago, but there are still rumblings in the distance. The air is fresh, vibrant. It was the potency of the air that drew Marcia out, something to quell the manic frequency that is thrumming under her skin. Always being awake is excruciating. Marcia often used to joke that she wished there were more hours in the day, or that she wished she didn't have to sleep at night. She knows now that this was wrong. There is something essential in those hours, something that keeps this craziness at bay. That's what she feels. Crazy. Cackling, humming to herself crazy. She doesn't even feel tired anymore. She feels like a hummingbird.

Marcia is standing on a bridge that connects the two halves of the city she lives in. The bridge spans a valley that wends its way north to the central east/west highway that tops the city. It takes drivers to the more affluent suburbs. It is the string that holds the hamlets and villages of urban sprawl like clusters of balloons. On weekdays it is a parking lot. Now, just before midnight, it is a fluid speedway, cars following the architecture of the valley. Mostly it's only cars that take the parkway, which gives it a different character than the other highways crammed with 18-wheelers. She is watching the steady stream. From her vantage point, she can see the red taillights snake their way north for several kilometers. It is quite beautiful.

She is looking out between two taut steel cables that extend from the edge of the pedestrian walkway out over the valley below. The cables are approximately eight inches apart and span the entire length of the bridge. They are held out on either side of the bridge by giant crosses that look like gallows' poles. The cables look like they should sing when the wind hits a certain frequency. Sentinels that line the road to the afterlife. It is part art installation, part suicide barrier. Prior to the installation, it was estimated that about ten to fifteen people a year took their life by jumping off the bridge, second only to the Golden Gate Bridge in San Francisco for suicides. Part of the bridge crosses over the yards of a private boy's school. Jumpers would sometimes land in the school's football field.

Marcia is imagining Frank's fall for the first time since his death. She works backwards in her mind. She allows herself to linger for a moment on the image of the crumpled body. How it must have hit. From the position of his body, he must have landed with the right side of his head and his right shoulder at the same time. The rest of the body followed. She knows that when she was looking into Frank's eyes, he was already gone. There was nothing. His skull split, his neck snapped, his bones broken and his organs separated from each other as they decelerated at different moments in time. He was gone. But lifting back from that in slow motion, she pictures him frozen a foot above the ground, eyes open, awake, five feet above the ground. Does he see her? Maybe he thinks the roses she's carrying are for him? Twenty feet above the ground. That's why his head's in the position it is – he's watching the ground approach. A hundred feet above the ground, maybe he's looking out across the lake. Maybe it hasn't registered yet, that he's about to die.

Marcia looks down at the freeway below. It's an indulgence, being able to stand here and contemplate suicide, all the while holding onto these steel cables. She can imagine herself in Frank's body, toppling out into space and falling onto the road below. When she was a girl, Marcia and her mother would visit an aunt who lived on the 16th floor of an old high rise. While her mother and the aunt were inside smoking cigarettes and drinking gin and tonics in plastic tumblers, she would go to the balcony and imagine falling. The railing was twisted metal bars, painted that Tremclad rust-paint brown. She would stand on the bottom railing and lean over from her hips. Imagine pushing herself up and over the top rail. She would be so frustrated with herself. It was stupid, she knew it, but she couldn't help feeling like a chicken. Sometimes she would simply imagine the old concrete of the balcony crumbling away and removing all choice from the matter. Here on the bridge, she feels it again, the rush of excitement that comes with allowing her mind to escape from the reality of her body, combined with the sense of shame at not having the courage to follow through with it.

She's been standing here for half an hour. It was a forty-five minute walk from her home to the bridge. The exercise and air felt good, but now it's getting cold and it isn't really a good idea to be out alone at this time of night. She'd watched the storm rage around the city from her loft windows. But the thought of her bedroom makes her want to vomit and going to an all night coffee shop seems maudlin. She thought about going into the office, but couldn't bring herself to do it. In the last few weeks, she has read, watched videos, masturbated, written in her journal, done her work, corrected the mistakes in her work, drifted off to sleep countless times and woken up nauseous and trembling each time. It is starting to make her crazy. Like solitary confinement in her own sleepless life. Tomorrow she goes to the sleep lab. Which leaves tonight.

Marcia is about to release the cables, let go of her thoughts and go home, rent a video, when she hears a voice. "Lady, you okay?" This is the second time this week she's been asked that question by a stranger. She turns and looks Frank in the eye.

"Thank you, I'm fine. Nothing to worry about with these cables." She slaps one of them, expecting it to vibrate at the contact, but feels no give. She suddenly feels very vulnerable stuck out here, halfway across this bridge. She sees a cab approaching from behind Frank and flags it. "Excuse me." As she steps into the cab, she turns to the boy with combat shorts and a mohawk and says, "I do appreciate your concern, though." She hands him a ten-dollar bill she had crumpled in her jacket pocket, then closes the door to the cab and gives the driver directions to the Summerview Centre for Sleep Therapy.

The boy with the combat pants and a mohawk uses the ten dollars to buy a loaf of bread, cheese slices, deli meat and a can of dog food at the 7-11 before returning to his girlfriend and boxer terrier in their tent below the bridge.

:)

"A couple of points above hospital, a couple below Best Western. No pool, but there is cable and air conditioning. Just don't make any long distance calls."

Marcia laughs. Liz's assessment is dead on. The room has a double bed, neatly made with a quilted, most likely acrylic, comforter. She's relieved to see that the bed is normal bed height, not like an elevated hospital bed. There are two bedside tables, one with a peach-colored lamp. There is also a long waist-high dresser along the wall. No alarm clock, no mirror. If you're lying in bed, the TV is mounted in the upper right hand corner of the room. The other corner has a video camera pointed at the bed. To the left of the bed is a stack of machines attached to rows and rows of electrodes. Marcia feels the bed. She opens one of the drawers to the bedside table. Gideon's Bible.

"Room service?"

"Sorry. There is, however, a continental breakfast included."

"I doubt I'll make it that far."

Dr. Schueller seems much more at ease in the laboratory setting. This is in contrast to her appearance, which is a caricature of the research scientist: lab coat, glasses, hair pulled back into a neat bun. Years of pseudo-pornographic advertising, sitcoms and simply growing up in the 70s trigger in Marcia a desire to seduce the doctor. It passes quickly, like the desire for chicken when driving past a KFC.

"I'm going to take a few minutes to talk through what's going to happen with you. I'll show you what all these machines do and I'll give you a bit of an understanding of what I'll be looking at. I believe in being straight with patients. Occasionally, I will not divulge certain things that might offer a risk of suggestion, as patients can sometimes create physiological symptoms if they know what the doctor is looking for."

"But I don't have any symptoms. I mean, not sleeping is the symptom."

"I think we know the cause, too. Right now, we're looking for the trigger, the link between the cause and the effect."

"I still can't believe he's dead."

Dr. Schueller is inspecting the stack of machines.

"I thought I saw him last night."

"You saw Frank?"

"I was out walking. I turned around and he was there, talking to me. It was so realistic."

Dr. Schueller continues working at her brisk pace, the lack of a pause in her work reassuring to Marcia. If she was worried, she would stop her fiddling, turn and look at her. But instead, Dr. Schueller continues her work of testing the connection of each wire to the central machine.

"One of the products of an extended period without REM sleep is that the mind will eventually start to dream while you're awake. Which is interesting, because the brain activity during wakefulness is actually remarkably similar to that of REM sleep. We call them waking dreams. Or hallucinations. For some reason, the brain needs to dream, and if the body doesn't create the conditions for it to happen, it will find other opportunities. Like that dog you saw. That's why I wanted to get you in here so quickly."

"I miss him."

There is a moment of silence while the confession hangs in the air, but Dr. Schueller has her back to Marcia. If she pauses what she is doing, it lasts only an instant before she stands and starts in on her description of the machines.

"All the more reason to take a look at what's going on. These machines are called polysomnographs. They track some of your key sleep indicators: eye movement, breath and muscle activity. Sleep patterns are remarkably similar from one human to another. While there is some variation in the lengths of the different stages, the same patterns are repeated by everyone. What I'll be looking for is the normal flow through the first four stages of Non-REM sleep, followed by the onset of REM sleep. The first four stages I will rely on brainwave readings and breathing patterns. For REM, we'll look more at eye movement and muscle activity. I say all this, fully aware that you've been waking up after the first ten minutes. I will obviously pay special attention to those ten minutes. I'll also be watching through the video feed."

"Thank you, Liz. You know, after our meeting yesterday, I felt like singing. It feels so good to have someone to talk to about all this. There's my mother, but she's my mother."

"And there are things we don't like to talk about with our mothers."

"Right." Marcia hesitates for a second before realizing that Dr. Schueller has made a joke, then laughs. There is another moment of silence. Something hangs in the air between these women. It sits on the lip of friendship and mistrust.

"I'm going to leave you some time to get settled in. Whenever you're ready to try, just push that button and a technician will come help you get set up. Please take your time. I really don't want you to feel pressured."

Dr. Schueller is at the door on her way out when Marcia stops her with a question that has been picking away at the edge of her thoughts.

"Doctor? Liz. Maybe this is a silly question. How much does that equipment let you see, in terms of content?"

"Can I plug you in and see your dreams on my monitor? No. In fact, it offers practically no insight whatsoever into the content."

"Imagine if it could."

"I have. For all my work in this field, that's one place I wouldn't want to go. My dream world's crazy enough as it is."

A pause.

"Perhaps crazy was a poor choice of words."

Both women smile. Then Dr. Elizabeth turns and leaves the room in silence. Suddenly alone in the room, Marcia sits down on the bed, bounces a bit, then lies back. She swings her feet onto the bed and puts her hands behind her head. In a strange way, this is kind of fun. Like the excitement of staying in a hotel with her parents when they would occasionally drive to Florida. She remembers lying on the bed with her father, pouring quarters into the Magic Fingers Massage box at the end of the bed, then shrieking with laughter as the bed would start to vibrate and dance under her. Those trips were like freedom, escape from the defined personalities and roles they had stepped into as a family, even at that age. How old would she have been? Eight? Ten? It was hard to differentiate the age for any memory between the ages six and twelve.

Marcia snaps her eyes open. She had begun to immediately drift in her thoughts when she laid her head back on the pillow. She blinks a few times, stretching her eyelids. She'd drifted enough for the taste of sleep to have entered her mouth. She looks up, first at the television, then at the camera. She waves quickly at the camera, then swings off the bed to get ready for the night.

:)

She spits the toothpaste out and rinses three times, before filling a glass and drinking it. She stretches her lips, looks at her teeth in the mirror, then pulls back to look at her whole face. It's difficult to imagine someone watch you sleep through a camera, through a series of lines on a graph scratching up and down. To Marcia, it feels like the worst kind of nakedness, the way she pictures a strip search under fluorescent lights.

The first time she truly fell in love was watching her boyfriend sleep. She'd had boyfriends, but this was her first love, the person she still dreams about to this day when she has love dreams. They'd been dating for a month. They made love outside under a tree. Afterwards they both fell asleep. She woke up before him. It was when she could still fall asleep with her head on a boy's shoulder, her arm across his chest. She watched him breathe in and out and saw how a person can be all ages at once. In his sleep, she could see this young man as a baby, as a boy, as a middle-aged man and as a stooped old man all at the same time. It was there, plain as day. And she fell in love with him then, when he had nothing to hide. Later, she slept with one of his friends. It made sense at the time. She was never in love like that again.

She puts on the pyjamas she brought. They are the pyjamas she brings home to wear on Christmas morning. She's been to the bathroom, brushed both teeth and hair, poured herself a glass of water. Nothing else remains to be done. The normalcy of her night time routine seems out of place in this context.

After peeing one last time, Marcia crawls into bed. Next to the bed on the night table is the book she brought, a Ruth Rendell mystery, which she regrets having chosen. It's not like she's going to the beach. She punches her pillows and pushes the button on the square box that sits on the table beside her temporary bed. Nothing happens for a minute or so. Then a broad-shouldered young man in what looks like his early twenties walks briskly through the door. He is one big smile, tousled brown hair. He, too, is wearing a lab coat.

"All set?"

"That was fast."

"I was just watching from the monitoring station."

Marcia looks up at the video camera. "That's kind of creepy."

"Don't worry, no cameras in the bathroom."

"No? I thought you might be running a voyeur website."

"Just to pay my way through med school?"

"Something like that."

"Sorry to disappoint. My name's John. I'm the lab tech here. I'll be helping Dr. Schueller with a lot of the monitoring. If you wouldn't mind lying back on the bed, I can start to get you hooked up here."

Marcia lies back on the bed. She isn't sure whether or not to shake his hand, but he busies himself by setting aside his clipboard and removing a tray of small soft circular pads attached to the ends of a bundle of transparent wires.

"Hello John. I'm Marcia."

"Yes. Thirty-six, recreational drinker, smoker, no allergies or family history of depression. Etcetera, etcetera." John waves his head at the clipboard while he begins readying the electrodes for application. "But right now, you're the person lying back and I'm the guy applying these so that we can have a looksee at what's going on. These may feel a little strange at first. And, of course, cold. Wouldn't be medicine if they weren't cold. Ready?"

John's manner puts Marcia at ease, like a small town gas attendant. The whole process takes less than five minutes. She keeps her eyes closed the whole time, while John swabs the area, applies gel, swabs again, then attaches the electrode.

"How you attach these little suckers is incredibly important. The biggest problem monitoring sleep patterns is if you don't get the connection right. Then you've gotta start all over again from scratch."

When Marcia breathes, she smells first the rubbing alcohol, closely followed by Boss cologne, then the starch of the lab coat and finally, the gentle, heavy smell of a young man's body as he works. She keeps her body relaxed, her breathing regular.

"Fantastic. We're good to go."

Marcia opens her eyes and looks into John's smiling face.

"That's it?"

"That's it. Anything I can do for you before I leave."

"No, that's fine. Thank you, John."

"Alright then. Sweet dreams."

John leaves the room. As soon as he is gone, she hears Dr. Schueller's voice piped into the empty room.

"Hello, Marcia. We're going to start monitoring now. If it's helpful, I'd like to take you through a relaxation exercise."

She can't see speakers anywhere, can't locate the source of the voice.

"Okay."

"Alright. I'm going to ask you to exhale completely. Empty your lungs of the day's tension."

Marcia breathes and realizes that she's been holding her breath, the air locked in the muscles of her chest.

"Good. Now begin to breathe slowly. When you feel your breath begin to drop in gently, automatically, I'd like to begin counting to twenty-five. Choose a point on the ceiling and let your vision unfocus. When you're ready, I want you to feel the heaviness of your eyelids and allow them to close."

Marcia closes her eyes and is immediately asleep.

:)

She is in an art gallery with its echoing stone floors and soaring arched ceilings. There is a red velvet rope that loops between three floor pedestals. This rope keeps visitors at a respectful distance from the art. Some visitors lean forward, straining to get close to the picture, as if it is a natural curiosity that needs to be placed under a microscope before it will release its secret. Others stand back, aloof but admiring, irritated by the rabble jostling to devour the art like some kind of fast food ,before discarding the wrapping on the marble floors. The room is littered with the detritus left by the voracious consumption of tourists. She is more aware of the people than the paintings. There are tour groups moving from section to section. Each tour guide holds a different color flag aloft, gathering their herd together before moving to the Baroque, or Mannerist, or the Illuminated Manuscript Pavilions.

Slowly, the clatter of heels and mumbling of various languages and squeals of children fades into white noise, like the hum of fluorescent lights, and Marcia is able to focus on what is immediately before her. A print, actually, not a painting. An Inuit print. There are four igloos depicted, and three Inuit men carrying home strings of fish. It seems out of place in this mausoleum of Western antiquity. A joke, or worse, tokenism. Not that Inuit art doesn't rival the great traditions. Not that she'd know. But certainly, not this one. As if the curator randomly selected a print to represent diversity. A nod of the head that is belittling in its indifference. Almost better to have claim to the noble outrage that comes with exclusion.

Marcia is standing, staring at the print. She feels unable to look away, although she feels nothing from the work itself. There is nothing, no revelation that comes from further examination. The work remains constant. But yet she is stock still, frozen, while the activity of the museum continues around her like time-delay video of traffic headlights whizzing along. She is distracted by the reflection. In a place like this, it is surprising to see the glare of light bouncing off the glass of the picture-frame. When she turns, looks up to find the light source, she sees nothing. There are no bright lights blasting away at the print. The frame itself, for that matter is a cheap black rim, the basic model found at any framing store. It's as if someone has stolen a famous work, and put this in its place as a joke on the fawning public, unable to tell the difference between greatness and a cheap reproduction.

As she stares at the light reflected in the print, Marcia leans in. There appears to be a smudge on the glass. She squints her eyes to see more closely, but nothing comes. "Breath slowly and count to twenty-five. Let your vision unfocus." The voice is a memory of Dr. Schueller coaching her to sleep. She begins to count. She can hear the air filling her lungs, like breathing in the bathtub with her ears underwater. At twenty-one, the image starts to dissolve. The print falls away, a layer of existence a million miles away, and the pane of glass fills the full plane of her vision. Slowly, a smoky image takes shape, as if the landscape of the glass becomes visible, like tipping it on an angle and seeing a profile start to emerge. First the eyebrows, then the cheekbones, followed by lips and hair. A man. Frank. She is about to scream when she realizes that this is a dream.

"This is a dream", she says.

Blackness.

"Yes." She hears this.

"Am I awake or asleep?"

"You are asleep."

"Where are you?"

"I'm observing you."

"Why can't I see?"

"I can only assume you are choosing not to see. Would you like to wake up now?"

"I don't know. I don't know the difference."

"I'd rather not interfere. Are you okay?"

"Yes."

With this answer, her brainwaves dip back into delta waves. Marcia's breathing becomes more regular, deeper. She passes through the first cycle of sleep, from REM back to Stage 2 for the first time since the accident. Dr. Schueller sighs, rubs her eyes. She doesn't understand. She changes tapes on the video feed and reviews the exchange. Nothing out of the ordinary leading up to it. Slight facial movements. Eye movement consistent with REM sleep. Then out of nowhere, "Am I awake or asleep?" Dr. Schueller stops the tape and rewinds to see if there's anything abnormal prior to this. Nothing. She plays it back. "Am I awake or asleep?" Dr. Schueller's response piped in through the speakers, "You are asleep." She knows the sound fills the room, like floating in an amniotic sac. No reason to turn her head. And yet, she's surprised to see the total absence of visual reaction on the patient's face. Just the next question, "Where are you?" She stops the tape, looks at the live feed. Nothing. Snoring lightly. Dr. Schueller decides to spend the rest of the night in the room with Marcia.

Dr. Schueller removes her heels outside the room and silently opens the door to the sleep room. She glides over to the bed, checks the electrodes, all the connections. She looks back at Marcia. The lighting in the room has been dropped to an ambient glow. Marcia's face seems soft and smooth. Dr. Schueller wishes she could touch her cheek, stroke some comfort into her troubled body. Instead, she crosses the room quietly and sits in a padded chair a few feet away from Marcia's bed. From this position, Dr. Schueller watches Marcia sleep through the night. At around five am Dr. Schueller's head slumps forward. She sleeps for forty-five minutes, wakes up and continues to observe Marcia.

In the booth, John keeps track of the recorded strips of electrical activity. He is now watching Dr. Schueller watch Marcia.

:)

Marcia's eyes snap open. The drone at the back of her mind shifts into focus.

"Marcia. Time to wake up. Marcia."

There's a hand on Marcia's shoulder. It isn't shaking her. It isn't doing anything except exerting a strong and steady pressure.

"Marcia. You're in the sleep lab. It's morning. It's Elizabeth Schueller speaking."

Marcia's eyes are open, tracking back and forth, scanning. There's a panic under the surface, waiting to bubble up. She isn't breathing. Everything is clamped tight.

"Marcia. It's time to wake up. Can you hear me?"

"Yes, of course I can hear you, Elizabeth. Thank you." This part is so calm, so nonchalant that it almost convinces both of them. Dr. Schueller's hand immediately relaxes and releases its grip on Marcia's shoulder. She stands swiftly, a crick in her ankle snapping quietly as she does. Physical contact is a last resort for her.

Marcia's mind is trying to grab hold of something concrete. She blinks several times, forces herself to breathe deeply and take in the room around her.

"What time is it?"

"Seven-thirty Wednesday morning. I let you sleep as long as possible. Your body desperately needs it, but I know you have work commitments to keep."

"I slept through the night?"

"Yes. Funny, isn't it?"

"You're kidding me?"

Everything is now in focus, clear. She slept through the night. That's why she feels this way, that's the source of the confusion. She smiles.

"It's actually quite common, you'd be surprised. Clients are often so relieved to be receiving treatment, that the lab provides a temporary relief from their symptoms. It is, however, only temporary."

"I'll take it."

"Of course."

She stretches muscles that have escaped the control of her brain for the first time in weeks, feels the welcome resistance.

"I feel like a million bucks."

"That's excellent."

"I feel like I just had the first sleep of my life."

The last wisps of sleep have blown away and she feels more fully present than she can remember. She feels free of the drag of sleeplessness that has weighed her down since the accident.

"I don't mean to be the voice of doom, but this feeling will wear off. You've been seriously deprived of sleep. You're not just running a deficit, you've got a rather large debt to repay. It will take more than one good sleep to get you back up to speed."

"I can't believe I slept through the night! God, it's almost embarrassing. Like when you bring your car to the mechanic to listen to the noise it's making and then it stops making it."

"Yes. Ironic, isn't it?"

The burden Marcia feels freed of is partially a freedom from the all-consuming self-absorption that has accompanied her state. In an instant, she sees Dr. Schueller not just as a doctor with the cure for her ailment, but as an individual, a person who needs caring and who has paid a price for Marcia's cure. The switch to outward concern is immediate, and so familiar to Marcia as to go unnoticed.

"Where did you sleep?"

"I caught a few winks here."

"Now that's ironic."

Dr. Schueller recognizes the switch that occurs in her patients. She understands that her patients have to create a role for her if they are to accept her help. She is adept at playing roles, sidestepping them when necessary. At the beginning of her career, she found this role-playing exhausting. By now, the shape-shifting is so fluid she is barely aware of it.

"I've often thought so. I sometimes sleep less than my clients. I do have an 8:15, so I should be on my way. Same time tonight?"

"You don't think I'm cured. My doctor seemed to think one good night's sleep was all I needed to get myself over the hump."

"He probably also believes most of his clients just need a swift kick in the pants. No, Marcia, I don't think this is over. I do think it's very positive. It shows that given the right combination of factors, you are able to sleep. But I haven't had a chance to hear the sound your car's been making yet, and I really would like to do that before I proclaim you cured."

"Okay. But you can forgive me being a little optimistic."

"I can forgive my clients almost anything."

Dr. Schueller is turning to leave.

"Thank you so much."

"I haven't done a thing."

"Still."

She leaves. The second the door closes, there's a knock.

"Yes?"

Expecting Dr. Schueller to refill the space she just left, Marcia is surprised to see John's form fill the doorframe.

"Oh."

"Breakfast. Coffee, juice, yoghurt, low fat muffin, fresh fruit and the Globe and the newspaper."

"What service."

"The 15% gratuity is included in the bill."

"I didn't think doctors were supposed to have a sense of humor."

"I'm not a doctor yet."

John turns on his heel and exits the room, leaving Marcia alone in this new world. She hadn't realized that the world had grown old and dirty without sleep. Today it's been taken down, shaken out, scrubbed clean and handed back to her, fresh as a daisy.

Marcia dresses carefully for work. She sits down to a cup of coffee and opens the paper. She reads each headline, the words crisp in her mind as she does. She eats her full breakfast, savoring the separation of morning from night, enjoying the breakfastness of the meal. When she finishes the paper, she folds it neatly into quarters and lays it on the tray. She looks at her watch. 8:42. Late.

Marcia Winters flies out the door of the Summerview Centre for Sleep Therapy and into the bustle of morning rush hour. She spots a cab, hails it and spills into the backseat. She frantically digs out her phone and dials her assistant.

"Hi Margaret? It's me. I'm on my way, be there shortly."

"Okay, you've got a 9:00 with George Stevens."

"Who?"

"I'm not sure, just says George Stevens, Program to Develop Leadership Capabilities. I'll tell him you're running a little late when he comes in."

"Okay. Thanks, Margaret." She ends the call and leans her head against the vinyl back bench, looking up through the back window of the cab. For this moment, Marcia feels fully herself once again. She smiles as she watches the skyscrapers file past, backwards into the past.

Chapter 11

George is standing in front of a bank of elevators. He is on the ground floor of the tower directly across the street from his office. It's 9:08. He is feeling very stupid. Somehow when he booked a meeting with Marcia Winters on the 34th floor of Centre Capital's south tower he forgot that he's been unable to enter an elevator for more than three weeks. It hadn't occurred to him when he had woken, showered, shaved or dressed in his work clothes for the first time in the past week and a half. In fact, George was feeling stronger than he had in a long while, as if a film of greasy doubt had been washed away by this decision to embrace the morning. Exiting the subway, he strode up the steps two at a time, anxious to meet this woman, anxious to retake control of his future. Maybe take control for the first time. He's not even sure what he's going to say when he gets there. He's been considering the recommendations in that first performance review: high-level thinking; becoming more proactive; taking on more responsibility. All of these things were driving him forward until he spun through the revolving doors and saw the bank of elevators sitting crisp and clean behind the central reception. This sight slams up against him and stops George in his tracks. Behind the twenty foot marble reception desk, a single security officer stares at him.

Everything is doubt. Not just about the elevators, about the whole thing, start to finish. "What the hell am I doing here?" bounces around the inside of his skull, punching holes through so many layers of his life. George is staring without seeing. His body is deflated, emptied out. He turns to leave the tower behind. Before he manages to put a foot in motion, he is stopped by the sound of his Blackberry ringing its antique phone ringtone. He didn't even realize he'd brought it, just part of the routine of getting ready for work. It sounds again, sharp and loud in the echoing lobby. He pulls it off the clip on his belt and answers, just to shut it up.

"Hello?"

"George Stevens?"

"Yes."

"Marcia Winters. We have a meeting booked for this morning."

"Yes."

"I just got in. Are you close?"

"Yes, very, but..."

"Yes?"

George is looking around the lobby, as if for some escape, some excuse he could grab onto. He had felt so confident, walking into this meeting as if stepping into some other life, but now the reality of his situation comes rushing back and he can think of no better excuse than the truth.

"I'm downstairs in the lobby. I'm sorry, I would have been on time. I was here, I'm actually still here, but I've been having some trouble lately. It's stupid, I'm sorry, but I've developed what seems to be a bit of a phobia about elevators. I saw a colleague fall out of a window and now I can't go up elevators. It doesn't even make sense, windows and elevators. Anyway, look, I'm sorry, I didn't mean to waste your time, but obviously I think I'm going to have to cancel. I'm sorry about that."

The phone is about six inches from his ear, his thumb is on the end button and he hears her voice.

"I'll be right down."

"Sorry?"

"I'll come down. What do you look like?"

"What do I look like?"

"What are you wearing? So I'll recognize you."

George looks down at himself. He's wearing what everyone else is wearing. His clothes are so nondescript, it's the nondescriptness that is the only dominant characteristic.

"I'll recognize you. I've seen you before."

"You have?"

"Yes."

"Okay then, I'll be right down. Don't go anywhere."

George doesn't go anywhere.

:)

"Frank Lewis. Your colleague who fell."

"Yes."

It's the first mention of anything serious. Their initial contact was hesitant and polite, Marcia emerging from the elevator, looking around expectantly, George standing across the lobby and waving, rather than walking over. Standing in line, waiting for coffee, they asked about each other's summer plans, Marcia mentioning she might go to her family cottage, George not sure what his plans are. But now Marcia has decided to get the ball rolling. She has developed the ability to confidently leave the niceties behind and transition to the real conversation without embarrassment.

"I'm very sorry."

"Thanks."

"You said you've seen me before. Where?"

"Schueller Management Consultants. You were waiting for Dr. Schueller as I was coming out. We passed by each other."

"Yes, HR has an excellent relationship with them. They've helped to groom some of our top executives."

George decides that honesty and directness are the right approach. Like playing a version of himself that might be true if he allowed it to be.

"I keep seeing Frank in my dreams. I think he's trying to tell me something."

They're sitting across from each other in a coffee shop. The table is low, knee level, and they are sitting in two large armchairs. George is sipping his coffee. He is physically relaxed now, in contrast to his rigid stance earlier in the lobby. His left arm is on the armrest, his right leg crossed over the left. He feels in complete control of the moment. Marcia is perched at the edge of her armchair. Her coffee is sitting untouched on the table. She is excited by this meeting. Increasingly, her work life seems abstract, like it's the hallucination, but this meeting feels very vivid and real.

"You booked this meeting yesterday. Why? Or rather, how? I spoke with my assistant and she said she didn't book it."

"Oh, the how's easy. I work in IT, I Just went in the back way. I guess I was a little embarrassed. I haven't been into work for a bit and I didn't want anyone to know I was calling you."

"Why not?"

"Really? Look, soft skills training is seen as a bit of a joke in my neck of the woods. It's just not something you talk about."

Marcia seizes hold of this. Everyone in HR knows that the rest of the organization looks down on them, but no one ever says it out loud.

"You see, that's it right there. People don't understand that as we move through our lives, we have to adapt to reflect our developing reality. As you advance, leadership doesn't become part of your job, it is your job."

George accepts the offering smoothly.

"I think I'd like to do something about that. I've always possessed excellent technical skills, but lacked the polish to take the next step. I booked the meeting with you because I think I might be ready to take that step now. And I was hoping maybe you could offer me some coaching."

At the end of this, George smiles slightly, raises his cup with both hands and takes a delicate sip. Amazing how easy the lie came, how quickly it became true once uttered.

"Absolutely. I looked in your file and you have a considerable stockpile of training credits available to you. We can use this meeting to assess your needs and when you return to work I can put together a training program to meet your needs."

"Oh."

"Were you hoping for something else?"

"Well, actually I... This is, look, I don't know what I'm doing. I thought maybe you'd be the coach."

"Me? Oh, well, no. There are people that are far more qualified than me. I'm usually just the person that sets it up."

George is on the knife's edge of honesty. A degree to either side and he knows he could spin out of control.

"This morning I felt as good as I have in awhile. I got dressed, I had somewhere to go, I made a decision to make myself better. I haven't felt that in a long long time. But when I got here I froze. Everything came flooding back. Seeing Frank burst out that window and that sick feeling in the pit of my stomach. I don't know, I just felt dumb. It took everything I could muster just to get here. I think this is as much as I can manage. I don't think I want to work with anyone else. You're very kind to have come down to meet me here, but I think I need to admit my limitations and move on."

"But a minute ago/"

George had begun to push himself out of the armchair, but sits back when he sees the look of genuine concern on Marcia's face. He is losing perspective on why he came here. The words are coming out of his mouth now and he is unsure if he's in control of them or not.

"Look, Frank was always trying to coach me. He was always pushing me to risk, to move beyond my comfort zone. That's part of why I'm here. You know he died trying to prove that point to me? He wanted to prove to me that the windows in skyscrapers are shatterproof. He said the only way to know is by trying. All this because we saw a couple having sex against a window and I said I'd be scared to try it. How stupid is that? And I think, the least I can do is try to live up to the potential he saw in me. But it's the elevator. I just can't do it. I can't confront the reality of all those floors, those cables taking me past floor after floor of cubicles and offices and computer monitors."

119

Marcia has lowered her eyes while George says this. When she brings her chin back up, her eyes are rimmed with tears, but the lines of her cheekbones and jaw are set and confident. "I didn't know how it happened. Nobody told me."

"So you knew him?"

She nods.

A wave of self-hatred hits George, realizing the self-absorption that brought him here, as if he's the only one that was affected by Frank's death, as if it were all about him.

"I'm sorry. I didn't realize. That must sound very stupid to you. The whole thing, I mean the whole thing is just so stupid. I always thought that there was a depth to life, to existence. And then something like that, so colossally stupid happens, and you can't help thinking that it's all stupid, that this whole drama we're swept up in is just so unbelievably simple and stupid. I'm sorry, Marcia. I didn't mean to drag you into this mess of mine."

Marcia is staring out the window at someone with a dolly overloaded with banker's boxes, trying to pull it up the ramp off the road and onto the sidewalk. She speaks without looking away from the scene.

"Have you ever noticed that we call optimists naïve and pessimists realistic? I think it's to protect ourselves against the terrible devastation of disappointment when things don't go the way we want them to. Hope is so tender and delicate that we grow tough shells to hide it. But it is the strongest thing we possess. I don't think it's all stupid. I believe that everything happens for a reason."

A man has stopped to help push the dolly onto the sidewalk. The first man mouths thank you and the two go their separate ways. Marcia returns to the coffee shop and makes eye contact with George who has been looking at her all along.

"You believe that?"

She nods her head, and they smile briefly at each other, faces unclouded and open. They are each surprised at themselves, surprised at the force of their emotion as they peel back the surface and reveal one of their fundamental beliefs, entirely by accident. Neither had meant to give that much away. They both look away again and allow their thoughts to flow. The silence sits for a minute, before composure sweeps back in to fill the moment, like silt oozing into a hollow scooped out of the sand.

"Would you like to talk about it? With me?"

Marcia is leaning forward, face open, unavoidable.

"What do you mean?"

"I mean, maybe it would help to talk. Not professionally, I'm no Liz Schueller, but I did know Frank. I knew him quite well. Sometimes it helps to talk to someone who knew him."

"Yes, I think I'd like that. A chance to talk about it. Dr. Schueller is very helpful, but it's not the same. I'd appreciate that."

Marcia smoothes back her hair and her smile transforms into the bright professional smile she brings to work.

"How about lunch tomorrow? I have an hour at noon."

"Okay. Sure. Thank you."

"Meet you downstairs in the lobby?"

George laughs in spite of himself. "Yeah, that would be best." Their eyes meet for one last real glimpse, a confirmation of what they've agreed upon, and then they break.

"See you tomorrow."

George has to stop himself from moving to hug her, and sticks his hand out abruptly. They miss, her fingers bunched up, her palm never getting in the action. "See you tomorrow." He watches her walk out of the coffee shop, turn right. For a moment they make eye contact as she looks back through the glass pane with the giant logo on the outside. She smiles briefly, then exits the tower. George watches her light a cigarette as soon as she gets outside the revolving doors. "She smokes."

He doesn't see her turn the corner into the same alley, lean against the same wall she leaned against the first time she felt dizzy walking back to the office after lunch with her mother. He doesn't see her shoulders drop and convulse, her cigarette hand go up to cover her face, the smoke stinging her eyes. He doesn't hear the choked moan, "Oh God", escape her tight chest. He doesn't know Marcia was at the bottom of Frank's trajectory, that she and George are connected by the fall, that they are held together and pulled apart by those four seconds of freefall. For the moment, he is simply lost in the delirious complexity of the moment. He smiles slightly, looks down at her untouched coffee. He is shocked with himself. Shocked at the lie, shocked at the ease with which it all unfolded, shocked how quickly it came apart and the truth came tumbling out, truth he was unsure of until he heard himself speaking the words, unsure whether his display of vulnerability was genuine or a ploy to get her to commit to him. He picks up a discarded newspaper and sits back in the chair to read. He stops for a moment and smiles. "I've got a date." He opens the paper and scans stories of government misspending, AIDS pandemics, alleged police corruption, American aggression overseas, China/Taiwan relations, battles over where to discard the city's garbage, a weekend nightclub shooting ...

:)

"I have to say that this is very exciting. I imagine you eat in places like this all the time. Power-brokering and all that. But for me it's very exciting. Oh!" Sybil is startled by the waiter removing the napkin from her water glass and placing it on her lap. "I'm sorry, I didn't see you there! Shame on you, sneaking up on me like that!" She smiles a little long at the handsome young waiter.

Marcia's stomach churns slightly. She is still digesting the morning. Remnants of her conversation with George Stevens, and an odd moment where she feels as if she is watching herself at the sleep lab talking with John, Dr. Schueller's research assistant, but slightly distanced, as if she were watching herself through the camera installed in the room. She forces herself back into the present and focuses on the waiter.

"...with a red wine reduction. Would you care for anything to drink to start with?"

"Oh, I don't know if I should. I'm seeing Mrs. Swift tonight, I wouldn't want alcohol on my breath! Although I dare say she gets into the sherry herself some days. Oh, why not, I'll have a gin and tonic. It's almost patio season. See? I'm even wearing white."

"A bottle of San Pellegrino. Thank you." The waiter nods, smiles, glides away. Marcia tries not to wince, tries not to make her mother feel self-conscious, outdated, overly-colorful, ashamed.

"I've embarrassed you, haven't I?"

"Of course not."

"I'm sorry, I'm just a little excited. I've said that, haven't I? It's just not every day that my workaholic daughter calls me up to invite me out to some fancy restaurant for lunch. It's exciting." Sybil is beaming. Composed and beaming, not asking, but waiting expectantly nonetheless.

"We had lunch last week."

"But at that little diner you keep me hidden away at. Not like this."

"I don't actually eat in places like this very often at all. My job's not quite as glamorous as you'd think. Mostly I sit at my desk, read files, talk on the phone, send e-mails and sit through presentations. I don't really deal with clients, so I don't really have an expense account. I mean, in a sense, my clients are the employees. And whether they're internal or external, I still treat them with/"

"Honey, I don't care. I was just going on, you know how I am. I'm just very happy to be here with you."

Marcia shifts slightly in her seat, pulls her skirt down a bit. Her mother can be very intense. When she speaks directly, she speaks the truth and she speaks it from a place of compassion, which makes it both difficult to avoid and deeply uncomfortable for the person it is directed at. She hides this in order to get by in the world because most people avoid truth-tellers. She knows this about herself and she knows this about the world. But she can't hide from the people she loves. And she loves her daughter more than she loves herself.

"I wanted to celebrate. And when I tried to think who I wanted to celebrate with, I thought of you."

"Celebrate what?" Sybil is nearly vibrating across from her. "Oh!" She jumps a second time as the waiter places a gin and tonic in front of her. He places a glass of ice with lime in front of Marcia, unscrews the cap on the bottle and pours a fizzing glass of water for her. He wraps a napkin around the neck of the bottle, places it on the table with two hands and steps back.

"Have you had a chance to decide what you'd like to order?"

"Oh, no, I'm sorry, we haven't even looked."

"A few more minutes, then?"

"Yes, thank you." This interruption has given Marcia a moment to collect herself and think through what she wants to say. "I know this doesn't necessarily mean anything, but I had my first full night's sleep in over three weeks last night."

"That's wonderful, honey!" She actually claps her hands together. "I've been so worried about you. I've wanted to call you every day, but I figured your mother calling every day to see if you were sleeping probably wouldn't help you sleep."

Immediately, Marcia is irritated by her mother's over-reaction, over-enthusiasm, her cloying desire to infiltrate every nook and cranny of her daughter's life. And deeply pleased by the unadulterated affection that pours off of her. As usual, Marcia's response is to be muted, rational, in the face of this ebullience.

"It took finally going into a sleep facility. As soon as I got there I must have relaxed. The doctor who is looking after me thinks it's just an exception, that we haven't discovered the underlying problem, but I'm optimistic. I think sometimes people just get better. My brain couldn't process seeing Frank die, so it kept me awake until it worked through what it needed to work through."

"Frank?"

Marcia glances down at the table, bites the skin inside her upper lip. She immediately regrets letting that slip. Amazed at the speed with which her mother locked onto the familiarity of her tone, the use of his first name. She knows she looks shifty. A caricature of shifty. She looks up at her mother and locks eyes. "We were lovers."

There's no challenge in this, simply the truth because in that moment there was no other option. Sybil understands this way of speaking, knows to jump straight in. While most people will talk around something, pretend not to understand, will the situation to be different, Sybil trusts what she sees and engages the situation head on.

"Oh no. Oh you poor thing. I bet you haven't told a soul, have you?" Any other question, she could have handled, but this cuts to the heart of her loneliness and Marcia feels herself beginning to dissolve. Her eyes fill with tears and the corner of her lips start to pull down as she clenches her jaw to contain the emotion.

Sybil reaches her hand across the table and holds Marcia's hand in hers. "It's okay, honey, I know we're in a restaurant. You don't have to do this now." Marcia looks up from her lap. "We're here to celebrate." Marcia nods weakly, gratefully. She uses both hands to wipe her eyes dry without smudging the make-up. Sybil squeezes Marcia's hand gently, brushes her hand softly with the back of her index finger and pulls back to her side of the table. "So let's celebrate. To sleep." Sybil raises her gin tonic in invitation.

"To sleep." Marcia laughs and clinks glasses with her mother. "Perchance to dream." Marcia pauses for a second, her face long, her glass suspended in air.

"It's bad luck not to drink after a toast, dear."

"Sorry. Yes, I was just thinking."

"I know you were, dear. It's still bad luck. I'm thinking about having the special. How about you, have you decided? I imagine our young man will be back soon."

"Yes, I think I'll have a steak. I never have steak." Marcia rubs her hands together, then closes the large leather-covered menu.

"I do think you should think about a little time off, though. If for no other reason than that you've earned it. I was thinking you might want to take a week up at the cottage. It's so beautiful this time of year. The water's starting to warm, the trees are exploding with that fluorescent green they get at the beginning of the summer. I could even come up for a bit if you'd like, take care of my daughter for a bit. I'd like that." Marcia opens her mouth, but Sybil overrides the objection. "I don't care what you decide, I'm just making a suggestion, do what you want. I know I can't tell you anything." Sybil turns and smiles at the waiter who has materialized at the side of the table.

"Have you had a chance to decide?" Marcia always mistrusts waiters in fine-dining restaurants. She can never tell if they're being snide or simply polite.

"I'd like the striploin medium-rare with garlic-mashed and my mother will be having the special."

"Very good. Would you care for some wine with your meal?"

"Absolutely. A bottle of whatever you have for a house cabernet sauvignon." Marcia collects the menus from the table and hands them to the waiter. "Thank you." She smiles confidently, starting to feel better. Simple things help Marcia manage her world, help give her a sense of control, like pulling back her hair, successfully hailing a cab, or ordering lunch for her mother. In fact, she feels even stronger than she did before for having been honest. Difficult, but as is so often the case, letting a little of the steam escape leaves her with a sense of calm. There is a quiet shift in the energy. The room is filled with mumbling, occasional bursts of laughter and the background sound of pots clanging and knives zinging. Marcia releases the breath she had been holding like a bubble in her chest.

"Well, isn't this something? My daughter." Sybil smiles broadly and holds out her arms as if to suggest there is something in the setting that Marcia should be taking credit for.

"My mother."

Both women smile and ease into a conversation steeped in the safety of their shared history. They are as essential to each other's happiness as clouds are to rain.

:)

He feels his temples throbbing as his feet thump down on the cement trail. His mind has grabbed onto a rhythm that fills the cavity of his mind. Three steps per exhalation, one two, three and three steps on the inhalation, one two, three. In this manner the breath and therefore the exhaustion remain constant, manageable. At the outset he'd attempted to keep his steps light, springing up again before the full weight of his body's trajectory made contact with the cement. But now after what seems like hours of running, the full weight of George's frame, heavy from years of sitting in front of monitors, comes crashing down evenly on each burning footpad. But he keeps his eyes set ahead, level on the trail as it snakes over bends and around trees. This eye contact with the future as it rolls up and under his feet, keeps George's mind separate from the increased pain in his lungs and feet.

When he comes to the beginning of the loop, he lets his arms sag, his head drop, his legs start to slow to a walking pace. Eventually he ends up bent over, hands on knees, the sweat flowing freely, dripping off his hair and forehead, running in rivulets down his chest. In contrast to the steady pattern he'd set while running, his breath now rips in and out in huge gasps, raging to replace the oxygen that's been sucked from the reserves in George's bloodstream. Instinctively, he looks down at his right wrist to check his watch, looking to quantify the experience. And remembers that he'd removed it before starting. That, in fact, had been the point of the whole exercise. To bludgeon his experience of time into oblivion by pushing his body, the cipher through which time flows, into auto-pilot, a state where his brain is too busy to assimilate and process experience. Too busy just trying to keep up.

George tilts his head back and gives a weak laugh. There is a euphoria flowing through him, an aliveness that comes in part from the blood and oxygen and adrenaline that is pumping through his veins for the first time in years, and in part from a feeling of freedom and escape from the parameters of his mind. When he goes home later, he falls into a deeper sleep than he has experienced for years, only dreaming in the morning hours.

:)

Heath

"Thank you for coming in, George. I've been going over things in my mind for the past several weeks and there are just a few things that I'm still not clear on. I'm hoping you can help me understand."

George is sweating slightly. He is sitting on an institutional metal chair with coarse black fabric on the seat. His hands are on the green wooden table in front of him, one hand nervously spinning the engineer's ring on his pinkie finger. Detective Mauritz is standing next to a window that is clearly a two-way mirror. There is a manila folder sitting on the table between them.

"What do you know about office tower windows, George?"

"I'm sorry?"

"You know, office tower windows? Like the one your buddy Frank flew out of a couple weeks ago. What do you know about those kinds of windows? Specifically, their installation?"

George is sweating heavily now. He knows that he looks nervous and that looking nervous makes him look guilty, which makes him even more nervous. He tries to answer calmly, but can only stammer. "Uhhh, uh, what do you, I mean, I dunno, uuhh."

"Let me help you out. We did some forensics on your computer and found these." Detective Mauritz pulls out a sheet of paper and shows it to George.

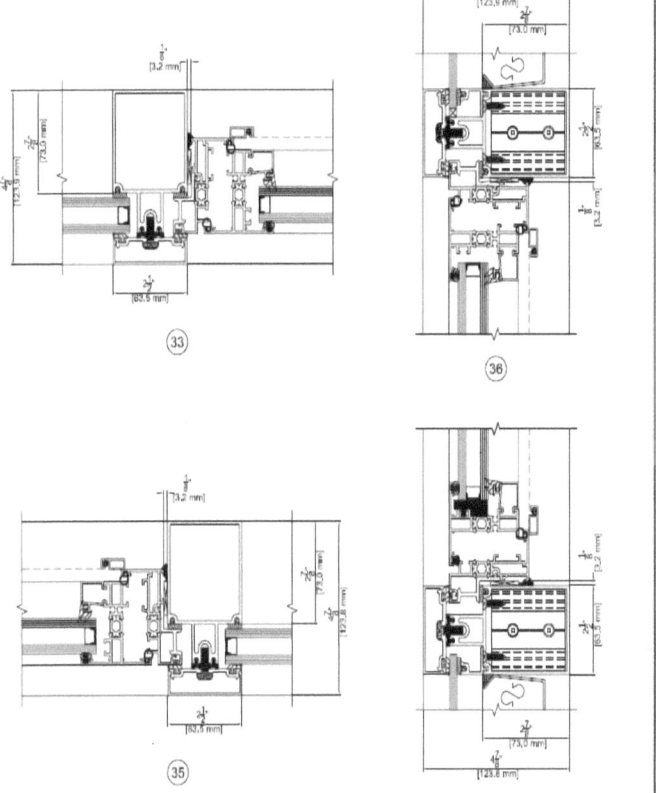

"These make any sense to you?"

George can hear a distant pounding, but can't tell if it's the blood in his ears, or something from outside. He leans in to look at the paper.

"What is it?"

"That's what I wondered when I first saw it, too." The thumping, or whatever it is, is getting louder. George wonders if Detective Mauritz can hear it, or if it's just in George's head. "These are diagrams of the silicone casings used to install high-pressure office windows. Now, when I came across these, I had to ask myself what these diagrams were doing on your computer. Do you have an answer for that, George?"

The sound is almost deafening now, a thick, heavy thumping that George can feel in his body. There's a higher, almost whining sound underneath the thumps and George is unable to form his thoughts clearly. He knows he needs to answer Detective Mauritz' questions, but he can't think straight.

"Can't you hear that?" he yells.

"Hear what, George?"

George turns his head slowly to look at the two-way mirror and through it, he sees Frank, pounding steadily on the glass. The walls are shaking with the force of the blows. George turns to Detective Mauritz. "I thought those two-way mirrors were supposed to be soundproof?"

"Why? What do you hear, George?"

George turns back to the mirror, back to Frank who is still pounding and screaming.

"He says he sees me."

Chapter 12

She's blindfolded. She can just barely see light through the gauzy weave of the fabric. Behind her she can hear the voices of all the other kids. They want her to fall back. She's the birthday girl and her mother has invited all the children from the cottages around the lake. There's a Safeway cake with blue icing. Now they're playing games. It's her thirteenth birthday and she's embarrassed by these kids' games. But her mother is looking at her with her neediness exposed and the other children are playing along. There are kids of all ages. One by one, they pick a slip of paper from a red plastic drinking cup. Each slip has a different game written on it: "Twister; Truth or Dare; Blind Man's Bluff". Marcia reaches in and pulls out a slip. She unfolds it and reads, "Trust Exercise"

A voice filters through. "I've been here. This happened. You're dreaming."

But Marcia is thirteen and blindfolded and nothing can stop the story from moving forward.

"Don't. They don't catch you. This is a dream. You can stop it."

She can't stop it. She sucks in a breath, holds it, rolls her weight onto her heels, holds her arms out and gives over to gravity, feels the lurch, arms windmilling. And then she's falling and it feels so bad. She screams.

It happened in a flash. Patient still for 15 minutes. Minimal visual movement. Normal readings. Breathing beginning to slow, becoming regular, brainwaves starting to lengthen. Patient begins to move through traditional brain wave patterns:

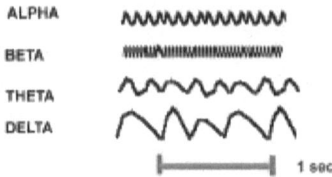

As the patient approaches Stage 2 NREM sleep, however, the brainwaves make a jump to slower delta waves (2 HZ or lower). This sudden jump, known as a K-complex, or sleep spindle, looks like this:

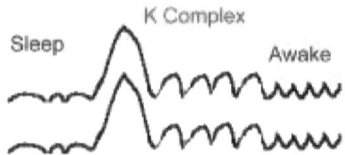

At that exact moment, when Marcia's brain is shifting gears, she sits straight up in bed and begins to scream. John continues to monitor. Dr. Schueller rushes from the monitoring station. It requires three steps, a door opening, seven steps, a swipecard and another door to open. As she enters the room she sees Marcia, ripping electrodes off of her scalp with one hand while swinging her left leg across her body.

"Marcia!"

She falls out of bed onto her knees. Dr. Schueller rushes to catch the polysomnograph before it hits the ground, dragged by the few electrodes still clutched in Marcia's hand. She doesn't get there in time. The state of the art 50-channel AS40 amplifier system is pulled off the IT9 mobile rack cart and lands on the ground with a plastic crunch. One corner of the durable plastic shell collapses inwards, sending a long fissure up towards the electrode receivers. Dr. Schueller races to the machine, picks it up delicately and replaces it on the bottom rack of the cart. She stops when she hears the sound of Marcia vomiting.

The door opens and Dr. Schueller sees John hurry past the bed and into the adjoining washroom. He knocks on the slightly open door and calls out in a moment of silence.

"Are you decent?"

Dr. Schueller can't help but feel the sting of the question.

:)

"Where are the rest of the readings?"

Dr. Schueller is in the observation booth with John. She sent Marcia home thirty minutes ago, while she and John began to sort through the damage. Marcia had apologized endlessly for the damage to the equipment, to which Dr. Schueller had smiled and laughed and made jokes about doctors being the most insured people on the planet, and insurance only being a good deal if you use it. Now she has turned on John.

"The last thirty seconds, where are those readings?"

John is sitting at a monitor, right-clicking files and reading the time-stamp.

"They get sent in batches. When the unit hit the ground, the last batch must have been interrupted. The readings stop just before that."

"What good is that? I need the readings from when it happened."

She is standing with her shoulders square to John, her full attention on him.

"The whole reason for having a sleep lab is to monitor people's sleep. I thought they trained you in this stuff at school. Don't they teach you how to use the equipment?"

John knows not to react. He has felt the brunt of Dr. Schueller's anger before. The danger being that she doesn't recognize the anger, sees only the object of her scrutiny and focuses on finding the error. Her intelligence narrows and sharpens into a dentist's drill and she will go at an issue until the abscess has been removed. He's seen her reduce many interns to tears. He knows not to defend himself, to simply weather it until it passes.

"Once I get the unit fixed, I'll hook it up again and try re-sending the batches."

"That could take weeks. What am I supposed to do until then? What would you like me to tell Marcia?"

He tries to keep his voice positive, helpful, as if unaware of the impending attack.

"We do have an older unit. We could try again. We know where the problem is now, when she wakes up. If we're watching for it, we should be able to capture it."

"Great. Why don't you tell my client that? That we missed capturing the results, that we have to put her through that again? Her number's in the file. Let me know when you've set something up."

Dr. Martin turns her back to John and walks to the door. She stops just before leaving, and without turning around says, "You know when I went school, failure actually meant something." And leaves.

John is left by himself, heart pounding and angry. Even when she's so blatantly wrong, he ends up feeling nine years old, reprimanded, sent to his room. He turns to the monitor in front of him and starts going through the recordings again.

:)

She slides her hand past the band of her cotton briefs. Closes her eyes, one hand up her shirt to play with her nipple. Feels the hot breath on her neck, the fingers on the soft skin at the base of her belly. Arches her back slightly, imagines kissing, full and soft lipped. Opening the white robe, pulling back the silk blouse to reveal a dark strong breast. The other hand reaching back, caressing his hard penis. Her fingers inside, then back out. Breathing's getting faster, and her hips are following the rhythm. Knots her fingers through the coarse hair, whispers her name, feels the cold hard vinyl against her back. Stomach in and out, rocking now, powerful surges are coming. She opens her eyes, looking for it, looking for the camera in the corner. Feels it coming through her, thrusting her hips forward, putting it on the display for everyone to see.

The pressure releases and Marcia drops her hips back gently onto the bed. She lies staring at the ceiling,

sweating slightly. Thinks maybe it will help her sleep
tonight. Surprised at the intensity of the fantasy. She
rolls over and sits up on the edge of her bed. She
smoothes her hair back and laughs quietly. She'll have to
do her best not to smile when she sees Dr. Schueller and
John in their lab coats. She looks at the time on the
birch veneer and aluminum alarm clock at her bedside.
11:12. On a normal night, this is when she would start
getting ready for bed, after the 10:00 police drama. She's
already gone through the ritual tonight, though, at the
sleep lab. She'd felt like a complete failure when they sent
her home. She'd failed at sleeping, destroyed their
equipment.

The phone rings, startling Marcia. It feels as if she
hasn't heard her home phone ring in months. She's been
in a bubble and the only people that call use her cell.

She answers, a question, "Hello?"

"Hi, Marcia? It's John from the Summerview Facility
for Sleep Therapy."

She feels an immediate flush, irrationally looks to the
corner, as if she was still on camera, as if he had seen
what she'd just done She dismisses the thought, shakes
her head, steadies her voice.

"Oh, yes, John. Hello. Are you calling to bill me for
trashing your lab?"

John laughs. "Not at all. In fact it's me that should
apologize. We need to capture some more data. I know
it's late, but I guessed you'd still be up."

"Very funny."

"I'm calling to invite you to come back in, if you'd be
willing. We have an older unit available and a pretty good
idea of what we're looking for now. If you'd be willing to
come back in, I think we can get what we're looking for.
We had some real promising results that last time, but
unfortunately some of the data got lost when the unit hit
the ground."

Marcia pauses, looks around her loft. There is
nothing that could keep her here, the prospect of another
night yawning before her uniformly unappealing. Every
inch has been pawed over in the past few weeks. There is
nothing fresh left in her life until she finds sleep again.

Heath

"I'll be there in half an hour."

Chapter 13

"The thing is that I'm starting to think that he might have been right. I never really had anything but contempt for him. We hung out but not really, mostly just because we were friends in grade school. But we were in totally different realities, him with his leadership skills, his 7 habits, his risk-taking. I mean, honestly? I couldn't stand him. He'd roll out that stupid speech about risk-taking and I could just picture him, scuff-kneed on the playground, crying 'cause some kid had finally stood up to him and punched back. He learned how to do it. How to smile, do the right things, say the right things, but he was still the same suck, the same bully. Just this time it's your bonus instead of your lunch money and nobody punched back 'cause he had the corporation standing behind him like some big brother ready to pound you if you talk back."

"Big brother?"

This time George is standing. His entire body is stiff from jogging. Even climbing the flight of stairs up to the Schueller offices had been an arduous and painful process. He's staring out the floor to ceiling semi-circle of a window in Dr. Schueller's office. She is seated, hands folded around her knees.

"Jesus. You know what I mean, don't get all George Orwell on me. I'm just saying I saw through him."

"And what did you see when you saw through him?"

George snorts.

"Frank was a bully. He wasn't smart, or nice, or interesting. He was stupid and he bullied people his whole life. He just got good at hiding it. The corporate world's full of people like him. It catches up to them in the end, just like Frank."

"How did it catch up to Frank?"

"See, that's just it, that's the irony. It's what killed him in the end. Always pushing everyone around. It was his speech on risk-taking that put him out that window. Genius. I guess if you're gonna roll the dice, you gotta expect it to come up craps sometimes. But, I mean, who does that? Throws himself against a window to make a point?"

Dr. Schueller, stops, cocks her head slightly to the right, like a bird.

"He delivered a speech on risk-taking before he died?"

George laughs.

"Him going through the window was the punch line. Couldn't have scripted it any better. And I think, "You know, maybe it was me." Maybe I was that thorn in his side, because I was the only one that didn't buy in. I'm the only one that wasn't whipped into a frenzy by his motivational speeches. Maybe I pushed him to that extreme."

"Blame is natural, but useless."

"Bullshit. Tell that to the Nazi hunters."

"That's justice, it's different."

"No, that's punishment. And some people deserve to be punished."

"Do you think you need to be punished?"

"Sometimes you're really interesting to talk to and sometimes you sound like one of the cops on CSI."

"I'm just following the logic of the conversation."

"I'm just saying that sometimes people are to blame for things. We console ourselves by saying that things were meant to be, or that everyone is ultimately responsible for themselves, that the universe is unfolding as it should. But maybe it's not. And maybe sometimes people are to blame and sometimes those people are us."

"Are you saying you blame yourself for Frank's death?"

"Absolutely not. Guy's an idiot. Who the fuck does that? Throws himself against a window, thirty-eight floors up? I'm just saying that maybe he was right about me. That maybe I do need to take more risks. And maybe if he'd known he was right, he wouldn't have pushed it so far. You know something can be my fault, but that doesn't mean I blame myself. I didn't push him out that window."

There's a long silence, where both George and Elizabeth decide how to deal with that statement, left floating in the air between them.

Suddenly, Dr. Schueller laughs. "No, George, it's not like you pushed him out that window."

George exhales against the window and traces his finger through the patch of fog his breath creates.

"He was going on about the guy in movies who gets left behind, the guy who's too scared to make a decision. He was daring me to throw myself against that window. In which case I'd be dead and you can bet your ass, he wouldn't be all messed up about it. He'd take two days off work, sleep with one of the women he's always having affairs with and be back at work the following Monday."

"Sounds like you made the right decision."

"Yeah, but if doing nothing is the right decision, then you can only ever know after the fact. Doing nothing can stop you from going somewhere bad, but it can't take you somewhere good. Only a conscious decision can take you somewhere good. So, in that he was right. Dead on. Sure, you run the risk of making some dumb decisions, but in the end, what's the alternative?"

"Seize the day."

"See, you're basically just repeating back to me what I just said and I still want to roll my eyes."

"George, what is it you're trying to say?"

George turns to Dr. Schueller. He throws out the next bit as if it had just occurred to him, as if it was the final approach as the conversation begins its descent.

"I think I met a client of yours. Marcia Winters?"

George's face reveals nothing. Nor does Dr. Schueller's. It is the quietest of moments.

"I passed her coming out of my session last week as she was going in with you."

Still there is nothing but a delicate silence.

"I've asked her to help develop my leadership skills."

The corners of Elizabeth Schueller's mouth are slightly raised. She blinks twice, three times.

"I'm meeting her for lunch in a few minutes."

Outside a seagull is catching an air current. It drifts softly up past the window behind George's head. As it reaches the top of the current, it's torso starts to lazily turn, almost in slow-motion like a roller-coaster cresting a rise, until it has rotated a full hundred and eighty degrees and begins to plummet down along the slick slope of cooler air.

"In fact, I should get going. She's meeting me in the lobby at noon." George laughs. He starts to cross the office.

"George?"

He stops. "Yes, Dr. Schueller?"

George waits.

"You can book your next session on the way out."

"Okay." Turns again, his hand on the doorknob.

"Oh, and George?"

"Yes?"

"It would be helpful to me if you could bring in a family photo album."

"You're kidding, right?"

"I'd love to see a picture of your mom."

Dr. Schueller stands, her back to George. Crosses to her desk. Wiggles her mouse to awaken her computer. Looks up.

"Thank you, George. I'll see you next week."

George opens the door, silently, walks out with slightly hunched shoulders, the victory of the moment suddenly evaporated like the patch of breath on Dr. Schueller's window, leaving only the smudge where his finger traced a line from the top of an office tower to the ground below.

:)

George has been gone fifteen minutes now. Dr. Schueller is sitting in her chair staring out the window where the seagull was previously. She had a call, but decided to cancel it. She's wondering if George is dangerous. Wondering if she miscalculated. Wondering if she should talk to Marcia.

She's trying to remember the speech she and Frank had worked out. She's trying to remember the words, how it ended. All she can remember is a single phrase. "Risk-taking means jumping and having the faith that if you don't land on solid ground, then you will learn to fly." It was something she'd come across on a quotations website and filed for future reference. When Frank had been working on accessing the leader within, she'd offered it to him. And he'd taken it. She's often felt uneasy when clients accept her offerings too readily, without any filter of analysis, without any filter of self. Frank had been like that, wolfing it down whole. She's wondering if it was ego, watching a client take her words so quickly, so wholesale, looking at her with absolute credulity.

But mostly, staring out the window at the skyscrapers in the distance, she's wondering if it was her fault.

Chapter 14

"That's Boba-fet."

"The bounty hunter?"

"Absolutely. Coolest character in the whole trilogy."

"You mean sexta-something."

"As far as I'm concerned, the other ones don't exist. Not after Jar Jar Binks."

She is wrapped in one of his sheets. A thin, white sheet with embroidered trim, obviously a gift from a mother, an aunt, or something purchased by a young man trying to emulate what he's grown up with. He is lying next to her. He is wearing a blue golf-shirt and boxer shorts. After making love, he grabbed the top shirt out of his dresser drawers in an attempt to cover his belly. These shirts are generally left untouched, the daily-wear clothes never making it out of the laundry basket. He's still young, the skin is smooth, but his belly is soft and drips past the elastic of the shorts. She is firm and strong from Pilates and the occasional hot-yoga session. They are both lying back in his bed, in his apartment, on his pillows, at four o'clock in the afternoon, looking at the shelf that runs the entire perimeter of his bedroom, about two feet from the ceiling.

"And what about that box?"

"Hockey cards. O-Pee-Chee. '78-79 season through to '85-86. Missed the Gretzky rookie, but got Mario. Not mint condition, but complete sets and at least I didn't play that game where you flicked them at the other guy's cards. All those ones have chewed up corners."

"Those've gotta be worth a fortune."

"Yeah, put all the things on these shelves on e-Bay and I could pay off this mortgage pretty quick."

George had felt almost drunk at lunch, like the time he traveled to England and met women in bars, drawn in by his exotic Canadian accent. They had talked well past a normal lunch, past when all the other diners had left the restaurant. Eventually, the waiters had asked to settle the bill, asked if they'd mind moving tables, so they could set up for the dinner rush. Standing on the street, it was clear they had nowhere to go. So he'd asked. "Did you want to come back to my place for a coffee or something?" And she'd said, "Yes, I'd like that. I feel like I've got nowhere to go." And that had been that. They were kissing by the time the door to his apartment was closed and in bed five minutes later.

"You always live here all alone?"

"I used to have a roommate, helped pay the bills, but he got married. You? Live alone?"

"Yeah."

The silence settles into honesty.

"I don't want you to think this is normal for me", she says.

"What do you mean?"

"Three weeks ago I went home from work early for the first time ever I think. Tried to have a nap. Now I'm here at your place in the middle of the afternoon. I'm supposed to be on a conference call."

"They'll never know you weren't on it. Just say you had it on mute and/"

"I was supposed to be chairing it."

"Oh. Yeah, that's a bit more of a problem."

They both laugh, enjoying the conspiracy of playing hooky, this room like their secret fort. There's a silence.

"I haven't slept since it happened. Since Frank fell."

"You haven't slept in three weeks?"

"I saw him land. I was rushing to meet him and I was on the street and I saw him land."

"Oh my God." George pulls the duvet over his boxer shorts. A sense of propriety in the face of grief. "Ah, fuck! Jesus fucking Christ, you've got to be kidding me." He's out of bed finding his pants on the floor, pulling them on awkwardly, both feet in one leg, then off, then back on. "You're fucking kidding me!" Half hopping, half walking down the hall as he tries to do up the button.

"George, what are you doing?" She feels stunned, not sure whether to be concerned, to be caring and open because of George's situation, or angry, slapped after opening herself up. She keeps her voice neutral until she can understand more. "What's the matter?"

He's in the kitchen now, the fridge door slams. In the hallway. "Fuck!" More pacing. Marcia is in bed. The sheet clutched in both hands beneath her chin. She is humiliated now, naked and blinking back tears. She can hear him outside the bedroom door. His belt scraping as he slides down the wall, ending up slumped, head on knees.

"George? You're freaking me out."

"I don't get away with anything. You know, some people do crazy shit and nothing sticks to them. Nothing. They walk away, back to their family, back to their bosses, doesn't matter if they just sold uranium to the North Koreans, they just keep going like God himself paved the way for them. Me? I do one fucking thing and it comes back. One fucking thing."

Silence from in the bedroom. George curled up with his back against the wall.

"George, what are you talking about?"

"I saw you at Dr. Schueller's."

Silence.

"What do you mean?"

"I saw you when I was leaving and you were on your way in. I heard you talking with her. I thought, I don't know what I thought, but I wanted to meet you. I thought I recognized you when I saw you at Dr. Schueller's office, so I broke into some files and found your information. I didn't set up the meeting to develop my leadership skills. I had this crazy idea that you were the woman Frank and I saw having sex in the office across the way. And, I don't know what I thought, but when we were in the coffee shop and we were talking, I thought, you know, Frank's always having affairs. He takes those risks and nothing catches up to him. And I thought maybe if I talked to you about what happened maybe you'd feel sorry for me and... God, I'm so fucking pathetic."

And then he's in the room. Moving around quickly, picking up clothes off the floor, grabbing empty cereal bowls, spoons clattering against the side, and taking them to the kitchen. She's still clutching the sheet, staring straight ahead when he returns.

"Good, I'm glad you're not saying anything, because I want to tell you what an absolute asshole I am. You have been nothing but kind and wonderful, and God, sex with you was, I can't even say what. I want to do something, I want to give you something that in some tiny miniscule way can make up for the colossal blunder I've made. I just want to make you aware, you, the one person out there who actually is probably more hurt, more fucked up about this whole thing than I am, I want to make you aware that I am so sorry if I hurt you or have made you feel used by this stupid, stupid, stupid/"

"Give me Boba-fet." She's surprised by the words as they leave her mouth.

"What?"

She's still there, sheet clutched under her chin, unmoving as if nothing was said.

"I want your Boba-fet."

George turns and looks at the shelf. He walks up to it, reaches up and picks it off the shelf. There is a square of pine shelf on the otherwise undisturbed sheet of dust. He holds it and looks at the box. He slowly lifts it to his lips and kisses it. Then puts it down on the end of the bed.

"Now go. I want to get dressed and leave here by myself."

"Sure. Okay. I'll leave the key on the kitchen table. You can slide it under the door when you leave."

"Okay."

"Marcia?"

"Yeah?"

"Nothing. Nothing."

He turns and leaves Marcia alone in his room.

Heath

When he's gone, she gets out of bed, naked in his adolescent's room, pulls on her bra, puts her underwear in her briefcase. Skirt, blouse, blazer. She picks up the Boba-fet off the end of the bed, puts it in her briefcase, walks down the hallway. She picks up the key off the kitchen table, locks the door behind her and slides it under the door. Her heart is racing. She knows she should be angry. Instead she's worried about this gentle, perverse man she has just made love with. Worried and unsure what to do next.

George watches from the bench in the park across the street as Marcia exits the building, looks both ways up and down the street before smoothing her hair back and choosing her left. His breath catches. He closes his eyes and imagines the nearly invisible hairs along her neck. He is very much in trouble. He's fallen in love.

:)

Marcia has opened the action figure and placed it on her desk next to the monitor. It is a detailed figurine, with a metallic helmet covering the head and a jet-pack on its back. The kind of toy that needs jet-propulsion sound effects and inevitably gets thrown at its destination, ending a fiery crash. She is doing exactly this. Definitely not working on a resourcing request she is supposed to be preparing for an executive council presentation next week.

Eventually she picks up the phone and dials.

"Hey Elana. It's Marcia. Yeah, I know, it's crazy, isn't it? I know, it's like you have to book an appointment or something. Listen, I know this sounds crazy, but you wanna go dancing? Yeah, really. Couldn't your James babysit? Well, they're his kids, too, aren't they? I know, I know. Look, it's fine if you can't, but I'm just going through some stuff, there's been some pretty big stuff and I could really stand to go out, you know, get loaded or something. Well, I dunno, maybe dinner and then that new club, Water. Okay, then after bedtime."

:)

146

There's a thump, a drop in elevation and a backlash before she's in the bathroom, retching violently into the bowl, whole body rippling like a wave, pushing the rot out of her. Then the shivering and soft rasping breath and the awareness of pain, massive pain in her head. One hand grips the edge of the bowl and she pulls herself up, looks into the mirror. Her eyes are sunken and hollow, over-emphasized by the mascara that has created dark lagoons around her eyes. She feels the rasp of liquor and cigarettes at the back of her throat and remembers the bowl of late-night noodles. Suppresses a retch.

In the shower she tilts her head back and lets the water ran over her face for a very long time. Eventually, she dries herself and dresses for work. Takes three Tylenol 3s, with codeine and heads into the office. She was unconscious for six hours, from three am until nine am. She arrives at work at 10:30. Her assistant lowers her head as Marcia passes, absorbing herself in an e-mail. Marcia says nothing, can't fathom the energy required to fight through the fog and find her voice. When she enters her office, something is different. On her desk is a beat up cardboard box. She calls Margaret to ask if she let anyone into her office, who tells her a bike courier came by. Not the usual one, a kid with a mohawk. Marcia looks at the box. It isn't secured, the top flaps simply folded over top of one another. There's no bill of lading, no return address. She briefly wonders if it's a bomb, thinks about calling security, then dismisses the idea. She draws in a breath and slides the flaps open. Inside the box are stacks of childhood items; a stamp collection in a faded yellow book; a box of certified coins; boxes and boxes of hockey cards; Battlestar Galactica memorabilia taken from Shreddies boxes; Fraggle Rock figurines from McDonald's Happy Meals; carefully cut out UPC symbols from cereal boxes; a ball of cigarette package tinfoil carefully separated from the filmy white paper. Sitting on top of it all, a note scrawled in erratic, adolescent handwriting: "It never added up to what I thought it would. I'd like to see you again."

Marcia folds the note in half and smiles. She places all of the items back in the box carefully, arranging each item neatly, then rearranging to make sure nothing will bang or roll about. She picks up the box and walks back out of her office, past Margaret, who looks up, starts to speak, then closes her mouth as Marcia sweeps out of the office. Outside, she hails a cab and places the box in the seat next to her. She directs the cab driver back to the apartment where she spent the previous afternoon. Walks up the stairs and along the carpeted hallway. The pain has crept back into the front of her head, spreading like a map across her face and forehead. When she reaches his door, she places the box on one hip and knocks. The door opens almost immediately. George is standing, half his body hidden behind the door. She jumps in before he can speak. "Do you want to go away?"

"What do you mean?"

"My mom has a cottage. She's always bugging me to go. And she always wants me to bring a nice young man along with me."

"Just like that?"

"I haven't taken my full vacation time in years. I've got it coming to me."

"You've got to be kidding me."

"Let's go. Pack your shit. Meet me at the Hertz rental around the corner in ten minutes. Any longer and I'm leaving without you."

The door slams, leaving Marcia in the hall. She grins gloriously, then leans her head forward against the door, feeling the coolness spread. Eventually, she turns and goes to rent the car that she and George will drive away from the city, through the traffic, up the highways and into the startling quiet of rolling forests and flashes of brilliant water that forms the undercurrent of her youth.

:)

Inside, George is frantically throwing any clean clothes he can find into an old Adidas gym bag. He remembers deodorant, a toothbrush, condoms. Grabs the latest copy of Scientific American off the kitchen table. As he is pulling the door closed behind him, he hears the phone ring. George hesitates, half his body in the apartment, half in the hallway. The phone rings again. George stands still. It rings a third time before George pulls the door closed behind him and turns the key in the deadbolt.

:)

Elizabeth Schueller slams the phone into its cradle.

She is starting to dislike him. Last night she woke at 4:17 am thinking about him and was unable to go back to sleep. So, she did what she does best when confronted with a problem: research. She spent the early hours of the morning searching through volumes of folders and directories, historical files, incident reports, thousands upon thousands of documents. At 5:52, she read the exact same performance reviews that set George in motion. She saw the arc of George's career, how it started promising, then stalled under Frank. She saw how other employees came and went from Frank's team, but George stayed on, stagnating. She read Frank's assessment of George: "Needs empowerment to take risks." And she was suddenly calmed by that sentence, the anger settling, the way forward clear.

"George doesn't need a cure. He needs a push."

The key to making money is in exploiting other people's problems. This is simple in business where everyone is engaged in the same pursuit of shareholder return. It is a simple calculation: does the return on fixing the problem warrant the investment in its cure? With people it is more complicated. Individuals are generally less profitable than businesses – in fact as wealth generators, they are less profitable to themselves than they are to the company. But they often have competing interests beyond generating wealth. In order to be successful in life, it is important to understand other people's problems. The more adept you are at pinpointing another's pain, the more likely they are to invest in you, personally or financially. Sometimes individuals mistake another's ability to identify one's weakness and pain as love.

Dr. Schueller is acutely aware of all this. There is no emotion in her acceptance of these principles. She simply understands that she runs a business, that many people depend on her running the business and the more successfully she applies these principles, the more successful her business will be. When Frank Lewis died there were three immediate concerns for Centre Capital: first, the public image of the firm; second, the stability and focus of the employees; and third, the smooth transition of Frank's internal and external client relationships. To help with these problems, Dr. Schueller helped construct communications reflecting the company's commitment to safety, rolled out a grief counseling program and created personal memos to each of Frank's key contacts. So far, his death has generated a little over $75,000 in revenue for her practice.

The thing that undoes success is failure. There is nothing that spreads more quickly than the smell of failure. The hint of it destroys reputations, spreads like rot through a client base. It feeds on itself, sours everything around it. Elizabeth can smell the whiff of it in her meetings with George. Something about how he avoids eye contact. How he avoids conflict, but never relinquishes control. There was danger in their last meeting, subversion. Like he had become aware of some truth and was holding it between them. Elizabeth Schueller is aware of this and thoroughly unwilling to allow failure to become an option.

She needs to get him back. Back into her office for one more meeting. She needs him to pick up the goddamned phone, is what she needs.

Chapter 15

They are silent through the snarl of downtown traffic and grinding stop and start freeways. It isn't until they are past the final highway narrowing with construction workers operating enormous machines, oblivious to the million cars sliding past, that they break the silence. They're flying now, the speedometer reading 130 km/hr as the pent-up frustration of the past hour's crawl unleashes itself on the highway. She's rented a Toyota Solara, the only sporty car the downtown rental company had available.

"Okay, talk."

"About what?"

"Everything. Tell me how you got the box into my office. I thought you were scared of elevators. Or did you lie about that, too?"

"I didn't lie about that."

"Okay, then tell me why you did it. Why you lied to me. Tell me you're not a stalker. That I won't regret this. That my instincts haven't abandoned me. That I'm not crazy. Just, talk."

"I don't think you're crazy."

"I don't find that reassuring."

"And I'm not a stalker."

"Just what a stalker would say."

George is gripping the hand rest on the door. He is trying to relax, but keeps glancing at the speedometer, keeps pushing himself back into the seat as if he could slow his body down, if not the car.

"Do you think you could slow down? I don't mean to be a backseat driver, I just get nervous. I start doing the math."

"What math?"

"Impact at 130km/hr. with stationary object. Impact at 130 km/hr. with object moving in opposite direction at 100km/hr, at 110, etcetera. I've got this thing with numbers. I think it's a way of distracting myself."

"Distracting yourself from what?"

"Good question. I don't know. Pain? Boredom? In this case, I'd say fear."

"I've never had a head for numbers." She has both hands on the wheel. George has barely finished a sentence before she is responding. Her energy is taut. But she eases her foot slightly off the gas and the car's speed drops to 115, George's body drops back down slightly into the passenger seat as she does.

"I've always done it, even as a kid. Like with my hockey cards. Each season had about 360 cards in the complete set. And you'd get master list cards where you could check off which ones you had and see which ones you needed. I remember lying in bed at night, trying to sleep and I'd go over it in my head. How many I had, how many I needed, what percentage of the total I had, how many more packets I would need to buy to get the whole set, getting exponentially more difficult the closer I got to a complete set, and how I could affect those numbers by trading my doubles for certain of the cards I had, assuming of course, that the company published the same number of each player. That one always drove me nuts, because it threw off all the calculations, if they printed fewer Wayne Gretzkys than, say, Rob Ramages. Also unfair, because they know you want Gretzky, so they're playing off your need. But then I wasn't even sure they were doing it, and if they were doing it, what the ratio of Gretzkys to Ramages might be, which made the calculations impossible. All I knew is that my friends and I had a lot more Rob Ramages than we did Wayne Gretzkys."

"Who's Rob Ramage?"

"Defenseman. Doesn't matter."

Outside the countryside has hit a regular rhythm of green swathes of corn fields, brick farmhouses with red barns and metal quonsets, patches of trees, which then repeats itself several times between each town. Their conversation is similarly settling into a less frantic rhythm.

"You can have your cards back."

"No, you keep them."

"I don't really want them. It's more the symbolism that I thought was sweet. I took it as an apology."

"It was. It is. I don't even know what I was thinking. This whole thing's kinda made me a little crazy."

"Try not sleeping. Half the time I'm trying to figure out if I'm hallucinating or really experiencing something. And I don't even feel that tired. Sometimes it feels like my body doesn't need the sleep, it's my brain that needs it, like I need to shut down or let go or just stop thinking."

Marcia is driving a road she has driven since it was a single lane each way, since she would get carsick and her dad would have to stop the car while she retched in the ditch. When she would start to feel bad, he would always say, "Look at the horizon and breathe deeply."

George hasn't seen the horizon in years.

"Why did you invite me?"

"I don't know yet. I just did it. Why did you say yes?"

George stops for a moment and seriously considers the question.

"I've lived my life playing games in my head. Making patterns and analyzing numbers and odds and I sometimes wonder if it's not me being too scared to live my life. You can control numbers. They're constant, and as long as you work hard enough, you can figure anything out. But then, things happen, people fall out windows, get in car accidents, fall in love and it's all so fucking random. Sorry. And I just don't get that. You look at the world and there's a pattern to everything. Electromagnetic patterns around the poles, electronic signals in the brain, even traffic has clearly observable patterns that reflect an underlying reality. There are patterns in everything and when we analyze them and break them down into their core elements we can understand and even replicate them, but then you live your life and you realize, no, there is no pattern, no logic, it's just random. And those two things, side by side, patterns and randomness, just don't make sense to me."

George is talking and it feels like the first time he made a friend. He's saying things he didn't even realize were true until he said them. Saying things he didn't know you were allowed to tell someone else.

"So that's why you said yes to my invitation?"

"You asking me up here seems like a random freak occurrence. But it's also part of the pattern that kicked into gear the moment Frank went out the window. And for me, I really only have two choices, yes or no. I've spent a lot of my life saying no. I thought that maybe I should just give up trying to make sense of it all. At least for a bit."

"I thought it was because you liked me."

She smiles to herself. Knows what she's doing and enjoys the play of it. Enjoys the gentleness and innocence of this unformed man.

"Oh. Well. That's the other thing."

"What?"

"I do. Like you. A lot. Which is crazy, because I don't know you. But ever since I saw you the other stuff in my head doesn't seem quite as important. That's why I want you to keep that stuff. Or throw it out. Whatever."

"Okay."

"Okay, what?"

"I'll keep them. Your collections."

"Oh. Right."

They fall into silence as the passenger side view opens into the first glimpse of an expanse of rock and water, a cottage with flaking red and green paint perched on an island with wind-bent trees. The layered blue water sparkles for an instant as the sun shines through a hole in the haze of clouds.

"How did you get that box in to my office? I mean, if you're scared of elevators?"

"I paid some homeless kid. Gave him 10 bucks, told him there was another 10 bucks when he came back. I waited for him in the lobby."

"Did he have a Mohawk? Green pants?"

"Yeah, why?"

"I thought I might have made him up."

The fields behind, they now pass gateways of rock that tower on either side of the highway, the road cut straight through the stone.

"Do you want me drive?"

"I'm fine. You can go to sleep if you want. It won't bother me."

Marcia and George fall back into silence, staring at the landscape approach and recede, approach and recede.

:)

George snaps awake as the car vibrates over the washboard gravel road. It feels for a moment like the car is being shaken off the road, before the tires find purchase again.

"Almost there."

"Sorry, I didn't mean to fall asleep."

"You were mumbling. I couldn't make out what you were saying."

They are driving down a long straight gravel road. On either side scrub brush encroaches on the road, a little farther back birches and poplars rise. Occasionally they pass an overgrown road with a family name, "The Jones'", carved on a wooden plaque, or a nickname like "Sunset Paradise" or "The Roost", or a pun like "The Greens' Green Grass of Home." Marcia turns at the road marked "Winters' Summer Place".

This road is narrow and rutted and not designed for a sports car. Marcia slows the car to a crawl and rolls down the window. Early summer comes blasting in, replacing the air conditioning with its thick warm air. She breathes deeply.

"God, I forget about this every time. Within twenty-four hours I'm usually itching to get home again, but that first blast of cottage, it's like time stands still."

"It's beautiful."

"Did you grow up coming to a cottage?"

"I grew up in the city."

Heath

The car follows a final bend in the road before slowly coming to a stop in front of a simple, single-story, 1960s cottage. It's in a small clearing, and behind it, a narrow path leads down to a slanted dock. A sixteen foot aluminum boat bobs in the water next to the dock. There's a large green propane tank next to the cottage and all the windows are covered in old, dark grey screens. There is a screened-in porch with a door that bangs loudly behind Marcia as she enters the cottage.

"Let me open things up. I'll just be a minute."

George is left standing next to the cottage. He can hear sounds from under the cottage somewhere. After a minute or two, he decides to walk down to the lake. The water is lapping gently against the shore, the aluminum boat making a hollow rhythmic thumping, then scraping sound. A breeze comes up, shaking the leaves so that the air around George is filled with it. He picks up a rock and throws it about twenty feet out into the lake. The lake swallows the rock with barely a sound, no ripples.

"Pretty isn't it?"

George jumps at the sound of Marcia's voice.

"Beautiful."

"I got the power on and the pump primed. We should go into town and get some groceries. We could get a movie. We've got a VHS player here and some old Paul Newman movies. My mom loves Paul Newman."

They turn and walk the path back to the cottage, Marcia in the lead, George following. As he walks the path, he is massaging the shoulder of the arm he used to throw he rock.

"Marcia?

"Yeah?"

"Maybe later, would you show me how to skip rocks?"

"You don't know how to skip rocks?"

"I grew up in the city, my dad worked fifty weeks of the year and I didn't have brothers."

Marcia turns to him, puts her arms around his waist. "I will teach you how to skip rocks." And kisses him. Like two people who love each other. "Come on, let's go into town."

:)

It's dusk. Marcia and George are sitting in the screened in porch, drinking Australian shiraz, listening. She's sitting in an old armchair with a pink knit cotton blanket covering her legs. He is leaning back in a cushioned glider rocking chair with his feet on a matching glider footstool, slowly rocking.

The conversation is gentle, meandering. It is part of the evening they are sharing, but by no means the most important part. Of equal importance is the rich eggplant color of the sky after the sun passes the tree line.

"I've never seen a bad sunset from here."

Or the drone of a floatplane landing on the other side of the lake.

"On Fridays in the summer, that's constant from about 3:00 until it gets dark. Executives who don't want to fight traffic."

Or the kerplunk of the bullfrog by the dock.

"What the hell was that?"

Or the shape that flits by in the almost darkness.

"Was that a bat?"

Or the touch of their skin as Marcia puts her hand on his.

"Do you mind?"

"No, I like it."

"I could turn on the light, but it's kind of bright. Would you like me to light a lantern?"

"I don't need it."

"Okay."

They sit in the darkness, holding hands, until everything else inside them stops - the thoughts, worrying about the other person, what to do next - eventually it all settles, and what's left is two people sitting in the darkness holding hands and breathing.

"You must be getting chilly."

"I'm alright."

"You want to share my blanket?"

"Thanks."

Heath

The vagueness of the shapes in the darkness allows the thoughts to emerge plainly. There is no urgency behind them, just the simplicity of truth.

"What was it like. Seeing him die?"

A pause. Marcia stands, hands the blanket to George. Walks to the screen door and leans her head against it.

"George, I haven't been completely honest with you either."

"What do you mean?"

"I don't even know how to say this, it's so insane." She pauses and takes a breath. "Frank and I were having an affair. The day I saw him, I was rushing to go meet him. I was late. We used to meet in an unused office in my building. I should have told you. How do you tell someone a thing like that?"

Suddenly, time speeds up again and George is pushing past her. He opens the screen door, lets it bang behind him.

"George?"

She hears his voice trail back to her out of the night.

"If I could do it all over I'd push him out that fucking window."

:)

She finds him sitting on the dock. She can hear the regular sploosh of rocks in water, with an occasional chink as it bounces off what they used to call the diving rock. The lake is calm, reflecting the bright light of the moon.

"You okay?"

"I'm trying to see how many times I can hit that rock in a row. My best is seven."

"Mind if I join you?"

"It's your dock."

When she sits next to George, he stops throwing the rocks. He has a small pile of them sitting next to him. He starts talking the moment she sits down.

"Frank and I grew up together. He was like a big brother to me. We competed with each other our whole lives. He was mean, though. He liked beating me, liked

158

rubbing my nose in my failure. But he took care of me, too. Most of the girls I knew growing up were his old girlfriends. He'd treat them badly, and they'd talk to me about it. I was the nice one. We went to different universities and took different directions. But when I came back with my engineering degree, he found me the job at Centre Capital. He took care of me, then made me feel worthless because of it. This just brings all those feelings back again."

George picks up a smooth, round rock and throws it at the rock rising out of the lake. A moment passes, then the tink! of rock bouncing off rock.

"I wasn't in love with him. It was just sex."

"That's supposed to make me feel better?"

"I don't even know why I did it. It's like I couldn't control myself. The danger of it was thrilling, knowing someone could walk in at any minute. It was like skydiving or something. Afterwards, I'd think about his wife, his kids, and I felt terrible. Every time I promised I'd break it off, but then it's like some primal thing would kick in that I couldn't control. It's scary not being in control, but when you give in, it's such a rush."

"I wouldn't have come here if I'd known."

"Do you want me to take you home?"

"No."

"Then I'm glad I didn't tell you."

George laughs.

"What?"

"This is insane. It's like this whole thing is trying to teach me some stupid lesson. I keep looking for the pattern. Random or pattern. It just doesn't make any sense."

"You still want to learn how to skip a stone?"

"Sure."

"Okay. There's two things: the shape of the rock and how you throw it. The rock should be as round and flat as possible. That offers the least resistance from both the air and the surface of the water. The key to throwing it is getting a good side-arm throw and snap your wrist at the end. That way the flat surface of the rock meets the flat surface of the water. The lower you can get to the water, the less friction there will be when it hits the water, so it will go further. Like this."

She chooses a water worn rock from the pile next to George that fits neatly in the hook of her index finger. She pulls her elbow back and snaps her forearm and wrist just before releasing the rock. The stone skims close to the surface of the water, barely touching down before arcing up again. It touches seven times, each time leaving only a small concentric circle of ripples where it bounced off the water.

George picks up a similar rock, pulls back and throws. The stone flies for a bit, before beginning to slice sideways. When it hits the water, the flat side of the rock is vertical and it disappears into the lake.

"Try this one. That one was too light." She hands George a perfect, smooth rock and picks up one of her own. "Let's do it together."

Like dancers, they pull back their elbows in unison, and snap their arms forward, stones flying out in parallel, skimming off the water at nearly the same spot. Marcia's skips eight times, George's six. Where they landed next to each other, the expanding ripples mingle. Where crest meets crest and trough meets trough the ripples make waves. Where crest meets trough, they cancel each other out. Marcia and George stand and watch the ripples expand, each ridge sparkling in the moonlight, until they become diffuse and the water returns to its glassy state. Marcia slides her hand into George's. They look at each other. George kisses her forehead.

"Let's not have to be sorry to each other for anything. Let's just forget the past, forget the future. Okay?"

"I like the sound of that."

"Yeah, me too."

As they turn to walk back to the cottage, the moon beats on their backs, pushing their shadows up the path ahead of them.

:)

Their lovemaking is slow and gentle, Marcia on top. Her hair hangs all around George's face, creating a hiding place where they brush lips and whisper secret sounds to each other. This is the bed where Marcia made out with her first boyfriend, let him touch her new breasts. The bed where she would lie and listen to her parents drinking with the neighbors. The bed where she would wake at three in the morning to the sound of a loon calling. It's the bed where, after their lovemaking, she curls up with George, and falls asleep for what feels like the first time.

:)

She's 13 years old and acutely aware of her breasts. Boobs, the boys call them. Bosoms, her mother says. She's in her first two-piece bathing suit. "What does she need that for? She's 13 years old for God's sake!" Her father had been violently opposed. Her mother bought it anyway, in town on one of her weekly trips to the general store for supplies and booze. She and her mother stayed the summer at the cottage with the other women and children, while the fathers roared in on Friday night and roared out again on Sunday. This Saturday is her first time wearing it. Her mother helped her put it on in the bunkie down by the water. Rather than witness it, her father slammed off to mow the lawn with his John Deere.

Now she's standing up to her knees in water on a wide flat rock buried a few feet below the surface.

"Jump!" screams the assortment of kidlets that amass at whichever cottage presents the best entertainment for the afternoon.

"Jump!" calls out Rod.

Rod is gorgeous. All the girls call him Hot Rod. His hair is long and curly and he wears mesh muscle shirts. He just turned sixteen and his dad bought him a Trans Am. He promised to take her for a ride sometime this summer.

"Go on, what are you afraid of?" teases Rod, splashing her with water.

A cool wind lifts off the water and gives her a chill, goose bumps lifting up off her arms. She hugs herself and looks down. To her absolute horror she sees two erect nipples, clear as broad daylight pushing out against the fabric of her swim top.

She clasps her hands over her boobs, closes her eyes and jumps into the murky green water.

She expects to full the cold air suck her breath out, but instead she feels only a stillness. In a moment, she has forgotten to anticipate the shock, has relaxed and let herself slip back into the comfort of drifting, held aloft and trusting her buoyancy. She spreads her arms and simply enjoys the feeling of floating.

It's the gentle breeze that wakes her, air that has been cooled by water. It rustles softly over her bare shoulder and cheek. She lifts up the corner of the blanket wrapped around her torso to cover herself and breathes in the musty damp smell of old cotton. She opens one eye to glance up at her shoulder and sees a corner of her grandmother's patchwork quilt. She opens the other eye and sees a rusty screen covering a chipped forest green frame. The window looks out over sun-dappled water. She lifts her head slightly and sees the lake, a willow bobbing its tendrils slowly over where the flat rock sits just beneath the surface of the water.

"I must have been dreaming", she mutters to herself. Sighing softly, she lays her head back on the pillow, pulls the quilt tighter, breathes in the smell of cedar and goes back to sleep.

:)

Marcia's body twitches. George, who has been listening to the silence that descends after the insects go to sleep, pulls back the hair that has fallen over Marcia's face and kisses her neck. He curls his front around her back, spooning their bodies so that he can fall asleep with the feeling of her breathing pushing outward against his chest and the smell of her hair in his dreams.

:)

"George! Get up! Someone's here!"

George blinks open his eyes and sees Marcia. He smiles.

"Quick, I heard a car on the gravel. Get some clothes on. I think it's my mom!"

George's smile dissolves.

"What time is it?"

"I dunno, late."

They both fumble frantically for their clothes. A car door slams. George is still sitting in the bed pulling on his jeans when the screen door bangs.

"Hallo-o", Sybil calls out in a singsong voice as she sweeps through the living room into the cottage's tiny kitchen. "This accident's done wonders for your sense of flair! First a chi-chi dinner, now a flashy new sports car! What's next, a weekend at the Ritz? I'm so excited. I brought some provisions. I got a Diane Keaton movie, enough Chardonnay to choke a horse, baguette, some of that French cheese you like, olives and of course, Rocky Road ice cream!"

With this pronouncement, Sybil turns majestically, one arm raised with expectantly, curled gracefully, and sees Marcia standing in the doorway, George coming up behind her. George is smoothing his hair at the back. Sybil's arm drops.

"Oh dear."

"Hi mom."

"I don't know who's more mortified, you or me!"

"Hello Mrs. Winters. My name's George."

"Hello George. It's a pleasure to meet you. I hope you like Diane Keaton. Marcia didn't mention she was bringing company."

"I didn't tell you anything, mom. What are you doing here?"

"Mrs. McReady from down the way called me this morning to tell me about the car in the driveway. You know, she always keeps an eye out for us while we're away. Well, I just thought you'd taken me up on my offer."

"What offer?"

"For a girl's weekend at the cottage? Don't you remember?"

"Remember what?"

"At lunch? I invited you up to the cottage. Said I thought it would help with your, you know, situation."

"Oh God. Yeah, I remember. Look, mom/"

"No, you know what? Let's pretend none of this happened. I'll leave the food on the counter, you go back to the bedroom, I'll vanish and it will be like the deli faeries were here while you slept."

"Mrs. Winters?"

"Sybil."

"Sybil. This is very awkward. I think you should stay. This is your cottage. If anyone should leave it should be me."

"Oh, I hate being alone up here. It's why I barely come up anymore. The woods spook me at night. Silly."

"Then maybe we should all stay."

Both women, mother and daughter, stop and look at George.

"Really?"

"Why not?"

"I like this boy already." Sybil crosses the room and gives George a giant familial hug, wrapping him in her shawl and rosewater scent. "Come help me unload the car."

:)

Marcia is sitting in the screened-in porch, fully wrapped in a fuzzy wool blanket, when George enters. She is looking out at the lake, which is lapping gently against the shore, mist hovering an inch or two above the water. It is preternaturally still. The sun is nothing but a warm glow and the birds are getting an early start. George stands for a minute in silence.

"What time is it?"

"Five thirty. I hope I didn't wake you."

"No. I think it was the birds."

"Quite a racket, eh?"

"Did you sleep?"

"Yeah. I mean, a little. I feel pretty good. I think it was a good idea to come up here."

"I'm glad." He kisses her forehead.

"Thanks. I don't know if I'm cured, but it's nice to have a break."

She looks into George's eyes. They are partners in this.

"Coffee's on."

George shuffles out of the screened-in porch and into the kitchen to pour himself a coffee. Sybil is already there, wrapped in a pure-white terry-cloth housecoat.

"Good morning", she sing-songs, tinking her spoon twice on the lip of her coffee cup. "Awfully early. I know my daughter can't sleep and I'm hitting menopause. What's your excuse?"

"Birds."

"Ah yes. Quite a symphony isn't it? It's actually something I've taken up in my later years. This place got awfully lonely for me after the divorce. I responded many ways, but up here, it was bird feeders. Just one at first. Then a few more. Different kinds: sunflowers and peanuts for larger birds, crossbills and grosbeaks. Then the suet for the nuthatches and woodpeckers. Then the sugar-water feeders for the humming birds." Before you know it, I had a bird sanctuary on the go.

She is holding the screen door open for him, ushering him into the porch where Marcia is still watching the water. She is in full flight on one of her favorite subjects.

"Good morning dear. But, it's the songs that bring it to life. This is the best time of day for it. I went to a Birding by Ear workshop this time last year, and it was just amazing. I mean, if I were to ask you, how many different types of birds do you hear right now, what would you say?"

"Mom."

"Just try it, dear."

George is amused, responds laughingly to the loud familiar call almost directly outside the porch.

"Well, there's that one."

"The robin, right."

"And that one. Sounds like a rusty hinge."

"That's a blue jay. And, of course that cawing is the crow. What else?"

Marcia is unsure how to respond. Embarrassed by her mother, enjoying watching George play along.

"I dunno, there's that bubbling song and the chattering."

He is starting to be drawn into it, enjoying the counting and categorizing of something he'd never thought to explore: sound.

"Well, the chattering's a squirrel, but the bubbling's a Warbling Vireo, I think. That's a beautiful one. Be still for a bit and listen a little deeper into the forest."

George sits quite still. His face is calm. Both women are watching him.

"Well, I hear that seven-note buzzing sound all around."

"Trust you to count the number."

"The redstart. And he's quite right, dear. The American Redstart is always seven notes."

"And a little further back, there's that one with those three repeated double notes."

"Very good, George. That's a yellowthroat."

"What is that nasal sound? Is it a baby animal or something?"

"That's the nuthatch."

"There! There's some drumming off in that direction. And a chip to my right. Wait. What was that?"

"Well, there's the woodpecker, but I'm not sure about the other thing."

"I'm not even sure I heard it, like a heartbeat or something."

His face is animated and alive. Not straining, but every pore open, like coral at night.

"There. That slow thumping, building in speed."

"You're right. I missed that. It's a grouse. They make that sound in by drumming their wings against a hollow log. Amazing isn't it?"

"That's incredible! It really is. How many was that? That's like nine birds, and there's probably more, but I never would have guessed it until I stopped and really listened."

The three of them sit for a minute, drinking their coffees, as the birds continue their morning chorus all around them. Sybil breaks the moment by standing, tightening her robe.

"Well, I'm going to get dressed. Maybe a little later we could go for a walk along the cliffs? There's some wonderful views and some different types of bird habitat."

George's response is immediate and genuine. "I'd like that."

Sybil kisses Marcia on the head and leaves the room, leaving a slight vacuum where she sat. Marcia sits staring after her mother, then turns back to George.

"What just happened?"

"What do you mean?"

"You just connected with my mom. Like really connected."

"She's a neat lady. What?"

"She's my mom."

"Well, it makes you think doesn't it? How much else do we miss? My ears pick up all sounds all the time, but until I focused on those birds, I never really would have been aware of them. It's like radio waves, frequencies. All this information is in the airwaves around us, but until we tune in to the right frequency we're completely oblivious to what's around us."

"Why don't you tune into my frequency for a bit?"

"I am. What do you mean?" He's immediately shy, bashful.

"I mean come here and cuddle with me. This is all so fucked up."

"What is?"

"You, me, my mom, the cottage, all of it. It's really messing me up."

She's smiling, though. George gets up, lies next to Marcia on her cracked vinyl lounge chair, and the two of them stop and listen to the birds, and the lapping of the water and they stop.

"You know what I like about listening?"

"What?"

"It's impossible to think. And as soon as you stop thinking, time stands still."

:)

It is noon and Sybil, Marcia and George are hiking a
section of the trail that follows along the face of a cliff.
The trail itself is humid and damp, with rich, dark moss
growing on boulders scraped clean by glaciers. The hiking
trail is rough but maintained. Windfall is cleared and
there are blue blazes attached to trees at intervals to
indicate the way. The forest is full of surprises. At once
deciduous with maple, birch and oak dominating, then
suddenly cedar and spruce as the trail climbs a few
meters. Sound is swallowed as they move along, Sybil and
George in the lead, Marcia bringing up the rear. They
have been hiking for an hour. When Sybil suggested it,
Marcia had initially resisted. "She can't help it. She
needs to be the centre of attention, even if it it's by acting
wonderful." But in the end, they'd decided to go. George,
having grown up in the city, was open and adventurous in
a way he hadn't been since childhood.

At the beginning, the three talked and stopped and
looked at every little thing: Sybil pointing out the poison
ivy, the ladyslippers; the porcupine George spotted
sleeping in the arm of a maple. George pushing ahead
excitedly, then coming back to check in with Marcia.

"It's like Endor! I keep thinking I'm going to see an
Ewok."

"You really are a total geek, aren't you?"

"Yep." Big grin. And bounding ahead to look at a
bright orange fungus growing on the side of a fallen birch.

"There it is! Our lunch spot!" Sybil is pointing to an
area where the trees are fewer and a thin blue can be seen
between the leaves. There is a boulder ahead that
requires hands and feet to climb. As they pull themselves
onto the rock, they each suck in their breath and hold, a
slight catch in their chests. The rock they are on is
enormous. It expands past them about twelve feet and
then stops. Beyond it is air. Beyond that, water with the
noon sun sparkling on it like's fool's gold. And beyond
that, trees and trees and trees.

This rock reaches out about a hundred feet above the
water below. The day is still and warm and clear. Sybil

walks to the edge of the rock, tilts her head back and stretches out her arms, basking in the sun.

"Isn't it glorious? It always makes me wonder what it must have felt like to be the first person here. If you ignore that radio tower, you can imagine how it must have been a thousand years ago. Looking out and seeing nothing but wilderness and space. Coming out here reminds me of my size and place in this world. No more and no less than what I am."

She is now chattering pleasantly and she begins to unpack lunch.

"But listen to me talk. You two, don't get old. The solitude drives you batty. Sometimes I can't believe the things I say."

George and Marcia have approached the edge of the rock. They are holding hands and looking straight out at the horizon. Their hearts are pounding, but they are quiet and connected.

"Now, I brought some of that baguette. It's a bit crusty, but it should be alright. Some nice cheese and apple, a few walnuts, olives, prosciutto, et voila! A feast!"

Next to George, Marcia is in transition. In slow motion, Marcia's head drops from level with the horizon at 90 degrees, down through 85, 80, 75 degrees, until she is looking down, through space, at the water below. George feels Marcia's right index lift up and settle against his hand several times. He thinks it is a caress, a quiet way of communicating, and he squeezes her hand in return. George is still looking at the horizon when he feels the hand go limp in his. He just has time to reach forward instinctively with his other arm as the body slumps forward, headed over the edge.

"Sybil!" Her head snaps up. It's the tone that speaks at a basic level, that says, "Danger!" She is moving forward before she sees George holding the limp body against his right leg, trying to push back from the ledge, but slipping on pebbles. She grabs George by the shoulders of his shirt and wrenches him onto his back, Marcia on top of him. They both haul Marcia up and off George, Sybil holding her under her armpits and George helping by awkwardly pushing her to the side while he slides from underneath her. When she is safely away from the edge, Sybil grabs the Nalgene water bottle and offers it to Marcia, who is starting to come around. George flips over onto his back and stares at the sky, chest heaving. Marcia drinks. Sybil is hovering, examining her daughter, ready to protect, rescue, heal.

"What happened?"

"I must have fainted."

"Are you alright now?"

"I think so."

"You almost fell. I think you scared George half out of his wits."

At that moment, there is a buzzing sound, an unnatural vibration that knocks George out of his reverie.

"Jesus!" George jumps up and pulls his Blackberry out of its holster. "I totally forgot I had this thing."

"You must be getting reception from the tower over there."

George looks down at the lit up screen. It's a message from Dr. Schueller. It is very short. It reads, "George. It's time to meet about your situation. I have information that will affect the outcome. I have time to meet tomorrow or the next day. Please confirm your availability with my assistant. Best regards, Dr. Schueller."

For a moment, George considers throwing it over the edge, like a toy soldier off the bridge, swirling and growing smaller until he sees the small white splash far below. But instead, he replaces it in his belt-holder and goes to Marcia's side.

"You must have gotten scared of heights. That's supposed to my problem. Feeling better now?" He smoothes her hair and smiles, but his eyes have gone cloudy.

:)

After a lengthy game of Monopoly, which Marcia won through canny trades and timely investments, she and George are lying in the squeaky, lumpy bed of her youth. Both are lying back, staring at the exposed joists of the ceiling. They have been this way for some time, quiet in their own thoughts. Outside, insects that look like giant mosquitoes are buzzing against the window screen.

"Something changed today, didn't it?"

"How's that?"

"When I fainted. It's like everything came rushing back. It's been nice, here with you, even with my mom. It's felt safe. But when I looked down at all that water below, everything came rushing back. Frank and work and the fear that's been following me ever since he died. It makes me think that all this is a lie. That maybe we're just hiding."

"The message on my Blackberry was from Dr. Schueller. She wants me to see her. That she has new information."

"And?"

"And what?"

"Are you going to go see her?"

"I don't know. It's hard to imagine going back. It seems to so far away. I'm enjoying this."

"Me too." She moves her head onto his chest. "But I don't think this is real."

"No, probably not."

"You're going to go see her, aren't you?"

George closes his eyes, holds Marcia close to his chest. He is holding onto the moment very hard, clasping the reality of the moment to his chest. But his mind is already starting to swirl downward, to disconnect from the muscles of his arms, the warmth of her body. Even as he holds on, he is slipping away.

:)

There is blackness and random images for a long time, like he is backstage at a movie theatre, walking behind the screens. He drifts in and out of realities, feeling dopey and heavy. Eventually, it's the sound of the flapping sheet that orients him. His peripheral vision starts to harden and he sees the familiar walls, furniture. He's back in the office. There is a glow through the hole behind the plastic sheet. Again, George feels the tug, the urge to see the other side of the sheet.

Frank's voice interrupts him. "Nice to see you George."

George turns to look at him. Frank is leaning against his desk, dressed exactly as he was the moment he exploded out the window. He is tossing and catching a small metal object with his right hand. George says nothing.

"So is that what this was all about? A girl?"

George is stalling, immediately scared.

"What are you talking about?"

"Don't pretend like you can't see what's going on, George, you fucker. Kill your best friend over a girl? Why didn't you just ask? I could have had anyone, didn't need to be her."

George is stumbling backwards, mind racing, trying to grab onto something solid.

"Frank, I have no idea what you're talking about."

"I've had a lot of time to look around here, George. Like I checked into the Hotel California. Can't seem to get away. So I started poking around. Kill some time. I found this. You know what this is? This is a half-inch flathead screw. The kind they use to secure the flashing that covers the silicone casings that hold these windows in place. You know where I found it? Your pocket in your pants in your laundry. You want to tell me how that got there?"

George is looking around for something to use as a weapon, something to fend off the impending attack.

"That's impossible. Frank, that's crazy, that's the craziest thing I've ever heard."

"When I looked at the silicone, the part that gave way when I died, there was a remarkably straight break. Almost like it had been cut."

"Frank, this is insane. Why would I want to kill you?"

"Oh, I don't know, maybe because you're a loser? Because you're a pathetic fucking coward that never did a goddamned thing for himself in his whole life?"

Frank is standing up now and walking towards George. George is slowly backing away.

"Maybe because you resented me for being everything you weren't? Because the first girl you ever had sex with

only did it because I gave her $20. Because I gave you
your job and you couldn't even do that right."

"That's not true."

He is close to the plastic sheet. There's nowhere else
to go. Frank's face is now inches away from George's.

"Don't you lie to me. Was it worth it? Was it worth
killing me to get in the pants of some girl from HR? You
can't hide from me. I see you, George. I fucking see you."

George suddenly screams, grabs Frank by his blazer
and slams him against the wall. He pulls him forward
then slams him again, Frank's head snapping back and
making a dull thud as it hits the wall. George pulls
Frank's slumped body away from the wall and throws him
on the ground. Pulls back his right arm and smashes his
fist into Frank's face.

"George!"

Someone's pulling on his shoulder. There's blood
running from Frank's nose. George pulls back his fist and
slams it into Frank's face again. He feels the cheekbone
crack under his knuckles this time.

"George! Wake up!"

The hand is shaking his shoulder, the voice belongs to
a woman. It is insistent. Frank's face is bloodied and
broken. A steady flow of blood runs from the smashed
nose, over the unmoving lips.

"George, wake up!"

George opens his eyes, stares without seeing. Marcia
is holding his shoulders, holding him down. There are wet
tears on his cheek.

:)

They are mostly silent for the drive home. This time
George drives, Marcia sits staring out the window to
prevent carsickness. George stares straight ahead, both
hands on the wheel in the 10 and 2 position. They are in
stasis, while the car, a pod made of plastics and metal,
hurtles them home towards the city. As they enter the
city they hit traffic. It is three o'clock in the afternoon.
Traffic no longer follows set patterns: before nine, busy
coming into the city; after four, busy heading out. Now

there is constant traffic both directions, the moments of clear sailing as unpredictable as an accident. They are silent as the car slows to a halt, moves forward a few feet, slows again.

The silence in the car is thick. It is as if there were a sheet of plexiglass between them. They watch the cars around them move and stop, move and stop. The lanes of traffic move at different times, but the cars that surround them remain the same. He gets to know the red Civic, the white grocery delivery van, the many BMWs and Audis. George resists the temptation to change lanes when the one next to him seems to start moving faster than his own. Statistically speaking, staying in the same lane should allow him to gain an equal or greater amount of ground than constantly changing lanes in an effort to exert control over an unpleasant reality. He is monitoring the cars around him, keeping mental tabs on them to try to test the theory.

A movement catches George's eye. He looks up and sees a hawk, floating above the traffic, circling, hunting, above the miles of grey pavement and idling cars. It is close enough that he can see mottling on the tail and wing feathers. An immature hawk.

"What are you doing?" he mutters quietly, leaning forward to look up at it through the windshield.

"What?" she asks, across the divide.

"That hawk. What does it think it's going to find on a freeway?" The hawk is still circling, wheeling on the air currents.

"Get outta here. Go on!" he cries. And honks the horn, as if he could startle the hawk into realizing it has lost its way. "Go on!" And he honks again, longer this time.

"George, it probably can't hear you." There is prickly irritation in her voice, the first time it has crept in between them.

"Get out of here, you stupid bird!" He is leaning on the horn, long and hard now. Other drivers are staring at him and are beginning to honk back.

"George, stop it!" She reaches for his hand, to pull it away from the horn and he uses the other to press against the horn, a constant blaring now, with the horns of other cars all around rising and falling in protest and harmony. They are fighting over the horn now, two adults wrestling each other, her trying to pull him away, him fighting to keep the noise going.

"Get the fuck out of here! Go!" The entire stretch of freeway is now filled with cars honking and blaring, a concert of car horns. George is leading the charge, his red car stationary, the horn going and going.

Eventually the hawk wheels around and soars off, away from the noise, away from the city, towards the waterfront that contains the city's sprawl.

George pulls his hands away from the horn, and watches it as it fades from view. He then puts his foot on the gas and pulls ahead, as if nothing had happened. Around him, the noise from the other cars eventually dies down, one car at a time. Marcia, beside him, is staring out the window again, livid, jaw clenched, arms folded.

"Just take me home."

Chapter 16

"Hello George. Please come in. I'm just finishing up here."

Dr. Schueller is facing her computer, her back to the door. George enters the room, sits in one of the chairs facing her desk. Dr. Schueller finishes typing, clicks Send and then shuts down her computer.

"Seems impossible to keep up with e-mail sometimes. The urgency of it, as if the world will come to an end if it isn't responded to by the end of the day. But then, you've been enjoying a bit of a break from all of the e-mails, haven't you?"

She turns to George, bringing the full weight of her attention on to him.

"Yes, I suppose I have."

"You missed our last appointment."

"Yes, I'm sorry about that. I was called away."

"Nothing urgent, I hope."

"I felt it was. Urgent."

"Ah, yes?" Dr. Schueller is still seated behind her desk. Her hands are folded in her lap. She is smiling that same enigmatic smile George has seen before, the corners of her mouth unnaturally curled up. Her eyes are dead. There is an awkward, stubborn pause, a gap which both momentarily refuse to fill.

"Your message said you had some new information."

George breaks the silence, and with this minor assertion of power, Dr. Schueller relaxes and switches into a lighter mode of conversation.

"Yes, my message. So you haven't completely stopped responding to e-mails."

"It came through on my Blackberry. I must have forgotten to shut it off."

"You know you can get a Blackberry massage? Eighty dollars to have someone massage the palms of your hands. I'm always amazed at what people will pay for things. I sometimes forget that value is completely arbitrary, that things are worth what people are willing to pay for them, nothing more, nothing less. But we're conditioned to believe that things, services, people, have an intrinsic value. Companies invest millions of dollars in this conditioning. It isn't so much advertising, as the building of a mental structure, a structure of valuation that we carry with us all the time. Everything we look at is seen through this filter. Take my job. Do you know what these sessions cost? Six hundred dollars an hour. That's ten dollars a minute. You were three minutes late and when you came in I made you wait another two minutes. That's $50 dollars before we've even had a chance to say hello. Was it worth it? Who even paid for it? The company. The company paid for it out of every service charge for every interaction one of its customers has, out of trading and buying and selling, shuffling the world's money around from one place to the next. So we don't even think about it. On the one side, it is made up of millions of pennies, accruing from millions upon millions of transactions. On the other side, a number so inflated, it's hard to place in the real world. Fifty dollars would probably buy 100 pounds of rice and you and I just spent it without a second thought. Was it worth it?"

Dr. Schueller is speaking casually, as if this is a conversation she has every day, but she is staring intently at George. George is fully engaged, appearing to take up more space in the room than he normally does. His answers are quick, crystalline, in contrast to the thick, swollen nature his speech sometimes adopts.

"I think so. I think I'm really starting to make progress here."

"Are you? Good. Me too. Have you been dreaming?"

"Constantly. In fact, I sometimes have a hard time telling the difference between dreams and reality."

"Really? Could you give me an example?"

"Well, the other night I dreamt about my father. He was helping me build a tree fort. The dream went on forever. We had to get his old table saw out of the basement. And then Dad went and got our old orange extension cord and ran it out from the basement. First we built the ladder up the trunk. And then a base for the fort and we even got started on some of the walls before it started to rain. Big warm drops of summer rain. Dad ran in to get our old blue camping tarp and he threw it over the table saw and we used some of that yellow plastic rope to tie it off around the base so the tarp wouldn't blow away. By this time it was really raining so we had to run inside."

"That sounds like a nice dream."

George notices that for the first time since they began their sessions, Dr. Schueller is taking notes as he speaks.

"It was. But it took forever. I mean, it was really long and detailed. But I read somewhere that dreams only ever last like a minute or something. You're the sleep expert. Is that true?"

"To the best of our knowledge, yes. From brainwave activity, it would appear that during REM sleep, our brain begins to function very much as if it were awake. These periods of increased brain activity usually only last between 60 and 90 seconds."

"So how does our brain do it? How does it experience such a lengthy dream in such a short amount of real time?"

"Well, that's hard to answer. It would seem that our brain collapses our perception of time."

"But for my brain, it's real. For all intents and purposes I experienced that afternoon with my father. The impressions on my senses, the feel of the raindrops, all of that is imprinted on my memory."

"Yes, I suppose that's accurate."

"In fact, it's all relative. What's real to me is what's real. It's the same as what you're talking about with the value of things. They're worth what people are willing to pay for them. If people collectively decided not to pay for those things anymore, they'd instantly become worthless. The economy is like a giant collective dream that we've all agreed to buy into. Pardon the pun."

Dr. Schueller stops writing for the first time since George began describing his dream.

"George, this is all very interesting. Truly, your mind seems to be very open and I think that's excellent. But I do think there's a danger of losing focus."

"Right. Our focus. What was that again? To help me stop being scared of elevators? To get me to want to build networks? To stop me from suing the company? What was our focus? I seem to already have lost it!"

"My focus is to try to understand why it is you're being haunted by the man you watched plunge to his death."

"You're right. You're absolutely right. That's why they pay you the big bucks. Let's see. The last dream I had about Frank I was bashing in his face because he accused me of trying to kill him to steal Marcia away from him."

George's energy is wild now, thrashing about like a sheet in the wind just before a summer storm. Dr. Schueller is grabbing at the edges, trying to put her weight on top of him, trying to prevent him from blowing away.

"But you said you'd never met Marcia until the day you saw her here at my office. Not only is he haunting you, his timeline is out of whack."

She laughs, lightly, but his energy bowls her over.

"You know the crazy thing? What drew me to her in the first place? When I saw her here I could have sworn she was the woman having sex in the office across the street that Frank and I were arguing about."

"Is that why you broke into her files?"

This works. George shifts slightly in his chair, the picture of guilt.

"What do you mean?"

"Last week. The day after you saw Marcia here, someone accessed three private HR files, George Stevens, Frank Lewis and Marcia Winters, using a System Administrator pass that was created as a backdoor by the architect who built the intranet. This was the first time the pass had been used since the network was launched. I'm assuming that it was you that used the pass. Is that right?"

George is silent. Since the beginning of the session, he has been animated, fiery. Each sentence popping out of his mouth the instant it is formed. Now, he is quiet. His shoulders curve inward slightly.

"George?"

"Is that the new information you were referring to in your message?"

"Yes. No one else knows. After our last session, I was concerned about your relationship with Marcia. I went back into the company files and noticed that both your files had been accessed on the same day. It seemed a bit of a coincidence. So I asked a client of mine in IT security to do some forensics."

"Are you going to have me fired?"

Dr. Schueller lets out a whoop of laughter. It is the first time George has heard this laugh. A noisy, boisterous, shriek of a laugh, the kind of laugh that would embarrass a husband at a dinner party.

"Good God no! George, is that what you thought? I couldn't be an executive coach if my first rule wasn't confidentiality. No, George, my worry is with yours and Marcia's safety. I'm concerned about your interest in Marcia."

"My interest in Marcia? How does that concern you?"

George is quiet now. His aggression replaced by the traditional uncertainty that has followed him most of his life.

"Well, you met her here at my offices. As a result of that, you broke into company files. One, that's a serious breach of one of my client's privacy, but more concerning is that it's fairly extreme behavior, George."

"I think I've fallen in love with her."

"Somehow I don't find that reassuring."

"I'm not a stalker."

"Just what a stalker would say."

"That's what Marcia said."

He smiles as he says it, her presence entering the room for the first time. He feels warmed by it.

"Don't you think it's a bit odd? This desire to connect with the woman who was on the street when Frank landed while you stood at the top of his trajectory? How long do you think it took him to fall?"

"Four point five seconds. Give or take."

"Just four and a half seconds separating you and Marcia. And for Frank, four and a half seconds between life and death."

"She said she was rushing to meet him."

"Well, then, she couldn't have been the person making love in the office across the street, could she?"

George's jaw has dropped open. She is drawing out the analytical part of him, helping him close the door on his confusing, undeveloped emotions. Using her understanding of who he is to control his reactions. She enjoys this part of the dance, where there is something at stake. Like a bullfight. A noble opponent. She smiles and moves in to seal off the disruption.

"George, I think we need to establish some boundaries around these sessions. If I'm going to help, I need to... George? Are you listening?"

George isn't listening. Slowly, he places both hands on either armrest and pushes himself into a standing position.

"George?"

George walks across the office, opens the door and starts to run down the hallway. He races past Agnes, past the painting covered in chicken wire, down the marble staircase and bursts through the revolving door of the lobby and into the street.

:)

Dr. Schueller walks across her office and closes the door. She crosses to her desk, picks up the phone and dials. Waits. "Yes, hi Marcia, it's Liz Schueller here. I'd like to talk to you about George Stevens. I'd appreciate it if you'd give me a shout. If he tries to contact you before we've had a chance to speak, I'd ask that you wait until we've spoken. George appears to be going through some kind of transition and I'm not entirely sure how he will emerge. Hope you're well. I'm looking forward to our next session at the sleep lab. Bye for now."

She hangs up the phone. Picks it up a second time. "Oh, hello Agnes. Yes, that was George. Well, it looks like I've got a gap in my calendar now, and I think I'm going to try to close my eyes for a few minutes. Could you hold my calls? Unless it's Marcia Winters, in which case put her through. Thanks, dear."

Dr. Schueller lies on the leather couch that is against one wall of her office. She chooses a spot on the wall slightly above her line of sight and closes her eyes while counting to three. Inside her mind, she is descending a set of stairs that go deeper into herself. This quick form of self-hypnosis has allowed Dr. Schueller to function on minimal sleep since she came across the technique while doing her Masters degree. Twenty minutes later, she opens her eyes, fully revived and ready to greet her next client.

:)

On the street, George raises his right hand and flags a cab. He jumps in the back seat, gives his address. He is leaning forward for the whole ride, elbows perched on the front seats as he urges the cab forward. His right knee is bouncing up and down. His condo is close, but traffic is slow. Construction has narrowed the street the cab must take to the condo to one lane. Eventually, he gives the cab driver a ten dollar bill and decides to run the rest of the way. He leaves the cab and sprints the three blocks to his complex, goes up the back stairs and down the hallway, reaching for his keys before he is halfway to his door, twirling the keys through his fingers until he arrives at the one with the round end. He slides the key in and twists, kicks his black rubber-soled dress shoes off, closes the door behind him, runs down the hallway and opens the folding half door that hides the apartment-sized washer and dryer stacked on top of each other. There are clothes piled on top of the washer, crammed between the machine and the wall. George sweeps the clothes from on top of the machine onto the floor and starts rummaging through them, frantically sticking his hands in pants pockets, turning dress shirts inside out and shaking them upside down. He sees a pair of khakis at the back of the closet, almost jammed completely behind the washing machine. He pulls these pants out and puts his hand in the right pocket and feels what he's been expecting, dreading to find. He closes his hand around it and pulls it out, eyes closed. He opens his palms, opens his eyes, and looks at the two, half inch flathead screws that lay cupped in his palm.

"Oh God." It's an exhalation and he leans his head back against the hallway wall. He shuts his eyes, thinking, mind racing. He is shuffling through options: call Marcia; throw the screws away and say nothing; call Dr. Schueller. Then he remembers the e-mail he received from Frank's computer. The Darwin award about the guy who fell out of that building in Chicago.

And George is up and running down the hallway. Slaps open his laptop, fidgeting while it boots up. His eyes fall on the Swiss Army knife on the coffee table and he lets out a groan. The minute he sees the operating system screen, he is into the program files, the annals of the computer's memory. He opens the Program Files, Temporary Files directory, Internet cache, scans through url after url of porn sites and science sites, every webpage he's visited for the past few weeks until he sees it: "Step by step window installation: http://www.starlingtech.edu/office/window_replacement". His breath catches in his chest as he clicks on the link. The page is from an online civil engineering course detailing the installation of office windows. George swallows several times, thin watery bile, before realizing he's going to be sick. He races down the hall and throws up heavily into the toilet.

After flushing the toilet, he takes a drink of water, head held under the tap. He stares in the mirror at the face staring back. He hasn't even shaved since the day before he and Marcia took off for the cottage, what seems like months ago now.

George goes back down the hallway, picks up his phone and dials. Waits. Hears her recorded voice.

"Yeah, hi, Marcia? It's me George. Look, I really, really need to talk to you. I'm at home if you want to call. Or better yet, just come over. Maybe you're at work, shit I forgot. I'll try your other numbers. Well, listen, anyway, if you get the message call me. It's George. Thanks. Bye."

George hangs up the phone, walks down the hallway and climbs into his bed. He places the phone on the night table next to the bed, pulls the comforter up to his chin and stares at the wall.

:)

It's Marcia's first day back at the office. The morning started off with a meeting with Carol about a change in compensation strategy, but had ended in Carol expressing her concern for Marcia. That people had been noticing a loss of focus lately. She's been late for things, nodding off in meetings, and then mysteriously missing a day of work, with no contact information, no Out of Office reply on her e-mail. Marcia said she appreciated the concern. That yes, she had been having trouble sleeping since the incident a few weeks previous, but that she's seeing a doctor about it and feeling much more in control. This seems to reassure Carol and the meeting ends with, "You know my door's always open", allowing them both to leave the exchange feeling that they've handled themselves well.

Instead of returning to her office, Marcia heads straight for the elevators and goes back down to street level. She steps outside the building and lights a cigarette right next to the Share the Air sign. She checks her phone, which she had put on silent mode and sees 2 Missed Calls. First she listens to Dr. Schueller's message, then George's. After listening to the messages, she finishes her cigarette, highlights one of the numbers and pushes Send.

"Hello, Dr. Schueller please. It's Marcia Winters. Thank you."

A pause.

"Hello, Liz. Good to hear from you. No, just a quick trip to the cottage to recharge. I thought maybe a change of scenery, and you know, I was actually able to sleep up there. But your call sounded urgent. Yes, now is fine."

There is a long pause while Dr. Schueller speaks and Marcia listens, during which time Marcia lights a second cigarette, something she normally never does.

The conversation is punctuated by the occasional, "I see" and "No, of course not."

Eventually, "Well, you don't think he's dangerous, do you? No, of course not. Well, I certainly do appreciate your call, Liz. Absolutely, I will call you if he tries to get in touch. Thank you again. Yes, we're still on for the sleep lab. I'll see you then."

Marcia pushes End, crushes out the second cigarette and approaches the first taxi at the cab stand. She gets in the backseat, gives the driver George's address, leans back and stares out the window at the countless people in business casual, full suits and courier uniforms rushing about like high relief sculptures against the endless sweep of office buildings.

:)

George is still in bed when he hears the double intercom buzz on his phone. He picks up the phone and pushes the button that opens the door without saying hello. He waits until he hears the knock at the door, then shuffles down the hallway and opens it on Marcia, who is standing in a charcoal skirt suit, framed by the door. After the intimacy of the weekend, there is an awkward moment where each assesses whether to hug, kiss or shake hands. In the end, George stands aside and mumbles, "You got my message. Come in."

Marcia enters and walks to the high counter that separates the kitchen area from the rest of the living space. She climbs onto one of the bar stools next to the counter.

"Do you want a glass of juice? All I've got is orange."

"No, thank you. Your message said you needed to talk. Is everything okay?"

"Oh, yeah, right. But not, like I need to talk, like we need to talk, I need to talk. Sorry that didn't make sense. I just need to ask, I just need to figure some stuff out."

"Sure, George."

George is inward, blurred, and Marcia is distant and wary. They are disconnected in this reality.

"When you said you were going to meet Frank. On the street, the day he died. Where were you meeting him?"

"I don't really want to get into all this, George. I don't know that going over it all again is helpful. I'm not proud of what Frank and I were doing, okay?"

"I just need to know where you were meeting. Please?"

"Fine. We were meeting in an abandoned office. The floor was being redone and eventually it was going to be Frank's office."

"What floor?"

"Why are you asking me all these questions George? He died before I could get there, remember?"

There is plain irritation in her voice. She is beginning to regret and the feeling is like milk curdling inside. But George is on his own track, insistent and demanding.

"This office, was it on the 38th floor?"

"Yeah, maybe, yeah, sure. Why?"

"Do you remember anything else about it? The decoration, the colors of the walls, anything?"

"I only ever saw it once. I showed it to Frank one day and we agreed to meet there the next time. That was it."

"Was there any art on the walls? Something from the corporate collection?"

This question sticks. It triggers her memory, stands out as significant.

"Yeah, I think so. One of those Inuit prints. I remember it because I was picturing it one night when I was trying to get to sleep, when I first got the insomnia."

So far, George has been facing the living area of his condo. He sits down, then stands up again. He goes to stand at the window to stare out before beginning to pace again.

"What's this about George?"

"What do you think the odds are that someone else was having sex in that office at the exact same time you were supposed to be meeting Frank there to have sex with him? 'Cause that's what Frank and I saw: two people having sex against the window in the office where you and Frank were supposed to be meeting to have sex. What are the odds of that?"

"But Frank was with you and I was on the street."

"I know."

"George." Marcia stands and walks to face George. She cups his face in her hands. "George, you're very sweet. You're a sweet man. But you have to let this go."

"Don't you find this all a little weird?"

"Yes, George, I do. This is all a little weird. And it's for that reason that I'm going to say what I'm going to say. I think we should spend a little bit of time away from each other."

"What?"

George snaps into the present, into the eyes that are looking into his.

"I loved our weekend together. This has been a lot of fun and I really like you. But, it's just all too confusing right now. It's all wrapped up in this Frank thing and I think we could both use a little space."

The wound is immediate and breathtakingly painful.

"She got to you didn't she?"

"What are you talking about?"

"Dr. Schueller. She called you, didn't she?"

"Dr. Schueller is just concerned for your well-being. So am I."

"That fucking bitch." George whirls away from Marcia and stares out the window, his back tensed. "Fuck!"

"George, I'm going to go now, okay? I think a little space will help. Really, I do. Then maybe in a little while we could grab a coffee? This is just for a little while. Okay, George? Okay?"

But George isn't answering.

"I'm just going to let myself out. Okay? I'll call you soon, okay? Alright. Bye George."

With that, Marcia grabs her purse and exits the apartment, leaving George, still as a statue, staring out the window, a sound like the breaking of thin morning ice ringing in his ears.

:)

George has been pacing his apartment for an hour. It started when he wrote down three timelines on a notepad, which read as follows:

George:

10:20 enters Frank's office. Asks Frank to get him a double double coffee.

10:30 Frank leaves Frank's office, leaving George alone.

10:36 an e-mail about a man falling to his death in an office tower is sent from Frank's account to George's account while George is in Frank's office. George picks up binoculars and begins to scan the horizon.

10:50 Frank returns with no coffees. Frank and George argue.

10:56 Frank throws himself against the window and falls out.

Frank:

10:30 leaves office to get coffees.

Does not meet Marcia at 10:45. Reports seeing a man who is identical to him.

10:50 returns to office with wet pants.

10:56 falls out window.

Marcia:

10:30 goes for cigarette.

Is late for 10:45 meeting with Frank.

10:56 on street when Frank's body lands.

George takes the porcelain buddha and removes the small bag of drying marijuana. He rolls the crumbly green and brown weed into a joint and lights it. The end flares into flame and burns until George blows out the tip and draws deeply. The smoke fills his lungs, scrapes the back of his throat, making him cough and gag. Immediately his head feels light and spinny from the combination of the drug and coughing. He continues to smoke while running over the list of timelines, which don't add up, don't make sense at all.

Why would Frank agree to get George a coffee at 10:30 if he was supposed to meet Marcia at 10:45? Unless he forgot? But who would forget that? Who sent George the e-mail from Frank's computer? Who was having sex in the empty office across the street if it wasn't Frank and Marcia? Frank's twin – the double he saw? But George has known Frank his whole life, knows he doesn't have a twin. Where did those two screws in George's pocket come from?

The questions revolve endlessly, eventually feeling as if his thoughts are being pulled apart like cotton candy.

There is of course an easy answer. That it's all true. It was George that sent the e-mail from Frank's computer. It was George that removed the screws from Frank's window and sabotaged the silicone seal, knowing he had a meeting about leadership and risk-taking with a junior team member that day. Frank was having sex with Marcia across the street. George did recognize Marcia as the woman in the window when he saw her at Dr. Schueller's office that first time.

Except that it can't be true. The timing's all wrong. And he can't remember any of it. And Marcia says it wasn't her across the street, that she saw Frank land at street level.

George's hands are shaking slightly. He is starting to panic. He rolls another joint and smokes it halfway through. Thinks about going for a walk, puts on his shoes and jacket. But when he opens the door and looks into his hallway, he experiences another attack. His heart starts to pound against his ribs, his perspective shifts as the hallway seems to expand and distort. Quickly, he closes the door, leans his back against it, staring up at the cheap flush mount half circle lighting fixture. He can see the carcasses of small insects that have somehow gotten into the fixture and died. He takes off his shoes, his jacket and goes to the fridge to pour a glass of orange juice. He paces the apartment, a captive now. Eventually he sits down again and turns on the TV, flips to the discovery channel which is showing a program about nuclear fission. He is drawn into the program, trying to understand how an atom can be split, how something so fundamental can be divided, how so much energy could be created from something so small, so basic.

He is very stoned, very tired. The muscles in George's hand begin to slacken, the remote control slipping slightly in his grip, his mind unresponsive to the sensation. He is beginning to drift, in the half world of wakefulness and sleep when he hears a knock. George stands and shuffles to the front door, barely able to lift his feet, like moving his legs through knee-deep water.

He opens the door and sees Frank. Frank is wearing a ball cap with mesh at the back that has a Flamingo on the front, its arched neck creating the P in Palm Beach, Florida and has several cameras slung around his neck.

"Come with me" he says. George follows Frank out the door.

It takes a moment for George to locate himself. At first, it's the heavy humidity of the air that triggers his memory. Then the background noise of children shrieking comes into focus. He reaches up, removes his fogged glasses and wipes them on his shirt. He looks around, sees blurry browns and greens, the soft edges of many people blending into a shifting mass. He replaces his glasses and looks around. In front of George is a huge, simulated rainforest, a pavilion at the zoo, with a family of gorillas lounging under a large rope ladder. The family clearly spans three generations: there is a patriarch, with his thick wrinkled leather face; the matriarch nursing a baby casually cupped in her long, long arm; and two young adults picking through the pile of fruits and vegetables, trying to ignore the infant who is hanging from the rope and attempting to grab the food before they can put it in their mouths.

Frank taps George on the shoulder, gestures with his thumb towards a strong, restless gorilla in a smaller area behind them.

"The guy in the cage behind us is the teenager. Too aggressive. They call him Zeus. Every time they let him in with the family, he starts to fight with the older one. He's spent his whole adolescence in isolation. Watch him. All he does, all day, is run to the gate, down to the swing, up to the window. That's what aggression does when it's got nowhere to go. See, in the wild, he'd have someone to fight. That's what he's supposed to do. But here, they can't allow that, so for the sake of harmony, he has to live in isolation. Funny isn't it? I mean, funny, like fucked up funny. You know what I mean George?"

Frank is staring at George very intently.

George moves away from Frank without answering. He goes over to a large plastic funnel, around thigh-high, the kind that's used to raise money for the zoo. There is a ramp on either side of the funnel, wide enough to hold a coin. Children hold a quarter at the top of the ramp and then release it, watching as it rolls around and around the funnel, the coin's speed increasing as it nears the center of the funnel, finally revolving madly around itself before falling into the void below. There are two young boys and a father next to the funnel. They look like twins. George overhears the man say, "I only have one more left." George puts his hand in his pocket, finds a single quarter. He hands it to the nearer of the two identical boys.

"What do you say?" says the man to the boy.

"Thank you", says the boy to George.

The two boys hold their coins at the top of the funnel. "One, two, three, go!" They both let go of the coins. The coins roll down the ramp and begin slowly circling each other. They are on opposite sides of the funnel, like two satellites orbiting the black hole in the middle. The ridged edges of the quarters make a noise on the hollow plastic funnel, the noise increasing in pitch as they begin to roll faster closer to the centre. By the end, they will almost be touching each other, madly spinning around the centre of the funnel for what seems like an eternity before/

"There's no stopping gravity is there?"

George turns and sees Frank standing behind him. "Eventually the coins are going to have to meet. It's just gravity." Frank removes the Palm Beach cap to run his fingers through his hair. A large clump of hair comes out in his hand, which he lets fall to the ground.

"What do you want to tell me, Frank?"

"I wanted to say thank you."

"For what?"

Heath

"When I fell, it was all reunited, all of me, every moment of my life, brought together."

"Why are you still here? Why can I still see you?"

"I just needed to pay you back." Frank reaches into the funnel and quickly pinches one of the rolling quarters between his thumb and index finger. He throws it in the air and George watches as it tumbles heads over tails in the air, its trajectory finally ending in George's open extended hand.

When he looks up, Frank is gone.

George shuffles back to his apartment, back to the couch, and slumps back down. His head drops to his chest and his hand goes completely slack, the remote falling from his grasp with a clatter as it hits the ground. George's eyes snap open again and this time when he wakes, he understands. Everything. Time is both particle and wave. Time is like gravity. Time can be divided and re-united. Time is life.

Chapter 17

It feels like a million years since the last time Marcia was here, irrelevant somehow, her sleeplessness eclipsed by the events of the past few days. She is answering Dr. Schueller's questions, but feels distant, removed from the moment she is in. She knows she's too slow to answer, her voice too soft around the edges, but she can't reel herself back in.

She and Dr. Schueller are sitting in reclining IKEA chairs, a white round plastic side table between them. The picture of a sci-fi sleep lab. There is a small video camera to one side and Dr. Schueller is taking notes. New age synthesizer music is playing repetitive sequences that tug gently at Marcia's attention. Her eyes are lightly closed.

"Marcia. Marcia?"

"I'm sorry, Liz. I'm just having a hard time concentrating. I think I fell asleep for a second."

"Understandable. But I think it's important you try to focus on my questions, focus on my voice. Now, with the sound of my voice you are going to go a level deeper. In front of you there is a set of stairs leading down and with each exhalation, you are descending these stairs. When you have arrived at the bottom of these stairs, I want you to raise your right finger."

There is a moment's hesitation in which Dr. Schueller wonders if it will work, if Marcia will be receptive to this type of work. Her breathing is deep and regular, the silk of her blouse gently rising and falling as the breath drops in and out of her belly. At last, her right finger lifts off the arm of the chair, softly but unmistakable.

"You were telling me about your hiking trip with George and your mother."

"At the cottage."

"Yes. Can you picture where you are?"

"We're at a look-out."

"What do you see?"

"I see sky and blue sparkling water until it curves over the horizon."

"Good. I want you to listen to my voice and I'm going to ask you to do something very specific. Can you do that for me Marcia?"

"Yes."

"Good. In a minute, I am going to ask you to look at you watch, but I don't want you to do it right away. I want you to look down, very slowly, in stages. If the horizon is a 90 degree angle to your body, I want you to lower your head very slowly, in five degree increments. Okay, start now by dropping your head five degrees. When you have dropped your head five degrees, I want you to raise your right finger. Good. Now I want you to lower your head another five degrees, raising your right finger when you have finished. Good. Now continue to do this, five degrees at a time, until you are looking down at your watch."

During this time, Marcia does not move. Her face is relaxed, the features soft. Perhaps it is Marcia's exhaustion that has made her so open to hypnotic suggestion. Weeks of sleeplessness have placed her reality firmly between dream state and full alertness. The hallucinations, while benign, are testament to this. While Dr. Schueller is jotting down notes and recording the time at set intervals, she hears a change in Marcia's breathing. Almost imperceptible at first, it's as if there's a catch in her exhalation, an extra step before the air is released. She looks up from her notes, looks at Marcia's face. Her breathing is coming faster now, the catch more pronounced. Dr. Schueller is about to say something, about to intervene, when Marcia's hands shoot straight out, fingers splayed, each muscle clenched.

"Okay, Marcia, you're okay. We're going to distance you now. I want you to feel yourself getting lighter, as if you can feel each atom of your body begin to fall away like grains of sands."

Marcia's hands and arms begin to drop slowly, like objects dropped in water, until they come to rest again on the arms of her chair. Her breathing falls back into the deep, regular pattern from before.

"I'm going to ask you to come back now and as I count to five I want you to become more and more alert. One, you're going to remember everything you just experienced, two, I want you to follow the sound of my voice, three, you will keep the memory but at a distance, four, wiggling your fingers and toes and five. Take your time to open your eyes whenever you feel comfortable."

Marcia takes a single, deep breath, smiles, and opens her eyes.

"How do you feel?"

"I feel wonderful. I really do. It was like the sound of your voice allowed me to let go. Like an anchor or something so that I could let myself float free. How long was that?"

"Everything included, beginning to end, about 20 minutes."

"You're kidding me. I would have said five, ten absolute max."

"That's one of the peculiar effects of hypnotism. There's an exercise practitioners of hypnotism frequently use with clients. They will ask them to put their hands in a bucket of ice water and hold it there for a full minute. As you can imagine, over time, this becomes extraordinarily painful. They then do it a second time, under hypnosis, this time for 90 seconds. Consistently, the clients will report no diminishment in the intensity of the sensation, but will vehemently deny that their hands were in the water for more than twenty or thirty seconds. Somehow, our mind seems to detach itself from how we internally monitor the passage of time."

"Why did you ask me to look at my watch?"

"That's simply an exercise to help put you in control of your non-physical self. It's a way of helping you to literally explore your subconscious. If you can control your actions, it allows you explore and potentially remember things that your conscious mind has overlooked. But in the middle of it something happened. What was it? Did you see something?"

"I felt like I was about to fall. I looked down and all I could see was water and air beneath me, and I felt like I lost my footing, like I lost my grip on the ledge."

"You did something quite fascinating. What we call Moro's reflex in newborns. After months in their mother's weightless, directionless uterus, babies all of a sudden find themselves lying on the flat ground with a definite up and down and sideways, all things they've never experienced before. And as they become accustomed to gravity and direction, they will sometimes suddenly shoot out their hands and feet, as if to prevent themselves from falling. It might be some vestigial reflex from when infants would have been carried on their primate mothers through the trees. That's what you did. As if you'd lost sense of direction, as if you were afraid of falling."

"You think I'm afraid of heights?"

"It would make sense. You saw Frank fall from a building. You recently fainted when put in a situation that would cause vertigo in many of us. And I think there is a connection to your sleep patterns."

"Sometimes when I'm falling asleep, I'll start awake because I feel like I've tripped, or I'm falling back or something."

Dr. Schueller is sitting up quite straight now, staring fixedly at Marcia.

"That's exactly it. That happens when your brain starts to slip into the slower brain waves. You're dropping down from the faster alpha waves down to the slower delta waves. But it doesn't happen gradually. There's a sudden jump that occurs – it's called a sleep spindle or K-complex. There's a lot of interesting work being done on this point of transition. This is also the point when sleep terrors occur in children. And it's exactly when you've been waking up. At the moment when your brain is receiving conflicting messages. It feels like you're falling, but you're not. It responds the only way it knows how – nausea. I think your insomnia is actually being caused by vertigo."

Dr. Schueller is flushed with excitement. It is the first display of emotion that Marcia has seen from her. She feels oddly disconnected from the discovery, as if Dr. Schueller owned it, as if it wasn't her experience that they were discussing.

"In other words, my mother was right."

Dr. Schueller laughs. Marcia doesn't.

"Well, in a sense. This does seem to be an aftershock of the event you were witness to."

Dr. Schueller leans in closer now, elbows on knees.

"I'm going to propose two solutions. One is very simple. These." She holds out two fabric rings that look vaguely like a bicycle-rider's pant protector. She pulls open the cuff with the tearing sound of velcro and holds it out for Marcia to take.

"This is a motion-sickness wristband. I brought them with me because I thought it might help with the nausea. It's very simple. It applies pressure to the appropriate points, which blocks nausea before it registers with your brain. I'm hoping that if you wear this it may allow your body to get over the hump of that first sleep spindle and allow you to get some rest. It's very simple. You just put one band on each wrist before going to sleep. That's the short term solution."

Marcia takes the cuffs and holds them in her hands, turning them over. Opens and closes the velcro fasteners a few times.

"And the long term?"

"Well, you seem very receptive to hypnosis. I'd like to go back to the day you saw Frank fall."

Marcia looks up at Dr. Schueller. Holds her eye. A large part of her simply wants to walk away: from George, from Dr. Schueller, from the whole stupid problem her life has become. She wants to get away from it, not go further into it. But she has made a decision. In leaving George in his apartment, she made a decision to trust Dr. Schueller, to throw her lot in with science, the lab, Schueller Management Consultants. It is the only way she can see to get back to her life.

She nods slowly.

:)

Inside her observation room, Dr. Schueller is observing the feeds. She is able to observe several versions of reality from this booth. One is the visual reality recorded by the video camera, transmitted through the cable and displayed on the television monitor. A second is the recording of the electrical currents traveling through Marcia's brain. Another records the subcutaneous muscular movement, another the rate at which Marcia's central muscle pushes blood out through her body.

From this perspective, Marcia has successfully passed through a full sleep cycle, from wakefulness to dream state and back again. All of these recorders and transmitters of reality confirm this fact. A fact made possible by Dr. Schueller's clever use of the motion-sickness band. She sometimes thinks that her job is to find ways to trick other people's brains into functioning in the manner which they were designed to function. That somehow, humans occasionally develop glitches that need to be corrected. At this moment, she is thinking of George, of the similarity in their work. If she were working on a network, she would describe the wristband approach as a work-around, a bypass that will allow for normal traffic flow, while the hypnosis is taking the system offline to correct the root cause.

Elizabeth Schueller observes Marcia through three complete sleep cycles before deciding she is satisfied and ready to call it a night. At 11:04 pm, she turns off the television monitor, closes the door to the observation room and calls down the hallway to John.

"I'm headed home, John. Page me if anything needs my attention. Otherwise I'll be back at 7:00"

Dr. Schueller puts on her overcoat, pulls her small purse over her shoulder, picks up her briefcase and exits the sleep lab. As she exits the parkade, she turns her Audi onto the usually deserted street without looking, only to see a flash of lights out of the corner of her eye and hear the sickening crunch of another car striking her passenger side. Her body is flung forward and sideways before snapping to a stop as the seatbelt locks into place, while her head slams into the side airbag that deploys with a loud bang at the moment of impact. Dr. Schueller hears the explosion of sound, sees the white airbag engulf her vision, and passes out.

:)

Inside Marcia is another reality from that which the doctor has been observing. The room is non-existent to Marcia's closed eyes and distant thoughts. Her body is soaking up sleep like a desiccated sponge absorbs water. Her mind is tripping and flying in and out of dreams, frantically scanning weeks of thoughts and impulses, fears and desires. Her heart is drawing oxygen and sending it out to every extremity. And deep, deep in the darkest place, a small fleck of life is hanging on to the edge of all it knows. This life that cannot see, cannot eat or breathe, and yet is engaged in a movement forward that it could no more stop or alter than the earth cease to revolve around the sun. At this point it is little more than movement, little more than a unit of infinite potential. Two cells that will become four, that will become eight, that will increase exponentially, beginning to turn possibility into reality. A split unit of infinity.

Chapter 18

D̲r. Schueller is sitting across from George, behind her desk. He is sitting in one of the office chairs positioned directly across from her desk, rather than in one of the more comfortable chairs where clients reveal themselves. He is sitting where she meets with colleagues, the director of finance, her assistant. She has a piece of gauze taped over one eye that can't completely hide the purplish bruising that is spreading from underneath. Her left arm from her elbow to just past her thumb is encased in a rigid, new-looking cast.

"I wasn't sure I was going to see you again. I found our last session troubling."

"Well, you didn't have to beat yourself up about it." A weak smile plays on George's face as he nods towards the cast.

"I appreciate your attempt at levity, George, but I'm afraid I find myself unable to match it. What can I do for you?"

She is fighting back tears. She is feeling overwhelmed and angry and doesn't want this man to be sitting across from her. The premonition of defeat she had is closing in on her, like the peripheral darkness closing in on a person in the early stages of blindness.

"In our first session you told me that I could always trust you to tell me the truth. That it's the truth that sets you apart."

"That's right."

She is feeling tired, her eyelids wanting to drop on their own. After leaving the ER, the adrenaline from the accident had kept her up well into the night. For the first time in years, Elizabeth Schueller slept in. Normally her eyes open a minute or two before her alarm goes off. This morning she finally woke to the sound of her bedside radio that had been playing classical music and updating her sleeping form to traffic and weather conditions on the tens for the past forty-five minutes. She'd sprung out of bed and raced to the sleep lab, arriving at 8:36. Marcia was long gone, as was John. A Post-It note was stuck to observation room that simply read "Slept great. See you for hypnosis at 6:00." Then when she'd arrived at the office, George had been waiting for her. Agnes tried to explain that she was booked solid all day, that he would need an appointment, but George had insisted on waiting. And now here he was, asking for the truth.

"Do you think I'm capable of murder?"

Dr. Schueller smiles without moving.

"Why do you ask that question, George? Surely, you must know how that comes across. If I had one of those secret red buttons that calls security under my desk, I'd be pushing it now."

A silence.

"I don't. Have a red button."

"Look, you've been profiling me, right? Gathering a psychological assessment of me. Do I fit the profile of someone capable of killing another human being?"

Dr. Schueller's voice remains impassive. She is still, afraid the slightest movement will splinter the air into a million fragments.

"Before I answer your question, George, and I will answer your question, but before I do that, I want you to be very careful right now. You and I have confidentiality. However, if you tell me of any action of yours that is against the law, it is my legal responsibility to report you to the police. Moreover, it is my ethical responsibility to encourage you to report anything to the police yourself. Have you killed someone, or are you contemplating the possibility?"

Each word is distinct and separate from the other. George's energy on the other hand is shifting and awkward, like snakes under his skin.

"No. I don't know. I don't remember. It's impossible. But you kept saying that I had to listen to what Frank was trying to tell me in my dreams. And then there's the screws and the window diagrams, but who knows, maybe someone's playing some weird fucking psychological game with me, or maybe it's the FBI, I don't know."

"Then, to answer your question, George, yes, I believe every human on this planet is capable of killing someone under the right circumstances. And frankly, I think it's the sophistication of our social structures that prevents murder from happening more often than it does. Do I think you specifically are predisposed towards violence or volatility? I don't know. I wouldn't have thought so, but your behavior over the past few weeks has been troubling. I have to ask you this. Is Marcia in danger?"

"Marcia? What? No! No. You don't get it."

"Then explain it to me, George."

She's too tired for this. She's being careful, choosing each word, doing her job. And yet, now, at the strangest of moments, she is distracted, drawn away from his words, his need. She is staring at George's face and a realization enters her mind: she doesn't like him. She's never not liked a client before. Clients are clients. They aren't to be liked or disliked. They are individual revenue-streams and need to be given the care and attention necessary to achieve the desired outcomes. Dr. Schueller is committed to excellence and excellence doesn't depend on personal preference. But it's undeniable. She is experiencing an intense and growing dislike of George Stevens.

"Have you ever heard of particle/wave duality in physics?"

"Tell me."

"At its most basic level, matter behaves as both a particle and a wave. Which is impossible. They're mutually exclusive."

"The idea of a paradox has profound spiritual implications."

George closes his eyes briefly, takes a calming breath.

"I thought about that for a long time. What you said about some God sitting at the bottom of the pile. That's not what this is about. That's a shortcut. Can't figure it out? Must be God. But it's not spiritual, it's a fuck up in the coding. Simple as that. If paradoxes exist, and they do, and if our brains can't accept them, and they can't, then there's something wrong with us. It means that what we experience is not everything there is. There's more out there that our brain simply doesn't process, that we're just not designed to understand. Which runs contrary to everything I've ever been raised to believe."

Pain is spreading from the back of Dr. Schueller's head, creeping around to the front. "Maybe we're not supposed to understand, maybe we should simply accept."

At this, the energy writhing under the surface explodes.

"What a stupid fucking thing to say. What an unbelievably stupid, irritating, Dr. Phil daytime television fucking thing to say. That's what you get for $600 an hour? Acceptance? Fuck you and your acceptance."

George stands, walks away from her desk towards the window. He stares out. He is throwing his anger at her, classic transference. These explosions are moments of opportunity, opportunities to redirect, to guide through careful questioning, but in this moment, she sees an opportunity to be rid of him, rid of the whole situation.

"What are you really doing here George? All you do is complain about your job. You want to get me to say your job sucks? At least you don't live in a village with no water, no money and a 75% chance of contracting AIDS. I gotta tell you George, you're running out of options here. Eventually I'm going to have to go back to your company and tell them that your profile no longer fits the company's. Having satisfied all contractual obligations, they will offer you a package, which you will take and that will be the end of the story. If that's what you'd like, and it sounds like it is, we can start the process right now, because frankly, I have a headache, you're not a scheduled appointment and I don't appreciate being sworn at in my own office."

She pulls out her handbag, fumbles for the bottle of pain-killers they gave her at the hospital, shakes two into her hand and swallows them dry, one sticking momentarily at the back of her throat, triggering a slight retching reflex.

Her anger calms George. He realizes it has always been her directness that's drawn him to her. Not trust, or even hope, but a grudging respect for the bluntness of her words.

"Look, you set me on this path. You told me to listen to what my dreams are telling me. Well, I have, I've listened and I'm not so sure I can look at the world the same way anymore. I think all of us might have made some kind of giant mistake about the way we live our lives. Some kind of giant mistake based on one simple, one very simple and one very wrong belief: that time moves forward and only forward."

"What are you talking about, George?" She is simply tired now, wants the conversation to end.

"I'm a computer geek. I work with binary systems. You know, it's one or it's zero, it's if or it's then. One or the other, with no in between. But that's not what you see. You see colors, text, graphics, animation. It's hard to believe that absolutely everything you see is actually just made up of ones and zeros."

"What, like the Matrix? Is this what's going on? Some kind of giant conspiracy theory?"

George is looking out the window, the ideas taking form as he speaks them. The experiences of the past month are opening and unfolding into a clear structure before his eyes, his mouth barely able to keep pace with the thoughts.

"It's not a conspiracy. It's a glitch. A glitch in our make-up, in our understanding of reality. As humans. It makes sense. We evolved to live in Newton's world. Of course we did, because we have to eat, we need shelter. So our brains evolved to deal with the world around us and anything not useful, it shuffled over to dreams, to the unconscious. Doesn't mean the other side doesn't exist, it just means our brains aren't designed to handle it. But the reality is that light is at the same time particle and wave. The reality is that the universe is expanding while at the same time it is in fact already infinite. Think of that: infinity is expanding. That'll give you a headache. So because we can't comprehend this, our brain splits reality into two. It divides time into the everyday reality of time, which is straight ahead, one unit of time after the next, and the other side of time, which is this river, this wave of experience which has no beginning, no end, it simply is. And since we can't understand that, we draw a line between awake and asleep, alive and dead, one and zero. But it's arbitrary, it's this totally fucking arbitrary distinction. That's what he's been trying to tell me in my dreams."

During this time that George has been speaking, he has had his back turned to Dr. Schueller. At first, she thought to check her Blackberry only to quickly check her calendar, to see her next appointment. But then it was in her hand, and she couldn't resist a quick glance at her e-mails. She's about to open an e-mail that's come in from a prospective client she's been waiting to hear from, when George finishes speaking. Dr. Schueller puts down the Blackberry and responds, picking up the threads of their conversation.

"And you think it's science, not the trauma of watching someone die that's brought you to this point? George, the brain is incredibly powerful. Entire worlds can be created. Take memory. Memory is an entirely subjective experience. We remember what we want to remember and forget the rest. And whatever doesn't fit with what we want to believe, we change. George, you have to consider the possibility that you're making all this up. That rather than experience the emotions that this incident has welled up in you, your brain has constructed an alternate reality in which you don't have to experience the pain you are suffering. Your brain is defaulting to what it knows best, what it trusts."

"In our first session you said you weren't going to tell me it was all in my head. That anyone could do that and that you were different from just anyone."

Dr. Schueller's headache has spread around her skull, applying consistent and painful pressure equally.

She reaches up with her index and middle fingers and begins to massage her temples in circles.

"Look, George, my question is this: How can you be sure this crisis you are experiencing isn't entirely of your own devising?"

"I can't. That's the point. That's exactly the point."

A moment of light as a different angle occurs to her, a chance to knock him off-track.

"What if I said it was all my fault?"

"What do you mean?"

"We like to say that blame is useless. That things were nobody's fault. But we're more and more likely to sue our neighbor, our boss, the government, the tobacco companies. But you know what? Sometimes someone is to blame. What would you say if I told you this was all my fault."

"I'd sue. Like that woman in Albuquerque who sued McDonald's for the coffee being too hot."

"Really?"

"No."

"George, I believe that your experience of the last few months has been in large part my fault. Frank was a client. A good client. He had a secret life. He liked risk, adventure. He would go skydiving, he loved boxing. Business trips he'd take an extra day to go white water rafting. He said those were the only times he truly felt alive. I coached him to use this as a leadership skill in the workplace, to lead his team by extolling the virtues of risk-taking. I helped him write that speech. I gave him the quote. I encouraged him to lead by example."

During this, George has turned again to look at Dr. Schueller. He is listening to her very carefully. The intensity of his stare almost makes her question this path, worried it might tip him over. But as she progresses, she realizes it is her only choice, to try to remove him as protagonist from this story he has created.

"You helped him write that speech."

"I did."

"Fear is the enemy of success."

"Me."

"Risk-taking means leaping with the knowledge that you will either land on solid ground/"

"/or you will learn to fly. You know what else? That memo that Bob Tillman sent out, the one you read to me at our first appointment?"

"You?"

"Yup. You've been obsessed by guilt. You've placed yourself at the centre of the universe, and no matter how earnest your quest, it is still an act of egotism. There is no fatal flaw, the world isn't broken, you are. But it wasn't your fault. Not because no one ever is to blame, as the song goes, but because it was my fault. Me."

"I'm glad these sessions have been helpful to you."

"George."

"My fee is six hundred an hour. But don't worry I'll hook you up with someone over at HR. Maybe you know her? Marcia Winters. I understand you've been doing some great work with her."

With this, George turns and walks out of Dr. Elizabeth Schueller's office. For a moment, she stands, staring at the closed door. She then picks up a glass paperweight with Centre Capital Official Partner etched into it, the letters white and opaque on the heavy, clear glass, and hurls it at the door. The paperweight hits the frame and, surprisingly, explodes into thousands of needle-sharp shards.

:)

Outside there is a man walking down the street. He is wearing khaki trousers and a button-down short-sleeved shirt. He is several blocks away from Dr. Schueller's office, completely unaware of the conversation that has taken place between George and Dr. Schueller. He is identical to George in every aspect. As George exits Dr. Schueller's office for the last time, the man turns from the northbound street he was taking, onto a westbound street. George clatters down the staircase of the office building, across the marble atrium and out the revolving door where he once watched Marcia smooth her hair. There is a chill as the wind tunnels down the street, and the man decides

Heath

to cross over to the sunny side of the street. As he exits the building, George sees the man that is identical to him in every way crossing the street. George is standing, staring at the man, when he is bumped from behind by someone trying to exit the revolving doors that he is now blocking. By the time he excuses himself, waits for the streetcar to pass and finally runs over to the sunny side of the street, the man is gone.

Chapter 0

Marcia is again in the sleep lab, again lying back in the plump reclining chair, again John is applying the electrodes and again she has the smell of Boss cologne wash over her. With the strangeness of the lab starting to dissipate, Marcia starts to feel something in the vein of enjoyment. Being fussed over, the delicate professional touch, the attention. Like the feeling of having her hair washed before being cut. She closes her eyes, exhales and smiles slightly. She remembers when her mother was in hospital, fighting the cancer. The hospital with its sounds of pain and smell of sanitizer and fluorescent lights and bile-colored clothes and flimsy curtains. There's something to be said for privatized medicine, she thinks as she squirms her back into a more comfortable position.

"Would you like a pillow to support your neck?"

More like a spa than a hospital, really.

"Yes, that would be lovely."

John offers her a grey, inflated travel pillow which she slips into place around the nape of her neck. This pillow is just the right mix of firmness and softness, not the kind you find at airports.

"Well, I think we're in the homestretch here, Marcia." Dr. Schueller has entered the lab where Marcia is lying back, fully attached to the electronic monitors. "Thank you, John. If you wouldn't mind recording the results from the booth."

John smiles at Marcia. It's a good job. He's well-paid, Doctor Schueller is offering increasing responsibilities and

209

to be honest, the class of patient he deals with at the sleep lab is a cut above what he would be dealing with in a typical residency. Occasionally, Doctor Schueller yells at him, but he's learned to keep his head down, learned not to offer too much information when asked a question, learned not to challenge, not to suggest, not to offer anything at all, except the odd smile and some tenderness that he slips to the patients on the side.

"Oh my goodness! What happened to your eye?" Marcia starts to sit up, but relaxes when she feels the resistance of the wires attached to her.

"The dangers of driving when overtired. Just stupid on my part. I have an unfortunate habit of not heeding my own advice. More importantly, how are you doing?"

"Fantastic! You're truly a genius, Liz. These wristbands have worked like a charm! I had an absolutely normal sleep last night. It's like all this never happened. I knew I made the right choice in coming to you!"

"I'm very glad to hear that, Marcia. Failing my clients is simply not an option for me. I see myself as a last line of defense for my clients."

Marcia is beginning to feel her old self. Feels the optimism that she has chosen for herself as a conscious approach to life return to the surface, the darkness of the past few weeks receding, like the backside of an eclipse. She's almost like her mother as she claps her hands together and asks, "So, what are we going to do tonight?"

"Well, the wristbands have dealt with the physical reality of your vertigo, but they aren't a long-term solution. To truly deal with the problem, I think we need to remove the trigger mechanism. So, I want to hypnotize you again. You were very receptive to hypnotic suggestion last time, and I think there's a dual benefit in your case. The first is that hypnotism can help us go back to the traumatic event and uncover details that may be overlooked or even blocked out by the conscious mind. Beyond that, though, hypnosis brings you into the realm of theta waves, what I think of as half-consciousness. This corresponds to the sleep stage where you are experiencing difficulty, and I think the controlled entry into that space will allow us to uncover what's making you wake up. John will be monitoring your readings, so we'll be able to gauge when you've entered the hypnotic state."

Marcia closes her eyes and smiles again. She wriggles slightly in the chair.

"Marcia, before we begin, did you ever hear from George?"

Her eyes remain closed.

"Yes, he called me right after you did. He still seems very upset about everything."

"Yes, I think you're right. And where are things now, if you don't mind me asking?"

"Well, I told him I thought it was best we didn't see each other for awhile. That I thought a little distance would do us both some good."

"Good. Good. Yes, I think that is probably the right answer. I had a similar experience and I reached a similar conclusion: that we should probably discontinue our work together."

Marcia pauses, then opens her eyes to look at Doctor Schueller.

"I thought you were the last line of defense."

Liz Schueller raises her eyebrows slightly.

"Sometimes this work can be a crutch and painful as it may be, the only way to truly move forward is to cut those ties. Certainly, we fulfilled the terms of the contract, there's no issue there. It's just that in this case, I believe George will be better off working this through on his own. Now. Let's focus on you."

Marcia closes her eyes once more.

"Yes, let's focus on me."

:)

At this moment, George is sitting in the living room of Sybil's two-bedroom condo, drinking lemon ginger tea. This is where she downsized to after the divorce. "Why do I need some big old empty place when I can go to the cottage anytime I want? Much better to be at the centre of it all." The condo is a low-rise in a wealthy neighborhood. The doorman knows everyone by name and is genuinely nice, not the unctuousness you'd expect from one of those expensive new developments. Outside the window are trees and just beyond the trees, the skyline of the downtown core all lit up like the world class city it always claims to be.

The walls are decorated with watercolors, washed out paintings of gardens and pastoral settings. If George were to venture into Sybil's bedroom, he would see a perfectly made bed with throw-pillows and the late afternoon sun streaming in.

When George arrived, Sybil had exclaimed with pleasure, hugged him with a kiss on each cheek. No questions, just tea and some Peak Freens. Now they are sitting drinking their tea in silence, staring thoughtfully out at the city.

"I keep thinking about what you said about the birds."

"And what was that, George?"

"That sometimes we just have to listen deeper into the woods. That when we listen more deeply, there are layers and layers of perception that very rarely enter our consciousness."

"I said all that?"

"I'm paraphrasing."

"Well, you make me sound very smart. Thank you."

At this, George lets out a loud bark of a laugh. "You're funny Sybil. You make me forget all the other stuff."

"It might be the tea."

George laughs again, then closes his eyes for a moment and breathes in. He's almost sad to let go of this moment of calm. Sad that things have to keep moving forward.

"I'm very sorry to barge in like this. It must appear very strange."

Sybil is sitting, unflappable.

"Not at all. You appear to be having a crise de coeur. And in the middle of the confusion, something jumped out at you that said you had to visit me. You don't know why, but you're in one of the rare moments of your life where you're following through on your instincts. It happens to all of us, George. It's just that at this time, it happened to be me."

During this, Sybil has been looking at George, while George has been looking out the window. The first tear that wells up feels like an accident, something that could be corralled and brought back. But it is followed by another, and pretty soon there is a wet stream of tears flowing down his cheeks.

"I don't feel lonely with you. I think I've been lonely all my life."

Sybil picks up the thread immediately, generously.

"I wonder when that loneliness starts. We're so warm and loved in our parents' arms and at some point, something happens that makes us aware of our aloneness. It seems to be at the heart of so many of our decisions, but I'm not sure we know why it's there."

She hands George a box of tissues. He pulls one out slowly, allowing it to unfold from the box. He wipes his eyes, his cheeks, sniffs loudly and exhales shakily.

"Have you ever heard of the term 'doppelganger?'"

"Well, sure, it's like a double."

"I printed this off Wikipedia."

He hands Sybil a piece of paper that has been folded into four, slightly curved from being carried in his back pocket.

A doppelgänger is the ghostly double of a living person, a sinister form of bilocation. In the vernacular, "Doppelgänger" has come to refer (as in German) to any double or look-alike of a person. The literal translation of the German word is "doublewalker", meaning someone who is acting (e.g. walking) the same way as another person. The word is also used to describe the sensation of having glimpsed oneself in peripheral vision, in a position where there is no chance that it could have been a reflection. They are generally regarded as harbingers of bad luck. In some traditions, a doppelgänger seen by a person's friends or relatives portends illness or danger, while seeing one's own doppelgänger is an omen of death.

Sybil reads the paper, then refolds it and hands it back to George.

"Yes, I read a book on Medieval European mythology awhile back that described something similar. I was doing some research on our family. It's so easy to do now with the internet, and it's amazing what you can find. I managed to go back thirteen generations. Imagine that! Did you know that I'm a distant relation of the Duke of Wurttemburg? Well, I suppose if you go back far enough we're all related to someone famous. Six degrees and all that. Would you like some more tea?"

"Yes, please."

He holds out his cup, which Sybil fills with still-steaming herbal tea from her Chinatown blue and white teapot.

"I'm guessing you saw your double."

George nods.

"I don't know if Marcia told you about a mutual acquaintance of ours falling out of a building."

"Well, of course. It's been all over the news. Very upsetting."

"When he fell out, I was in the room with him."

George pauses, expecting Sybil to interject, but she is sitting still, smiling at him, waiting.

"Just moments before he fell out the window, well, threw himself out, he told me he saw his double. That was why he spilled coffee on himself, which made him late, which made him get a new pair of pants from the dry cleaners, which led to our argument, which led to him throwing himself against the window, which led to him dying."

"I think all tragedy hinges on the simplest of completely avoidable events. But hindsight is 20/20, George. You know that."

"But I don't know that. That's the root of the problem. If seeing your double is an omen of death, and it's seeing the double that is the cause of death, then it signals that the death has in some way already happened. Time moves forward from the event and runs its course, but the mere fact that the future has been predicted suggests that it's always been."

"Yes, I can see why you're upset. By your reasoning, you're already dead, from the moment you saw your double."

George turns and looks at Sybil. "Thank you for not arguing with me. Anyone else would try telling me why I'm wrong."

"George, I've felt like I was already dead since the day I was diagnosed with cancer. I remember everything about the moment my doctor told me. That's the day that the shadow of death attached itself to me and it's never left. You never lose something like that."

George breathes in, a shaky breath that rises upwards, pulling himself together as the breath fills his body. He stands. Sybil stands, too, and he reaches out his arms. She walks into them and he wraps his arms around her old woman's body. She is tall and strong, but the bones have been hollowed by the battle that's been waged.

He whispers, just past her ear, "I wish you were my mom."

:)

Marcia's breathing is regular, barely perceptible. She is lying back, eyes lightly closed. Dr. Schueller is at her side. Inside the observation booth, John is recording the regular feed of electrical activity produced by Marcia's brain at regular intervals. There is a peacefulness that has descended upon the lab. Everything seems in its place.

Doctor Schueller is speaking in a measured but confident voice. "You are calm and relaxed. You will follow the direction of my voice and my voice will serve as a focal point for you. We are going to go down a level into your memory. You will experience your memories as they occur, but you will be removed from them, as if you were an observer of the memory. The sound of my voice will be your focal point. If you are ready to move into your memory, raise your right finger."

Marcia's breathing remains steady. Very slowly, her right index finger lifts off the armrest and then settles.

"Good. Your subconscious remembers and records everything you experience, whether you are aware of it or not. We are going to visit the morning of April 27th, at ten thirty am. Where are you?"

The clarity of her speaking voice is surprising, coming from a body that appears to be asleep. While Dr. Schueller has become accustomed to this mixed reality of the hypnotic state, in the observation booth, John is surprised and fascinated. He stops watching the video feed, and moves to the electronic feeds, learning to trust the readings that show what's happening below the surface.

"I'm in the elevator going downstairs for my morning cigarette. I'm watching the television in the corner of the elevator. The TSX is down twenty-eight points, Teck Cominco is up thirty-two cents and Telus is also up fourteen cents."

"Okay, we're going to move forward in time. It is now 10:45. Where are you?"

"I'm in an unused office on the 38th floor. Frank and I are embracing. His arms are strong, stretching against his dress shirt. I'm undoing his buttons, rubbing my hands across his chest."

"What?"

Dr. Schueller stops writing. She is starting at Marcia's impassive face.

"I'm rubbing my hands across his chest." She repeats this with the same expression, the same rhythm as the first time she said it.

"Stop, Marcia." She looks to the observation room. "John, can you pull the last minute of readings for me? I want to see if there's a jump in the readings. This isn't right. Okay, Marcia, I'm going to ask you to move a few minutes forward, to the moment when/"

And now she is screaming, her arms thrashing as if she is hurtling backwards through space, desperate to grasp the receding ledge. Doctor Schueller whips back to Marcia.

"Marcia! This is Doctor Schueller. I want you to use my voice as a focal point. Listen to my voice, Marcia, I'm going to ask you to distance yourself from your sensations, to pull back as if you were hovering slightly above the events you have been experiencing."

Marcia's breathing stabilizes immediately, her body relaxes, her arms fold once more across her stomach. John enters the room, printer paper in hand.

"There's no change, Doctor. Theta all the way."

"What do you mean? Did you get the part where she's screaming?"

"Theta. She's never not been hypnotized, this is all part of the same thing. This is what's in there."

"Okay, go back. I want to pull all the data from the beginning. The video feed, too."

She says this as if it were his fault. John quickly exits, his absence leaving a silence in the room. Dr. Schueller closes her eyes for a moment. Marcia's soft breathing is like a baby's, her stomach rising and falling, her face relaxed and beautiful.

"Okay, Marcia. We're going to slow this down. One beat at a time. It's April 27th, 10:45 am. You said you're in an abandoned office with Frank, your hands on his chest. I want you to describe, very slowly, what you see and feel."

"We move across the room. Frank pushes into me against the window. I move my hand down, hold his penis/"

"Okay, we can move forward a minute. Where are you now?"

"We're against the window. Frank is pushing into me. I can feel my orgasm building. I am looking over his shoulder, digging my nails into his arms. I'm looking at an Inuit print. There are three fishermen moving towards two igloos with strings of fish behind them. The light from outside and the city beyond is reflected in the glass. He's moving faster now. He's going to come, I can tell. I bite into his shoulder to stop from screaming. I see something in the reflection of the print. Oh God!"

Marcia's body shudders and she falls silent, her breathing still rising and falling. An eerie silence enters the room, pressing in on the doctor and patient, one strapped to electrodes, one lost and blind, asking questions to escape the darkness.

"What do you see Marcia?"

"I see a body fall past. I look and see a body reflected in the print as it falls past. And then he comes inside me and/" And again she starts screaming.

John's voice pipes in. "No change doctor. She's screaming, but there's no change in her electrical readings."

"If I want something, I'll fucking ask!" She yells this over shoulder, in the direction of the two-way glass. Then, "Marcia. Talk to me. Focus on my voice. What do you see?"

"I'm looking into his eyes. I hear a smack and turn around and there's his body, twisted and bloodied on the pavement. His eyes are open, staring into mine, but he can't see me."

"Who Marcia? Who are you seeing?"

"Frank. I'm looking into Frank's eyes."

"Where are you?"

"I'm on the street."

:)

The date is May 25th. Detective Jerry Mauritz of 55 Division is sitting at his desk. He's responding to as many of the over two hundred e-mails he has yet to address as he can, when the mail cart rolls by. Three envelopes are dropped on his desk, two manila 8 ½ X 11s and one standard white envelope. The white one catches his eye. It is hand-written, scrawled, with a lump in the middle. He rolls away from his computer, picks up the letter, turns it over. No postmark, no return address, just George Stevens handwritten in the upper left corner. The name sounds familiar, but he doesn't place it.

He hesitates, but the envelope is much too small to be a bomb. He slides his finger under the flap of the envelope and slides. The envelope tears at the top. He reaches an index finger in and scoops out the two flathead screws that formed the lump. There is a single sheet of paper in the envelope. He unfolds it and reads.

Dear Detective Mauritz,

You told me to contact you if I thought of anything else that might be of relevance in the death of Frank Lewis on April 27th.

In the past few weeks I've come to realize that it was most likely me that was responsible for his death.

While I can't completely prove this, I hope you will consider the evidence. I found these screws in the pocket of the pants I was wearing the day of Frank's death. These are screws from the flashing surrounding the window in question. I later found a link to a website describing the correct installation of office windows. I can only assume I used the knowledge to make the window structurally incompetent. I also had previous knowledge of Frank's habit of throwing himself against his window as a part of an inspirational speech he would give new members of the team. The final piece of evidence is an article I e-mailed myself about the Darwin Awards, an annual award given to the most stupid deaths of any given year, describing how a man fell out of a Chicago office tower by falling against a window with degraded rubber casings. I can only assume this was my inspiration.

I understand that my tone may be puzzling to you. It's true that I don't have any direct memory of these actions. I certainly did have moments in which I experienced hatred for Frank, though even I'm surprised I would have taken it to this extreme. I have dreamt of murdering Frank. I have also dreamt of flying, killing my parents and operating as a secret agent, but I don't believe any of these to be true. I believe that my doppelganger is responsible for these acts. My shadow self. I know this will sound ludicrous to you. I am doubtful that I will be able to convince you or anyone else that this is anything but delusional rantings. But I believe there is scientific evidence to support this theory.

I believe each of us exist simultaneously in two separate realities, one linear, one not. I believe that one reality begins at birth and progresses forward until it ends at the time of our death. I believe there is another reality that is a separate non-linear existence, with no beginning and no end. Birth and death are simultaneous. There is a scientific basis for this. At the quantum level, matter is both particle and wave. This seems scientifically impossible, and yet is absolutely true. I believe we are also both particle and wave. We are matter and as such, subject to the laws of matter. Because the brain can't understand this, it separates the two realities. These two realities exist separately for most of our lives. Our realities circle each other like quarters in a funnel, until we are revolving around and around, almost aware of the other, almost there, until we explode into the infinite. We are stars, who over time collapse upon themselves. Death is a black hole from which no light can escape.

I don't truly believe that I will be able to convince you of this theory. It sounds crazy even as I write it. And yet, I am utterly convinced that this explains all the mysteries of life from a valid scientific perspective. It is the point of union between quantum mechanics, psychology, spirituality, software engineering and the paranormal. It is the last secret on earth.

The trick is that it is impossible to prove. The only way to verify it is through experience, and of course, that is the point of no return, the point where gravity collapses in upon itself and no light can escape.

I do apologize for the pain I have caused. I write this to you in the hopes that it will explain my death. Not grief, or anger, or remorse, but enlightenment.

George Stevens.

Detective Mauritz finishes the letter. He's not entirely sure what to do with it. Rather than go through his files, find George Stevens' contact information and bring him in for questioning, as he probably should do, he sits down at his desktop, calls up his browser and Googles Particle Wave Duality. He gets 428,000 results (in 0.28 seconds).

:)

"Okay, Marcia. I'm going to bring you out now. As I count to five I want you to become more and more alert. One, you're going to remember everything you just experienced, two I want you to follow the sound of my voice, three you will keep the memory, but at a distance, four wiggling your fingers and toes and five. Take your time to open your eyes whenever you feel comfortable."

Marcia blinks twice, then tries to sit up quickly.

"It's okay, Marcia. We're going to deal with this."

"Deal with what? What just happened?"

"I'm not entirely sure. It seems that in your subconscious you were two places at the same time."

"But that's impossible."

"Yes, it is. Perhaps your mind has fused two memories. I don't know, but we'll find out."

"Oh my God. George."

At this, Marcia starts pulling the electrodes off her skin. She swings her legs off the chair and runs to the cubby where she puts her personal belongings while at the lab. Her purse. She pulls out her phone, turns it on, impatient for the screen to boot up, then scrolling, scrolling, until she hits it, Stevens, George. She pushes the green button and waits. It goes to voicemail immediately, "Hi this is George's cell. Leave me a message and I'll call you back as soon as I can."

"George! Whatever you're doing, stop. Call me. It's Marcia. I'm on my way to your house. I'm sorry, George. I believe you. You hear me? I believe you." She says this last line holding the phone directly in front of her mouth, as if the extra emphasis could reach through the phone, grab George and shake him.

"Marcia." It's Dr. Schueller. She is using her professional voice. The stern one that lets patients know they need to get a hold of themselves. That they're acting out and need to have an external awareness of how they must look. "Marcia."

Marcia is fumbling with her jacket, trying to get her arms in at the same time as she is putting on her boots. She turns to Dr. Schueller, slinging her purse over her shoulder and hisses at her, "This is all your fault!" With that she walks out of the sleep lab, leaving Dr. Schueller by herself, staring at the door.

Inside the observation room, John is watching Dr. Schueller watch the door. After a moment, he reaches over to the monitoring equipment and shuts it off.

:)

George stands at the bottom of the bank of elevators on the concourse level of his former place of employment. He is waiting for the elevators to arrive. He has guessed that the second elevator to his right will be the first to arrive. He is calm. After a moment, the arrow above the second elevator to his right lights up and the doors open. Two women in skirts, blouses and sneakers exit, while a middle-aged man in a charcoal suit holds the door for them. George waits for the three to pass and enters the elevator. He is surprisingly alone in the elevator. He is glad for this. In the event of another panic attack, he would much rather be alone. He pushes the button for the 56th floor, two floors below the top level. The top two floors are the executive floors that open directly into a highly secured reception area. The 56th floor houses many of the company servers and is generally abandoned.

As he passes the 32nd floor, a signal from a nearby cell tower is unable to locate his handset in the heart of the office tower and sends the call directly to voicemail.

At the 56th floor, the doors slide open and George exits the elevator, calm and clear-headed. He smiles. Overcoming his fear of elevators is a clear indication of the rightness of this.

Rather than enter either set of glass doors that bookend the elevators, George turns down the hallway that flanks them, walks past the men's washroom and to the beige metal door at the end. He opens his wallet and removes his ID card that has remained unused for the past month. He holds it to the card-reader, sees the small green light and opens the door into the concrete stairwell that runs like an artery through the building. He takes these stairs until they reach the top. The stairs lead to a metal box that opens onto the roof of the building. George opens this door and immediately is blasted by cold wind. He puts his shoulder into the door, forces it open and steps onto the concrete roof.

The centre of the tower is a professional running track, sloped towards the middle. It has its own entrance and is separated from the area where George is standing by a chest high wall. The side he is on is industrial, cement and steel. But the view, the immediacy of the landscape of towers that rise like mountains around him and streets that fan out in every direction as far as the eye can see, makes him stop and turn slowly, 360 degrees. George is surprised by the visceral reaction he has to the power of this landscape that surrounds him, like the Grand Canyon, or the Columbia Icefields. He had never thought of the city as terrain until this moment. It is the first time a city has made sense to him. City used to mean an absence of terrain when seen from the ground, or a sprawl of circuitry when seen from an airplane approaching the airport. But from here, he can feel the strength of the girders that hold the buildings against the wind, he can see into the windows of offices around him, he can look down and feel the distance, the sheer height of these monsters that erupt like fungus from the centre of the city. It is a powerful feeling to be standing at the top of this building, at this moment in time.

George feels privileged, alone. He is standing at the very edge of the building. The wind is whipping his pants against his legs. George closes his eyes, thinks of the hawk he saw, floating on thermals above the freeway. He draws in a deep breath, pulls his arms straight above his head, and with perfect form, swan dives off of the ledge and out into the air...

Inside the cab, Marcia is stuck in traffic, headed to George's house. She is too late, headed in the wrong direction, headed away from where George has learned to fly.

Inside Marcia, the floating collection of cells finds the puffy pink walls of its home for the next nine months and implants itself. There is no up or down, no light or dark. There is only the absolute.

The tower eventually locates the handset, as it plummets from the top of the building and sends the signal. The cell phone vibrates and chimes, the lit up screen reads, "Message waiting."

:)

Heath

Somewhere else a newborn baby is sleeping in its mother's arms. It has finished nursing and is deeply asleep, its impossibly large stomach rising and falling like a bellows. Occasionally the baby surfaces, finds its own hand and sucks the soft skin before dropping back down into the rhythm of its mother's rocking.

Eventually, the mother goes to put the baby down, hoping it will sleep long enough to allow her to get a few things done before the next feeding. When the baby's back touches the solid unmoving plane of the bassinet, the baby startles, shooting its arms out wide. Until now, its world has been one of constant movement inside its mother's womb. The shock of the stillness is the hardest adjustment.

The baby's mother leans in and whispers, "Shhhh, it's okay, shhhh." The baby settles, sighs and drops back into sleep.

0110

About the Author

Simon Heath has worked as a playwright and theatre director for the past twenty years. Doppelganger is his first novel. He is currently working on a trilogy of novels called The Power Trilogy, based on a worldwide power outage caused by solar storms. Samples of his work and links to future novels can be found on his website at www.simonheath.ca. He lives with his family in rural Ontario, Canada but travels the continent as an executive communications consultant. If you would like to be notified of the release of Escape, the first book in The Power Trilogy, please e-mail the author at simon@simonheath.ca. Your e-mail won't be used for any other purpose.

The Power Trilogy Synopsis

The Power Trilogy is built around a single event – the collapse of the majority of the world's electrical grids. The trilogy is the story of a family and their struggle to survive in a world without power. Brian, Karen and eight-year old Robin live a comfortable, modern life in Toronto. Karen works in Business Process Outsourcing, a corporate role focused on process and efficiency. She is also 33 weeks into an unplanned pregnancy. Brian recently left his job as a Water Infrastructure Engineer with the City of Toronto. He used a severance package offer to fulfill his dream of buying land in the country and building an off-grid home. He left the job before they knew Karen was pregnant. Their relationship has become increasingly acrimonious over the years as Karen has become more and more involved in her career and Brian has become more and more involved in building a new, different life in the country. Robin is eight years old, first one up in the morning, smart as a whip, and caught in between. Increasingly, she is siding with her father with whom she has spent weekends fishing and canoeing the past few years while Karen finished an executive MBA. Then the power goes out. And stays out.

When the power goes out, the world shrinks. With no internet, no cell phones, no television, no available gas, no running water, no lights and no grocery stores, priorities change. The world shrinks to the people and things that immediately surround the family. There are the basics of survival: enough food for three meals a day; drinking water; dealing with an end of term pregnancy. But there are broader questions as well. How does this family, this failing marriage, respond to the crisis? Who do they trust? Do communities join together or turn on one another? Is there chaos or structure? What role does morality play in a world without power? Who will live and who will die?

Escape - Chapter 1

Sunday, India

She's never felt so white before. Standing in the middle of a dirt side street, with her maternity business suit and shiny leather briefcase, thousands of brown-skinned people moving past and around her. She is thirty-three weeks pregnant and her large belly is hidden under her stylishly cut grey business suit. Another few weeks and she wouldn't have been allowed to fly. She's been alternating this and another maternity suit for the past two weeks of her pregnancy. She is hot in these clothes, in this temperature. It's still only ten in the morning, but the temperature has already risen to around 28°C. Bikes and rickshaws, a camel, two oxen, and whining motorbikes whip in and around the constantly shifting mass of humanity. A bead of sweat runs between her shoulder blades, the length of her spine, before being absorbed by the elastic waistband of her skirt. She had stopped to buy a bottle of water. The guide had told her not to stop, told them all not to go off on their own. But she'd been followed, handled and guided since the moment she got off the plane and driven to her opulent hotel. The hotel where a few years earlier, masked men and teenaged boys walked into the lobby, restaurant and upper floors and started shooting white people. A simultaneous attack to increase the body count before its inevitable and brutal suppression, carried out at several hotels, nightclubs and public locations. An attack targeting people like her, people doing what she is currently doing: business. The hotel that costs 11,581 rupees a night, the equivalent of $C300. A bargain by Canadian standards, given the splendor of the hotel, the services provided, cloth not paper towels in the marble bathrooms, the attention to detail at every turn. But this is where the division of the country becomes clear. The average person in India makes 20,000 rupees. The average person working on the call centre systems integration project she is here to lead makes about 600,000 rupees. As her Indian counterpart on the project had explained it, "India is not a poor country, it just has a lot of poor people in it." She is currently carrying 15,000 rupees in the leather briefcase that she has clutched against her side, along with her passport, Visa, laptop, Blackberry, iPod and hand sanitizer. All of a sudden she feels very far from home.

She tries to swallow the panic that is rising in her. She is white and rich and pregnant and lost and completely dependent on her tour guide remembering her, having counted heads, like taking children onto public transportation for a school trip. She volunteered recently to be a parent on her daughter's class trip to a local heritage museum. Took the day off work to be a good parent. She and the other parents were responsible for three children each, getting them on and off the subway, keeping them close crossing the street. The trip had left her exhausted, amazed at what teachers do every day. The whole trip she was terrified that she would lose one. Even then, she had brought along her Blackberry. At one point she found herself reading a message and when she looked up, two of the children were gone. She started to turn, was about to call out, when she heard the giggles from behind the fence they were standing next to. "Don't you ever do that again!" she'd said, suppressing the guilt, vowing to turn off the Blackberry, to pay better attention to the things that really matter. What she hadn't said, was "Don't you know that at any second you die? You could be shot? Run over, abducted? Don't you understand how vulnerable you are?" She doesn't want to pass her fear onto her daughter.

And now here she is. Standing somewhere in Agra. Lost and vulnerable. One breath away from being kidnapped, killed. She could simply vanish and it wouldn't matter.

"Excuse me, madam?" The voice behind her is impossibly polite, with the extra peaks and valleys of the Indian intonation. "You are looking lost. I am guessing you are looking for the Taj Mahal."

"Yes. I managed to get myself separated from my group. I can't remember the name of the tour company."

"It is okay. Please, let me show you the way."

She is hesitant, suspicious. She has heard too many stories: people swindled, framed with drugs by the police, drugged and waking up in a bathtub of ice with their kidneys or ovaries removed. Trying to compare the risk of being on her own with the risk of trusting this man standing in front of her, with loose white dhoti wrapped around his waist, cotton kurta open at the side, leather sandals, mustache, clear brown eyes, smile, hands clasped behind back.

"Thank you. That's a very kind offer."

"I am practicing speaking with foreigners. I hope to leave this place someday. Please, follow me."

He walks quickly, several feet ahead of her. She has to walk quickly to keep up as he darts around people, avoiding collisions effortlessly while she waits for the ox cart, or group of people, or motorcycle, or canvas-covered truck, or group of children, or gangly pack of rusting bicycles that never seem to collide, to pass before rushing to catch up with him. Her ankles throb, she holds her belly as she hustles after the man who is able to remain impossibly white in the midst of the dust and animal shit. Her own shoes are dusty and scuffed. She is breathing heavily, her gait erratic as she tries to contain her fear.

She loses sight of her guide as an old man leading four oxen crosses her path. When the way is clear again, she has no sense of where he has gone. None of the streets are straight, no grid system here. Her chest is starting to tighten when she sees the man waving from next to a building. She hurries after him as he once more disappears around the corner. She is becoming irritated, in spite of the generosity, and is about to call out to the man to slow down, please, when she turns the corner onto a larger street and there he is again, standing in a small archway.

"It's hard for me to keep up. You move so fast!"

""Come this way."

He leads her down a small passage way that ends in a metal gate. He pulls out a long spike that is holding the gate closed and swings it open, indicates for her to go ahead. She walks through the gate, out of the passageway and into the grounds of the Taj Mahal. They've come in from the side and she is completely taken off guard by the sheer beauty of it. The noise and chaos of the Agra street falls away as the white and brown marble building rises above.

"It is very beautiful, is it not?"

She is speechless for a moment. Unable to cut through the moment of pure, genuine awe, in order to reach out and grasp, then form, words that might in some way relay the incredible experience of taking in such crystalline, sparkling, aesthetic perfection.

"I don't know if I have ever seen something so beautiful. It takes your breath away."

"Yes, it takes your breath away." He is repeating the phrase, turning it over in his mouth as if to taste the meaning.

They share a moment, side by side, looking at the magnificent building, he in traditional Indian garb, her in classic business suit.

She snaps out of the moment, looks at her guide. "I'm sorry, I think I see my group up ahead." She pulls her wallet out of her shoulder-strap briefcase and unsnaps the lid. "I can't thank you enough", she says, pulling out 100 rupees, wondering if 100 rupees is enough. She hesitates, sees the picture of Mahatma Gandhi's smiling face, then pulls out another 100 rupee note.

The man holds up both hands and shakes them at her vigorously, "No, no, no, missus. I am happy to bring you to this place."

"Please. I don't know what I would have done without you." She holds out the two 100 rupee bills between them.

The man smiles, sadly maybe, and shakes head. "No, thank you missus. I am practicing my English."

"Well. Thank you. I didn't even ask your name."

"My name is Hardeep. And what is yours?"

"Karen. My name is Karen."

"It is a pleasure to meet you Karen."

"You too, Hardeep."

They turn from each other, the Indian man back into the dense jungle of diesel fumes and street stalls, the business woman towards the pristine lines of the Taj

Mahal. Suddenly she turns and calls to the man. "Hardeep?"

"Yes, Karen?"

"Have you ever worked in a call centre? Answering phones?"

"I have studied to provide in-depth IT support to challenged end-user groups." He smiles.

"Really?"

"Yes." He stands, smiling.

"Could you write your name and a way of getting hold of you on the back of one of my business cards?" She is fumbling in her briefcase, trying to find a card, a pen, worried about losing her group once again. "I'm sorry, I can't find a pen."

"Perhaps I could e-mail it to you?"

When she looks up, a Blackberry has appeared from the folds of his clothing.

"Yes, why don't you do that?" She hands him a business card. He smiles. She grimaces, feeling stupid, Western. "I'll look forward to hearing from you, Hardeep."

They turn away from each other. By the time she looks over her shoulder in the direction he went, he has disappeared, reabsorbed by the life of the street. She stops for a moment, looks at her hair in the mirror in her wallet, pops a mint into her mouth and hurries to rejoin her tour group standing on the steps of the main building, about to enter the mausoleum. She leans over to a colleague, the consultant helping to structure the outsourcing deal.

"What did I miss?"

"Oh, not much, just a bunch of history and dates and stuff. Where'd you go?"

"Oh, nowhere. Just discovering a bit of the off-the-beaten-track India."

"Yeah, well, I'd watch that. It's not always all that safe here. It's not like back home."

"Right. Thanks."

They both turn their heads to the front again, where the tour guide is speaking.

"... an architectural expression of eternal love. When his second wife died in childbirth, The Shah was so overwrought at the loss that he built this building, so that he, and others would always remember the purity of their love. Some say that when you enter the building you can actually feel the power of that love. Marriages have been saved and families re-united by the beauty of this monument ..."

Karen looks up at the perfect white cupola, tilts her head a little to the side, then smiles to herself. She takes out her Blackberry, does a quick mental calculation for time difference, then hesitates with her thumb over the dial button. Instead she pushes a different button and keys in the following message:

At Taj Mahal. Amazing. Thinking of you building house for us. Love and miss you. Please kiss Robin. See you soon. Karen/Mom

When she looks up, she has fallen behind again, the group having moved into the inside of the building. Karen puts away her device and hurries after them.

Sunday, Simcoe County

"Dad! Dad!"

Robin is the first one awake, as always. Just like her name.

Their bed is a foam mattress on the plywood subfloor. They tried an air mattress, but it sprang a leak the first night they used it. They woke up in the middle of the night flat on the hard ground.

"Dad!"

Sleeping with his daughter is one of the pleasures of these weekends in the country. He knows this is probably the last year before she no longer wants to sleep in the same bed as her dad. She already wants privacy in the bath. He'd been shocked the first time she covered up when he'd walked in on her changing for bed.

"Come here! You gotta see this."

He understands that there is something outside, that this is why she is whispering so urgently. He rolls off the mattress and crawls on his hands and needs over to where Robin is looking out the window.

"Look!"

He peeks his head above the bottom of the window ledge – the wall of windows for passive solar heating that went in last week, finally completing the shell of the house – and sees, not ten feet from the house, eight wild turkeys, walking around the place as if they owned it. There is some low-lying mist hovering about six inches above the ground, so that all they can see are the feet of the turkeys, and then the upper parts of their bodies, heads and necks sticking above the fog.

"What are they?"

"Those are wild turkeys."

"There's no such thing!"

"Okay, they're red-chinned dallywappers."

"Da-a-ad." The exasperated voice.

"You asked."

"They look so weird!"

"Yes. Yes, they do." Long stick legs, bare heads and bright red wattles hanging down. When they hear Brian and Robin, they startle, walking quickly away in zigzags, leading with their strange bare heads. Within seconds, they have disappeared into the mist and undergrowth. Amazing that such huge, awkward birds could disappear so completely, so quickly. Amazing they've survived evolution.

"My coffee ready yet?"

"Da-a-ad."

He and his daughter are at the country house. Brian finished putting up the bales a few weeks ago and he and Robin are working on the adobe stucco. Mostly he is working on the stucco while she reads, plays her Nintendo DS, or goes crawling around looking for bugs or cool sticks or fossils. She has yet to find a legitimate fossil, but Brian hasn't had the heart to tell her that what she finds are probably nothing more than funny shaped rocks. She had wanted to take the last specimen to the Royal Ontario Museum, because it was shaped like an arrowhead. He's just been stalling on that one, coming up with lame excuses not to go, without flat out refusing. And what does he know, maybe it is an arrowhead and he's just a cynical grown-up. This is where he usually stops the train of thought and focuses his attention on something else.

Heath

This is the first weekend that the electrical system is fully up and working. The propane stove got hooked up the week before and the tank filled. There had been a bill for $1000 worth of propane slid under the front door. There's a composting toilet and woodstove for additional heat. It's the May long weekend and the two are celebrating. They've gone up while Karen is away in India. The nights are still cold, but the days are warming up and there's a loosening, a feeling of ease that comes with the warmth.

"Can I have some hot chocolate?"

"Sure thing, Beaner. We're living in the lap of luxury now. What do you want for breakfast? I have cereal, toast, bacon and eggs, you name it."

"Can I have pasta?"

"Sure. You can have pasta. Why don't you go get some wood from outside and we'll fire up the woodstove?"

"Okay!"

Robin skips out the side door. Brian watches her as she goes. Tries to remember what it feels like to skip. Then turns his attention to the stove. He fills his only pot with water from the tap, his water, the well drilled, the pump powered by the solar panels and a small wind turbine, puts the pot on the stove and turns the knob to the right. The stove clicks several times before the blue flame flares from the burner and spreads out across the bottom of the pot as he puts it down. He goes into one of the back rooms of the house, the cold storage which he has already stocked with Mr. Noodles, pasta and sauce, rice, pickles and giant Costco containers of salt, oregano, coffee, olives and every other imaginable staple. The back rooms are away from the wall of windows. When he sat down with the architect to design the house, one of the things he'd said was, "I want this house to run itself." The design had used the heat of the sun as the main energy source. Facing south on the side of a hill, they'd built it to absorb every last ray of heat in the summer when the sun was low, with an overhang that provided shade when the sun was high in summer. The rooms at the back, away from the windows, were for laundry, cold storage, and one guest bedroom they could close off in winter.

When he returns with the pasta, the water is boiling on the stove. This simple thing, water boiling, gives Brian enormous pleasure. Water boiling on the stove he put in, in the house he is building, on the land he chose. He can't wait to put in the garden – it's his surprise for Robin this weekend. In his bag he has several packets of seeds: lettuce, carrots, beans and peas, even some red pepper and cantaloupe he'd bought on a whim. They've never had a garden in the city. He's always been afraid of what's in the ground, what toxic substances might have been leaching into the soil. Here, he and Robin can plant a garden and watch it grow. What could be better than that?

-

It's been a long journey getting here. Brian is a Water Infrastructure Engineer for the City of Toronto. Was. He still forgets that he no longer works for the City. Holding together the leaking pipes, keeping the water pumping and the shit flowing for a city of 2.5 million people. It was a frustrating job. He spent more time finding ways to cut budgets than to do what he was actually trained for. For years he raised the alarms about the state of the infrastructure. By the models he ran, more than half the water pumped at source escaped through cracks and leaks in the pipes. Fugitive losses, they're called. Which is significant given that a full third of the City's power bill goes directly towards keeping those pumps running. The entire underground system is held together with binder twine and duct tape, but nobody wants to hear that. Nobody wants to hear that we'll all be wading in our own shit within five years if we don't invest in infrastructure. And that's in a Business as Usual scenario, never mind that every time there's a major rain storm it overflows capacity and we dump raw sewage into the lake, never mind that the number of severe rainstorms has been rising steadily over the past few years, never mind that we have an aging population and a shrinking tax base, never mind that the fastest growing source of water pollution is pharmaceuticals, including estrogen from birth control pills being peed into the water and that while we have water treatments for harmful bacteria, we don't have treatments for pharmaceuticals, we don't even measure that. Never mind all that. He often thinks of Cassandra. In his degree program, he was forced to take one humanities course, and he had chosen Greek Mythology. Cassandra's punishment for having offended Apollo was to be able to foresee the future, but never have anyone believe her when she would raise the alarm about her premonitions. That's what working for the city was like.

Six months ago he took a package. He had seen the writing on the wall and it spelled collapse. The new mayor planned to save hundreds of millions of dollars through attrition – encouraging people to retire and not hiring anyone to replace them. Smart.

It seemed fair. He had held up his end of the bargain, working a job he hated for the good of the family. At first, when Karen was home for the year after Robin was born, her company topped up the first six months, but after that, only what the government provided. And then childcare, on top of the mortgage, a second mortgage, really. After her first year back, his wife decided she wanted to do her Executive MBA. It was a huge commitment, but it would position her for promotion. They'd decided on a live-in nanny, while Karen studied. She promised to finish it in two years, but in the end it was four. At one point she'd threatened to quit the program, because she hated what it was doing to them. It was the only time he really lost his temper. "You'd better finish that fucking degree, because I am never doing this for you again." He instantly regretted the words, but there it was. Robin was six by the time she finished. Halfway through grade one. She and her father had taken to fishing to pass the time. Weekends when Karen was in a classroom, running the numbers on financial models and reading case studies of strategic mergers and acquisitions, Brian and Robin would head out into the countryside surrounding the city. At first, they would visit the local streams and rivers that dotted the countryside north of the city where he grew up. He knew that each of these streams funneled into the various rivers that flow through, and in many cases under, the City of Toronto, where they eventually emptied themselves into Lake Ontario, where each particle of water could spend up to fifty years before eventually making its way to the Atlantic. When Robin was four, they would look at flowers and collect smooth rocks in the water, or look for frogs, or spend the afternoon flipping over larger rocks to look for crayfish. When she was five, he bought Robin her own fishing rod. It was a plastic Spongebob rod that got hopelessly tangled the first time she tried to cast it. The next day they went to Canadian Tire and bought an inexpensive collapsible rod with a pushbutton reel. That day, she caught her first fish, a nice-sized small mouth bass. When she saw the fish, she shrieked and dropped the rod into the water, Brian having to run out up to his thighs to catch it in time before the bass dragged the whole rod and reel down under. They spent the summer packing up first thing on a Saturday and heading out to fish the day away. The next spring, Brian planned a weekend fishing trip. He rented a canoe from an outfitter, went to the local Canadian Tire for some supplies and headed out for the opening of trout season. It rained the whole time. Couldn't light a fire. Didn't catch any fish. So, he went back and bought proper gear. A camp stove, a proper 120 litre canoe pack, waterproof everything, an emergency kit, even a little backpack for Robin to carry on portages. He bought a used canoe off of Craigslist. The next trip he planned for the whole family. At the last minute, there was a network outage at the contact centre and Karen had been forced to stay behind. So he and Robin went on their own.

Every trip they took, they would drive down a different side road to get home. In the back of his mind, he was dreaming of an escape. Looking at houses, looking at land, imagining what it would be like to wake up in the country, drink his coffee looking over a rolling landscape, watching Robin be picked up by the school bus at the end of the road. At the very least a weekend place. Robin's job kept her tied to the city, and frankly so did his. So he dreamt of a piece of land. He tried not to let Robin in on it. Tried to hide that her mother's dreams and her father's dreams were growing farther and farther apart. So, of course she knew.

"Daddy, if we move to the country, I'm coming with you." She was six when she said that.

"What do you mean?"

"I mean I don't want to stay in the city with mom."

A pause to assess. He is caught off-guard, feels foolish that he doesn't give his daughter credit for her intelligence. He always tries to treat her like a full person, not like a kid, but then something like this happens and he realizes that she has continued to grow and he's barely keeping up.

"We're a family, Beaner. Whatever we do, we're going to do it together."

"Okay." They spent the next fifteen minutes driving in silence, staring out their respective windows at all the land passing them by.

One weekend, they stayed out an extra day. He managed to get a signal in the park and sent two text messages: one to his wife, the other to work. Both said the same thing. "Extending absence. Unavoidable. Back tomorrow."

When he got home, there was an offer waiting for him at work. Six months' salary, lump sum payment with a little extra for accrued vacation pay and whatnot. He took the package. Formed his plan on the way home, shaped the arguments, thought through what he would say. He would take the cash and use it to buy land. Then he would take a year to build the house. He'd been researching straw bale houses and felt confident he could build one. The six month's pay would cover the land and letting the nanny go would save enough each month to make it manageable. In one year they could have what they always wanted – a country place, very little debt, off-grid, so very few maintenance costs, and a chance for him to spend more time with Robin, spend a little time thinking about what he really wanted to do with his life. How could she refuse, after he'd supported her through the EMBA?

She wasn't happy about it. Joked about his midlife crisis, that it was better than becoming a coke addict and buying a sports car. But underneath there was an uneasiness. A feeling that the tectonic plates of their marriage were shifting. She started to feel judged, as if the things she believed in no longer fit his view of the world. He got into an environmental kick, as she described it. Started researching how to go off-grid using wind turbines and solar panels and micro-turbines for run of the river power generation. All the things that made him want to be an engineer in the first place. They fought more often than not.

He found the perfect land. An hour from the city, 20 acres at the headwaters of one of the major tributaries to Lake Ontario. Perfect for fishing. Conservation land on two sides, farmland on another and a bush lot on the fourth. Just far enough away from the city as to be affordable. There had been a squabble with the township about zoning and as a result there was no electrical service to the lot, which had dropped it into his price range. The property had been on the market for over a year with no offers. He came in low and they accepted. And if he did most of the work on the house himself, dipped into the secured line of credit, not much, they could just afford it.

Of course, he was away more and more. At first he would drop Robin off at school, drive straight to the property, work until four and then drive back in time to pick her up from after school care and make dinner for the family. But eventually he started spending more and more nights on the land. The winter was mild, so he was able to work most days. Once the foundation was in, and the in-floor radiant heating in place, he and a friend did the framing and laid the subfloor. He ran the in-floor heating off the woodstove. He put the wiring in himself, the plumbing, too. He was happy up there. And then he'd come home and things were hard. The freedom, the forgetfulness of the day up north was replaced by stress: stress from traffic, stress about picking up Robin from daycare before 6:00, after which they charge a dollar for every minute you're late, stress about dinner, stress about stress. No wonder he wanted to be up north. But the more he went up north, the worse it got.

Heath

Until she discovered she was pregnant. Seven years after Robin was born. After they'd decided they were through, that one was enough, that they couldn't imagine loving another child as much as they loved Robin. They discussed terminating the pregnancy. Karen was almost forty-four. Did they want to risk a Downs baby? Who was going to work if she took a year off again? How would it affect her career? Three months into his year off. Which put a hard deadline to the project. Because he wasn't going to be running off to some unheated grass hut once the new baby arrived. Her words. They had just poured the foundation when she found out. The road had gone in the month before. He started to think about the gestation of the house in parallel with the gestation of the baby. He was running out of time.

Now, thirty-three weeks pregnant. The shell completed, the windows in, the grey water system in place, the solar and wind hooked into the batteries that are wired into the outlets and switches. Now it's the final touches: the floor, the kitchen, the cabinets, the fixtures, the paint, the furniture. He's way behind and he knows it.

-

He's disturbed by a loud thumping by the side of the house. When he opens the door, he finds Robin standing there with a load of logs in her arms so high that her chin rests on top. She is kicking the door.

"For God's sake, don't kick the door!"

"My arms were full"

She walks in and dumps the four logs next to the woodstove.

"I don't care if your arms were full, I don't want you kicking the door of our brand new house!" Sometimes he thinks all he does is give his daughter shit for not picking up, not saying please, not listening, not...

"Okay, fine. Is my pasta ready?"

"Not yet."

"Your phone's blinking. Can I read it?" She has already picked up the phone when he snatches it away from her.

"Just let me, okay?" He is still irritated. And feeling guilty for being irritated.
"It's a message from your mom. She says to give you a hug and a kiss and say she misses you."
"Where is she?"
"India, remember?"
"Oh, right."
They're like this. They bicker constantly, father and daughter. A displacement of roles, maybe, or just their way.
"Water's boiling."
"I know."
"Can I play my DS?"
"Sure."
She opens her video game and a cheerful sound greets them. She is drawn into Mario Kart.
"Could you turn off the sound?"
He dumps in the spiral pasta, then turns back to the phone. Closes his eyes for a second, then keys a message back.
Beautiful morning. Mist and wild turkeys. Hope the trip is going well. We're good. Robin sends kisses back. See you at the airport. B.

Friday, India
The pitch had been summarized in one slide:

Offshoring Benefits
Op/ex reduction of $120M annually
Removal of non-core activity allows for redeployment of key resources
Seamless integration
o Technical JVM-based platform
o Cultural – accent and cultural training
Partner with proven industry track record
o 10 year track record in Business Process Outsourcing (BPO)
o High Cust Sat scores
o Access to talent pool with high level of technical proficiency

Scalable solution allows phased migration
o Level 4 requests (Q2)
o Level 3 requests (Q4)
o Level 2 ???

Nobody asked what would happen to the people who
would lose their jobs. Nobody even considered it. Except
Karen, and then, hadn't her own husband taken a
package and wasn't he happier than he'd ever been?

The entire front lobby of the building is strewn with
orange, yellow and red flowers. A woman with a small red
dot on her forehead, a bindi they said, is handing a thin
taper to Karen, Jim the CEO of InfoSys who has flown in
for the event, the CEO of BPO International the Indian
company that is taking over the customer relationship
management function being outsourced and the project
leads from both the North American and Indian sides.
They have all been given flower wreaths and bindis to
mark the occasion. All five hold the candles and smile for
the cameras that are there to capture the occasion. A
copy of the photo will be printed in the business section of
the local newspaper, as well as in Karen's company's
internal newsletter and annual general report. When the
event coordinator gives the signal, all five lean in to light a
large candle symbolizing the partnership being
inaugurated at the event. Again, they hold the pose and
smile for posterity.

When the candle is lit, the two CEOs move to a large
button that has been built for the event. The Go Live
button has been set up to establish the routing link to
begin transferring calls to the new centre. On two large
monitors, rows of call centre employees with headsets can
be seen waiting to start taking calls. Again, the CEOs
pause to have their pictures taken, before both placing
their hands on the oversized button. A countdown has
begun, and Karen joins in the chant,
10...9...8...7...6...5...4...3...2...1!" The button is pushed
and a moment of silence follows with all eyes glued to the
monitors. After three seconds that feel like an eternity,
there is the sound of a phone, and the Indian man in the
foreground pushes a button, and says, "Thank you for

calling InfoSys, my name is Jason, how may I help you?" There is another brief pause before the man turns to the camera, smiles and gives a thumbs up. Inside the lobby a cheer erupts from the thirty or so people who have gathered for the event.

Karen is ecstatic. This is the successful culmination of six months of work, work that had been placed under her executive oversight. A significant placement of trust in her, and the fact that she was able to bring the project in on time and on budget before once again going on maternity leave is an enormous relief. She is smiling and shaking the hand of everyone around her. She makes sure to talk to everyone on the project, thanking them for their commitment and dedication and wishing them all some well-deserved rest. She is shaking Jim's hand, hearing him praise her with words that make her swell with pride, "commitment...stick-to-it-iveness... very impressive, Karen, very impressive indeed", when she sees Hardeep standing to the left of the entrance. She continues to watch as a security guard, in a SIS jacket grasps him by the elbow and begins to escort him towards the entrance. Karen breaks into Jim's monologue, "Thank you, Jim, you don't know how much that means to me. I have to apologize, but there's something I need to deal with, I don't mean to be rude", and slides through the crowd to the lobby entrance. The guard and Hardeep are just outside when she catches up to them.

"Excuse me! Excuse me!"

They both turn to look at her.

"It's okay. He's with me. I asked him to meet me about a job. I'm VP Call Centre Service Delivery, see?" She holds her badge towards the guard, who studies it for a moment, then releases his grip on Hardeep's elbow.

"My apologies."

"Nothing to apologize for, that's your job."

The guard moves back into the building, leaving Karen and Hardeep standing on the steps leading up to the five story office building they have just exited.

"Hardeep. I'm glad you came. I'm going to introduce you to someone who can take care of you."

"Thank you Miss Karen."

She is still flush with the event she has just been a part of and feels enormous affection for this man. She wants to share the feeling. She wants to help.

"I feel like you helped me find my way, Hardeep. Which you did, in a literal sense. But more than that. I'm sorry, I'm not making sense. But I just feel very grateful to you. I feel like through your kindness, you helped lead me back to myself. It's silly, I know."

"The Taj Mahal has that effect on people." She stops, struck that he clearly understood what she was saying. She feels connected for this instant, to him, to India, to herself and her future, to her family who will be waiting for her back home.

"Maybe you're right." They are smiling at each other now, looking into each other's eyes in a way that Karen is unaccustomed to.

"Would you mind waiting for one second?"

"Of course."

She pulls out her Blackberry and texts another message.

Project completed. Feeling top of the world. Was lost but now I'm found. Can't wait to see you and Robin. Let's start fresh? Love you, Karen.

She puts her phone away and smiles broadly at Hardeep.

"Okay, now let's see what we can do for you!"

www.ingramcontent.com/pod-product-compliance
Lightning Source LLC
Chambersburg PA
CBHW050508260626
47157CB00004B/1233